Agent Red Boxset 4-6

Teagan Stone Series

Ava S. King

304 Publishing Company

*I want to dedicate this book to my family and friends.
You are always with me, no matter where I go, and
everything you've taught me has made me a better person.*

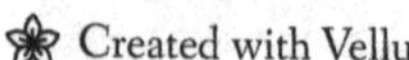 Created with Vellum

Latest Releases: Ava S. King

Agent Red Fatal Memory Teagan Stone Book 1

Agent Red Fatal Target Teagan Stone Book 2

Agent Red Fatal Crime Teagan Stone Book 3

Agent Red Fatal Justice Teagan Stone Book 4

Agent Red Fatal Enemy Teagan Stone Book 5

Mirror of Lies - A Jessica Smith Book 1

Agent Red Fatal Death Teagan Stone Book 6

Mirror of Lust - A Jessica Smith Book 2

Ruined: Andi Easton Book 1

Agent Red Fatal Revenge Teagan Stone Book 7

Agent Red Fatal Pursuit Teagan Stone Book 8

Upcoming Releases (2024)

Restore: Andi Easton Book 2

Christina Harris Mystery/Thriller Series

Agent Red Fatal Attack Teagan Stone Book 9

Agent Red Fatal Mission Teagan Stone Book 10

Disclaimer

This work of fiction contains strong language and explicit content and is only intended for mature readers. The story may contain unconventional situations, language, and sexual encounters that may offend some readers. This book is for mature readers (18+).

Introduction

Sign up for Ava S. King's mailing list for news, new releases, and special offers.

www.authoravasking.com

Part One

Agent Red (Fatal Justice)

By
Ava S. King

Synopsis

Teagan Stone is out of options and quickly running out of time. She must find the creator of America's most sought-after device to save America from a potential attack. But devious Russian forces with deep pockets are impenetrable.

The seasoned spy will stop at nothing to find the creator, bring his kidnappers to justice, and prevent a bombing—even if it means she has to risk her life.

She refuses to let evildoers take innocent lives. Not on her watch.

Chapter One

The alarm blared, and the team secured their masks and guns within five minutes to save the hostages from a terrorist attack. Teagan stood behind the two-way mirror and watched the clock run down with top members of the president's cabinet as Spider, Daughtrey, Gregory, and a few other seasoned team members rushed through. After climbing in from each side of the plane simulation, her breathing stayed elevated. Seeing Gregory lift the bottom shaft of the plane near the rear door, dressed in all black, he signaled to Spider that he would take the right side of the aisle. Spider strolled down the walkway with his gun ready to claim a terrorist. Soon as he hit the second row of seats, a man jumped up in camouflage, reaching for a hostage. When Spider raised his gun and shot at his chest, the red dye exploded.

"One down, two to go," Spider whispered through his headpiece.

"I got first-class secure," Daughtrey muttered back, opening the door of the bathroom.

Teagan gleaned at the clock, and it read two minutes left.

"Keep it moving," Teagan mumbled to herself.

All eyes were on them, and if they wanted to continue The Firm, they needed to show it was worth paying over five hundred million dollars a year to keep them running.

"It's a waste of money," Duncan Brooks, Deputy Secretary of Defense, said. The blond blue-eyed, skinny, cocky, five-eleven, preppy boy was a pain in everyone's ass. He crossed his arms and shook his head. For his entire career in politics, Duncan had taken every chance he'd gotten to shut down the agency. A few of the guys chuckled at his comment when he announced another call that a second guy was taken down. With forty seconds left, every breath was held in the room as Duncan and Teagan exchanged a look. Accomplishing this task of securing more funding, eventually picking someone to take over as director would help Teagan get closer to finally head into retirement officially. She was still grappling with some of her memories. Life had gotten only more complicated after the death of Abe Price. Sandra Gregg made it her mission to make Teagan aware that she was on to what The Firm did with killing, kidnapping, and brutalizing enemies of the United States.

"Time," Teagan called out, releasing her hand from the buzzer. Clapping in accomplishing her goal, Teagan smirked, seeing Duncan roll his eyes and gaining the needed funding for another five years.

Duncan cleared his throat and extended his hand for a shake.

"Good job, Stone."

Teagan looked down at his hand and backed up to Duncan.

"Thanks." She reached out and clasped his hand, then turned toward the door and headed to the room with her crew.

Spider removed the headset, wiping the sweat off his brow.

"What did they say?" Spider removed his gloves.

"Nothing yet." Teagan motioned at the two-way mirror.

"Funny how the guys in suits determine if we get to do our jobs, one they're too scared to do," Gregory complained, shaking his head.

Teagan thought the same thing as the email came in yesterday morning while working on a fresh case. Before she could call the president to discuss the budget renewal, grumblings throughout Congress put them in Duncan's crosshairs.

"I'm starving; how long do we have to wait?" Daughtrey pointed at the window as the door opened, and Duncan, followed by the other top aides, came back into the room.

"Gentleman and lady, you've shown your skills, and the president, as you know, is fond of whatever it is you do here." Duncan waved his hand around.

"You mean saving lives?" Gregory's brow lifted in confusion.

Spider and Daughtrey chuckled as Duncan cleared his throat.

"If that's what you want to call it. If it were up to me, I would shut this entire organization down." Duncan shrugged, sliding his hands in his pocket. All eyes looked around the room, then back at him in surprise.

"Are we free to go or not?" Daughtrey crossed his

arms over his chest. Teagan put her hand on his chest, stepping in front of him and facing Duncan.

"What's your problem?" Teagan asked.

"My problem is people like you come in and use up resources that could be used for actual work to get done," Duncan argued, pointing his finger in her face. Teagan held a harsh glare, picking up on every little detail of Duncan's face and demeanor. Something about the crust wedged in the corner of his eyes let her know he wasn't getting enough sleep. The wrinkled grey coat that was two sizes too big hung from his tall, thin, lanky frame. The yellow color of his teeth, unshaven beard, and dirty nails screamed the lack of detail to his hygiene and appearance of a man either going through a divorce or about to lose his job.

"When did she serve you papers?" Teagan questioned.

He looked her up and down, nose flared.

"What did you say?"

"I asked when did your wife serve you papers for a divorce?" Teagan repeated, not backing down. The guys sneaked behind her.

"My private life has nothing to do with this shitstorm of a team. Do you know how many times we've gotten calls about a corporation or unlawful detainment?" Duncan blurted out.

"Either we get the budget, or we don't. You have too much on your plate at the moment. The president will reach out when he needs us," Teagan replied, walking off and nodding for the guys to follow as she went around Duncan toward the front entrance and pushed it open.

"Agent Stone?" Duncan called out. Teagan stood face forward with her back to him. "Don't get too comfortable." Duncan left through the other side of the office. Teagan headed to the truck, opening the door as Spider came up beside her.

"You playing dirty now, Teagan?" Spider removed his vest and helmet and passed them to the cleanup detail of the facility, loading up the truck as the driver started the car. Gregory and Daughtrey followed.

"Spider, you know me better than anyone. Duncan is the one playing dirty."

"That doesn't mean we stoop to his level." Spider sighed, buckling his seatbelt.

"Are we going to eat? I'm still hungry from breakfast." Daughtrey stood at the second SUV, waiting to get in the driver's side. He hated being driven around like the rest of the team, even though Teagan constantly fussed about them getting more and more notices.

"Keeping my eyes open. Let's go so we can feed this big baby," Teagan kidded, smiling at Daughtrey. Until she learned something different, Duncan would be on her list of people who might become a problem.

"Did you get any more intelligence on Maksim?" Spider inquired, loosening the seatbelt over his chest and checking his messages. Teagan looked back at him through the rearview mirror, raising a brow.

"No, have any of your contacts turned up?" Teagan thought, tapping her fingers on her thigh. The last known contact after Maksim getting away after the shootout was months ago, and Russian intel dried up, so Teagan focused on other open cases of potential threats to the country.

"Soon as I get back to the office, I'll put in some calls." Spider stretched out with his arm on the back of the seat.

* * *

Seeing the stack of papers on the Petrov crime family, Teagan flipped through files and reports the FBI tried to keep hidden. Most of the details were blacked out in Sharpie or classified but pinpointing the death counts amassed with his family getting away made her heart pump faster.

"Bastard."

Maksim was last known in Russia, and not having any guidance from their government on turning him over would make the task of getting him stateside even worse. Grabbing her cup of iced latte from Starlights Cafe from the local café, Teagan sipped on her drink, staring at photos of Maksim talking with another man in front of a car.

"Where are you?"

Gritting her teeth, Teagan sat back in her seat, studying the photos for any hint that would give her something to go on. Her first case a year ago was Diablo, moving right into stopping an assassination attempt, to being accused of killing a reporter, and now handling a corrupt gun ring in New York. Taking her skills to the streets and talking with local gangs and police officers might benefit from getting Maksim in custody faster. His facial expression looked stark, determined, and ready for war. Knocking at her door, she turned in her seat. The door opened with Broderick progressing inside.

"Yeah."

"I think we've walked on eggshells, and I wanted to come to some agreement."

She motioned for him to take a seat in front of her desk.

"Speak." Teagan put the photos down on her desk.

"You probably have an idea about me being some corrupt asshole."

"Pretty much."

"Noted, but you have to understand after you left, they put me in charge."

"Are you telling me you didn't enjoy having the responsibility to call the shots?"

"I regret some choices and believe Stanton was one of them."

"He played everyone. Then sleeping with Leah caused me to look the other way." Broderick clasped his hands together in his lap. Broderick was clever and careful with his words. Teagan would keep watch on how Broderick moved forward but let him take on more responsibility unless he made another move on her family.

"We'll never be friends, Broderick. You broke that trust." Her phone ringing interrupted the conversation.

"Director Stone."

"Am I speaking with someone from The Firm?" a whisper-soft voice said over the phone.

Teagan's brow rose in confusion.

"You're on with Director Stone. How can I help you?"

Broderick stood to leave, but she waved him to stay and put the call on speakerphone.

"I can't talk long, or they'll know it's me," she responded.

"Who is this?" Teagan picked up her pen and paper to take notes.

"I know who's helping Maksim Petrov."

Broderick and Teagan's eyes locked in sync at the statement.

"What's your name?" Teagan questioned.

"Sorry, I can't tell you that," the voice whispered slowly.

"What can you tell me?"

"All I can say is he can't be trusted. My brother got into something stupid, and now I'm worried about him," the girl said.

"Who is your brother?" Teagan rose out of her seat, hovering over the phone.

"He doesn't understand that the money comes with loyalty to the Petrov family."

"Tell me your name," Teagan replied. Broderick crossed his arms over his chest. Her door opened again, and Spider walked in with Tony behind him.

"I need to go," she said, rushing off the phone. Teagan's eyes closed shut, her head lowered in frustration.

"Interrupting something?" Spider asked.

"You want me to trace the call?" Broderick inquired.

"Please and make sure you keep it under wraps until we know for sure who's behind this call. It could be a setup."

Broderick picked up her phone and called Gregory. For a second, Teagan estimated the person had to have known her schedule. Often, her lunch break would be right around this time. Broderick ended the call, holding a piece of paper.

"It's untraceable," Broderick said, and Teagan cursed under her breath.

Spider started to speak, and Teagan raised her hand, cutting him off.

"I just got a call from some woman who said she knows about the Maksim Petrov family."

"She didn't give a name." Spider's face wore a scowl.

Broderick shook his head.

"By the time Teagan tried to get them to give a name, they hung up, and we didn't have time to set up any tracing capabilities," Broderick said.

Teagan moved toward the stack of files and passed over half of what she was working on toward Spider. Until they called again, it'd be back to the simple task of reading and studying what they knew so far of Petrov and reports from her contacts in the city.

"Broderick set up a meeting with Malcolm Holmes of the Third Street gang," Teagan explained, writing something on a piece of paper.

"Are we ordering lunch in?" Spider questioned.

Teagan glanced at the clock on the wall. She had promised a family dinner tonight. Burying herself deep in work lately, she would make it up to them with pizza and a movie.

"I can't today. I promised the kids pizza and a movie." Teagan lifted her jacket off the coatrack and picked up her purse and some files to leave for the rest of the day.

"Should we expect you tomorrow?" Spider asked.

"You can handle one day in charge. Call me if you need me." Teagan patted him on the chest and strolled out of her office.

"Tony, let's go," Teagan called over her shoulder.

Chapter Two

An hour later, Teagan slid her key in the door of the quiet house and tossed her purse on the couch, releasing a breath over the long day. Heading to the kitchen to grab a bottle of water, she heard laughter coming from the backyard. The kids were playing with Christian on the swing set. Grabbing the cordless phone off the charger, she went out to the backyard and chuckled at Tatum, screaming at how high she was on the swing.

"Mommy." Cole ran toward Teagan and hugged her legs.

She lifted him up in her arms and kissed his cheek.

"How's my baby doing?"

"Good," Cole replied and kissed her cheek, and she put him down on his feet.

"You're home early," Christian observed.

"Yep, pizza and movie tonight." Teagan raised the cordless phone in the air. All the kids screamed in excitement.

"Who wants pepperoni and cheese pizza?" Teagan asked, dialing the local pizza shop.

"Me! Me!" Cole and Tatum jumped up and down.

Teagan leaned over to cup Tatum's chin and inhaled her baby girl's sweet vanilla scent from her hair shampoo. Christian stretched his arm around her neck when she stood and pulled her into his arms, kissing her behind her ear.

"How was your day?" Teagan tucked a piece of her hair behind her ear and followed the kids into the house. Christian shut and locked the back door, turning to Teagan.

"Mostly researching potential clients I could bring with me if I start my own company."

He released her from his hold and opened the fridge to grab a bottle of water.

"Do you want anything specific on your pizza?"

"Meat lovers and hot wings." Christian leaned against the counter. Tatum ran back into the kitchen, reaching her arms out for him to pick her up.

"Make it two large pizzas and hot wings."

"Mommy, can you do my hair tonight?" Tatum asked.

"Yes, baby. Just let Mommy finish her work first."

Heading back into the living room, CJ and Cole were searching through the stack of movies. Teagan was proud to see her family content and happy that she was home with them.

"The pizza will be here soon." Teagan sat on the couch with CJ laying in her lap, stroking his head.

"Mommy, are you a cop?" CJ questioned, eyeing her.

"No, why would you ask that?"

Cole turned on *Spiderman* and sat in front of the

coffee table next to Tatum. The doorbell rang, and he popped up, running to beat Christian to the door.

"Pizza!"

"You know better than to answer the door," Christian said, pulling his wallet out of his pocket. Taking the pizza from the driver, he let Cole handle the bag of hot wings.

"Set it on the table, and I'll grab some plates." Christian placed the pizza boxes down on the coffee table, ignoring the conversation between Teagan and CJ.

"Some of the kids at my school talked about seeing you in the news," CJ explained, rising from her lap and scooting close to the pizza.

"Ignore those kids. I have a job that's important and protects you."

"So, something like a cop?"

"Eat your pizza."

"Who's ready to eat?" Christian came back in with a gallon of lemonade.

"Don't get any grease on the table, you guys." Teagan helped to plate their food with equal slices of pizza and wings. The kids giggled as Teagan sat back on the couch, eating a piece of pizza. She cuddled up next to Christian again just as the house phone rang.

"I'll get it," Christian said, reaching around her and grabbing the phone off the end table.

"She's right here. Hold on," Christian's low voice hissed in annoyance as he passed her the phone.

"Who is it?"

"Work."

Teagan caught the hint of annoyance in Christian's response and rose off the couch, heading toward her office.

* * *

"Hello."

"Sorry to bug you, Teagan, but I thought you'd want to know what's happening," Gregory said. Teagan locked her office door once inside, taking a seat behind her desk. Turning her computer on, she logged into the database of The Firm.

"What do you have?"

"The call wasn't traceable, but we have other information from Malcolm," Gregory answered.

"How did that conversation go?"

"He wasn't on board at first, but after a little persuasion and threatening to lock his people up, he agreed," Gregory hinted.

"So, is he dealing with Maksim?"

"He told him he wasn't, but I don't fully trust him."

Teagan opened her desk drawer, removing the black binder with every contact with criminals she'd come across in her line of work. She wanted to check her files on Malcolm from the last time they'd spoken.

"Malcolm's still running illegal gambling rings." Teagan clicked on the photos of Malcolm talking with other men surrounded by women in skimpy lingerie. The images brought back memories of her time with Diablo in Spain. The amount of attention he poured on her that night made her heart swell in the thought that he was really in love with her and wanted a future, but she knew it was all make believe for a mission.

Gregory brought her out of her daze. "What are you thinking?"

"Make the call and get him to meet with me."

"In public?"

"At the park."

"Should I have Spider with you or—"

"Call Broderick."

"All right."

They hung up, and Teagan went through her updated emails from Spider about the budget numbers. She desperately wanted to hire more security and get training to add to the team for missions. In her vision, it would be best to have the top people recruited so she could officially step back and put someone else in charge. A knock at her door came, and she jumped up to open the door. Pushing the door wider, he stepped inside, passing her favorite lemon and honey tea toward her.

"What's this?"

Christian leaned against the corner of the desk, watching Teagan drink her tea and closing the space between them. Staring into her eyes, Christian lifted her chin and ran a hand down her arm.

"I knew you'd be up all night working. We haven't had a second to connect."

"How is everything going?"

"Busy."

"I know you're building your business. Do you think it's too much?"

"Not really; I have a few partners that I'm bringing on to invest."

"Does this mean we're going to have less time together? The kids are getting bigger."

"Maybe a family vacation should happen."

"CJ wants to go to the opening baseball game. Maybe we could do that first."

"He'd love that, and Tatum wants to go to Disney World."

Teagan placed the tea on the desk, reached up to hold the back of Christian's neck, and pressed a kiss on his lips.

"Let's go to bed."

"Reconnect." Christian tapped her on the nose.

"Mmmm... Big time."

* * *

Two days later, Teagan stepped out of the dark-tinted van holding a cup of tea in her hand, wearing her black shades. She approached Malcolm sitting on top of the park bench, smoking a cigar with his security surrounding him. Malcolm Holmes was thirty-eight years old, five-ten, dark-brown skin, bushy brow, thin nose, and muscular build. He was known in the city as the Godfather for helping local kids get into school and donating money to local businesses to keep them afloat. People didn't know he was the biggest ringleader over guns and gambling in the city. Crime was at an all-time high in New York, specifically Queens, and many times they'd arrested or buried people who had some affiliation with him.

"Mr. Holmes." Teagan lifted her shades to the top of her head.

He grinned, stepping off the bench and puffing on the cigar as he extended his hand.

"Teagan Stone."

"You know why I'm here."

"Gregory told me."

"So, are you going to help?"

They walked down the walkway toward the pond as the security followed them. The weather was cool and breezy with the sun streaming down. A few people were out playing, and mother groups exercised with their babies.

"You know Maksim and what he's capable of doing." Malcolm stopped moving and turned to face her with his hands in his pockets.

"We can protect you." Teagan sipped on her tea.

"How long have you been married?" Malcolm questioned.

"Stick to why we're here."

"The loyalty you have with your husband is the same thing I have with my team."

"Do you know why you're able to run around right now?" He scoffed and ran a hand down his face.

"Does that make you feel good to threaten me?" Malcolm stepped in closer to her face.

"If you're scared, say that." Malcolm laughed, clapping his hands.

"Agent Stone, we're done here."

"We're done when I say we're done. You will help us, Mr. Holmes."

"If I don't?"

The unfortunate thing about her job was to threaten people she felt weren't necessarily guilty, but she needed to show that she was in charge to get her point across.

"Teagan, everything all right?" She noticed the grimace across Malcolm's face when Broderick came up beside her.

"He's your backup?" Malcolm pointed at Broderick.

"Broderick is going to be your contact from now on. If Maksim so much as breathes, I want to know about it."

"What am I getting out of this?"

"Staying out of jail," Broderick said.

Malcolm's security tried to lunge at Broderick, but Malcolm held a hand up to stop them.

"Let me get this straight. You want me to help you capture a Russian terrorist and not care about my safety."

Even though he seemed confident in his words, she could tell Malcolm was scared shitless. Maksim was a more significant threat to him. He could wipe out his entire bloodline with one phone call.

"All we need is for you to tell us when he makes contact with you," Broderick replied.

Malcolm glanced over at the group of moms holding their kids and dumped his cigar on the ground, stomping the fire out.

"I'm not wearing a wire," Malcolm said.

"I want Broderick to be there with you, and he'll wear the wire. Assume he's one of your security guys," Teagan explained.

"He's going to know something's up if he was on my security detail. He looks like the police," Malcolm complained, throwing his hands up.

"Don't worry about what I'm wearing. Just let everyone know I'm your new guard," Broderick stated. The male ego between the two of them had Teagan shaking her head in disbelief. No matter what, men always wanted to be the top dog in any fight.

"Broderick will be fine. Keep us updated." Teagan extended her hand out for a handshake.

He nodded, reaching out his palm to seal the deal, and grunted at Broderick as he walked off. She peered at Malcolm and his team as the car drove away, finishing off her drink.

"Are you up for this?" Teagan studied Broderick. The small scar over his brow still stood out even after five years. Why couldn't she forgive and forget? They'd been at odds since she joined the team and believed all those years it was a true friendship, but the kidnapping of her family changed everything.

"Don't tell me you're scared for me." Broderick glanced over, joking. Teagan smirked and strolled to her awaiting security detail. She lifted one leg into the car, turned to her right side, and watched Broderick grinning as he walked backward toward his red Range Rover. They'd been enemies for the longest time. His irresistible grin kept women falling at his feet. Not Teagan Stone. Behind the mask was a man who only wanted things his way, and in time, this case would show what his next moves were.

Chapter Three

A *week later.*

Malcolm sat in a room with his team surrounding him as Broderick stood to the side with a wire on him, capturing everything they talked about. One of the conditions he made after leaving the meeting with Teagan was that any discussions beyond Maksim weren't used against him and his men. At first, Teagan wouldn't agree, but Malcolm was adamant about not letting Broderick in on anything if his people got arrested. They even agreed to allow deals to go down and not interfere unless Maksim was a part of everything.

"Who's this guy?" Ishmael, one of his lower-level dealers, motioned at Broderick.

Malcolm looked over his shoulder.

"This is Brody, one of my new security men."

"Is something going on?" Ishmael's brow dipped in concern.

"Nothing beside us moving in higher rank with some new clients." Malcolm moseyed around the table of men. They were all inside the backroom of Sammy's restaurant, a local cafe that Malcolm invested in when they went under. With the investment, he was allowed to use their back room anytime he wanted without argument. Now five of his top lieutenants sat waiting to get word on any updates. He cut his eyes toward Broderick, standing like a statue, not saying anything.

"How is the money looking on third and bankman?"

"I picked up a hundred thousand from Beans earlier today," Ishmael replied, lifting the bag off the floor and throwing it on the table.

"What about you, Ralph?" Malcolm said, checking the bag of money.

Ralph was older. He recently got out of prison for drug trafficking after five years and came out wanting to make money again to take care of his family.

"We brought up two hundred thousand. I need more of the Glocks," Ralph responded, passing over two duffel bags.

"Have Dorian load you up with some new pieces. I called you all here for a reason."

"What's up?" Ishmael called out.

"I got a phone call from Maksim Petrov." Malcolm tapped his finger on the table, peering a look at Broderick.

"Isn't he the Russian dude?" Ishmael said.

"He's interested in doing business together."

"How much is he paying?"

"He wants a cut on gambling and gun traffic." Everyone in the room grumbled, talking all over each other.

"We run the gambling, and we're not working for

some Russian family," Ishmael barked, jumping up out of his seat.

"For real, boss. We have the entire west and east on lock," Declan said. He was one of his lower soldiers who stayed on top of his gambling business.

"Exactly, why bring more noise on us and put the DEA on our asses for fucking with Russians?" Ishmael argued, pacing back and forth.

"Do you trust me?" Malcolm questioned the entire room, staring at each man he brought on throughout the years. The community of kids looked up to him, but the older men and women knew Malcolm wasn't any good, and he only continued to hurt the community with the influx of drugs, gambling, and guns.

Ralph cleared his throat.

"Who do we report to if he comes onboard?"

"Nothing changes. I'm still holding all the cards," Malcolm explained.

Ishmael nodded, leaning against the wall with his arms folded across his chest.

"Then let's make this money," Ishmael committed, eyeing Broderick closely.

* * *

Two hours after the meeting, Broderick sat in the front seat of Malcolm's limo as the driver rode through the streets, heading to a local mom and pop restaurant. Broderick continued looking out the window as the car turned down a familiar street.

"My men don't trust you."

"Your job is to get them to trust me," Broderick replied, expressionless and steadily looking forward.

Malcolm chuckled.

"This isn't a bad area; the Bronx is home. We take care of each other."

"Taking care means bringing guns and drugs around."

"Touché."

The driver stopped in front of Eloise's. Everyone knew this was the clear zone; nothing happened when you stepped through those doors out of respect for the couple and the family that built the restaurant over fifty years ago. Currently run by the grandchildren and close friend of Malcolm, Jersey Hanson, a woman who was interested in more than a one-night stand. Broderick and Malcolm stepped out of the car, with more security following behind as they marched inside, nodding at the hostess and knowing who they came to meet. Broderick held his hand out, halting Malcolm's steps.

"Remember we need Maksim to trust you."

"Obviously, I'm in this to make sure my people don't get harmed," Malcolm spat back, treading to the table of men sitting down.

"Keep it that way," Broderick reminded, following toward the crowd of security standing around the table. During the afternoon hour, they closed the place down for private conversations between mafia families.

"Mr. Holmes, finally we've set something up," Maksim's second lieutenant said.

"Where's Maksim?" Malcolm asked, staring at two men sitting with four bodyguards behind them; neither one looked like Maksim Petrov. It was eerily silent for a few minutes as all men wanted to come across as the top boss throughout the entire meeting, but Broderick studied each man and kept his shades on, while Gregory captured the camera footage back in the Agency.

"Maksim will make contact soon, but for now, we come with good news," Saveli said, giving Broderick a long look.

"Do I know you?" Saveli chucked his chin up at Broderick.

"He doesn't speak," Malcolm said.

"You have them trained well." Saveli grinned.

Broderick clenched his teeth in aggravation.

"I'm open to giving Maksim five percent of gambling business."

"We were thinking fifty," Saveli remarked, leaning back in the chair.

"That'll never happen." Malcolm started to rise out of his seat.

Saveli held his hand up, stopping him from leaving.

"Twenty percent?" Saveli asked.

"Five percent, and that's me being generous. Before we start, let's be clear. I run everything here. Won't get out of hand, Saveli." Malcolm leaned forward, peering into Saveli's eyes.

Saveli' held his hands up in surrender.

"No problem, that's what you Americans say, right?" Saveli clenched his hands, leaning forward on the table.

"As long as we understand where things stand."

"The guns?" Saveli inquired.

"What are your plans for the guns? I heard your boss has a lot of issues."

"What issues?"

Malcolm shrugged.

"His name is on the streets over some agent getting shot," Malcolm brought up.

"We've not heard of this before." Saveli curled his lip up.

"So you have no clue about the police looking for your family?"

"None, but we know how your name is always run around here."

"I can handle my business, but I'm not getting my people sucked into some international bullshit." Malcolm narrowed in frustration.

"I'll inform Maksim of your concerns, but we'd like to move forward."

Malcolm nodded.

"Set up a meeting with Maksim, and I'll see about agreeing." Malcolm stood straight up, never leaving the Petrov family to stew if they'd have to make an example out of Malcolm Holmes. All the men stalked back to the car, heading back to the warehouse to reconvene. Malcolm didn't ask any questions as they arrived back to their cars at the warehouse, and Broderick hurriedly jumped out. Watching as he got into his car, Malcolm was slightly impressed that Broderick wasn't trying to demand any more information from the meeting and let him lead.

* * *

Twenty minutes later, Broderick pulled up to the security garage in the back of the building, waiting to be approved for entrance. Something that had been playing over in his head made him think that Maksim was closer to them in the city, maybe even watching as they talked. Saveli kept his eyes focused on him rather than Malcolm, causing the hairs on the back of his neck to rise. He rubbed a hand down his face as the garage door opened, allowing him to park in the usual spot. Climbing out, Broderick nodded at another soldier coming out of the elevator. He stepped on and hit the floor for his team. The low music of jazz playing kept his mind clear and intent on what needed to happen.

"I need a life," Broderick mumbled to himself, stepping off the elevator a few minutes later.

Strolling down the hallway, Broderick appeared in front of Teagan's door and knocked.

"Come in!" she called out.

Pushing the door open, he was waved in to sit down as the TV played in the background on CNN.

"Any updates?" Teagan sat back, crossing her legs, tapping her middle and index fingers on the desk.

"I had a meeting with Saveli."

Teagan's eyes rose in surprise.

"What about Maksim?"

"My guess is he's either still out of the country or watching from a distance."

"You suspect he was there, not showing his face?"

"Yeah, it just felt off, and Saveli specifically asked if he knew me."

"What did Malcolm say?"

"He kept the conversation about the gambling fee and guns."

"Is he signing off?" Teagan wondered.

"Yeah, but hesitant on guns."

"We need him to be all in on this, Broderick. Remind him of our deal."

"I will, and I got the footage for Gregory."

"Good. I believe Maksim is coming hard, and we need to be prepared."

"I agree. Are you going to meet with the president tomorrow?"

"Yeah, and I'm not looking forward to dealing with Duncan." Teagan blew out a breath.

"When do you fly out?" Broderick questioned.

"Early morning."

"Try not to get in the news again." Broderick rose out of his seat.

"Depends on if someone pisses me off."

Chapter Four

The next day, Teagan sat in the black Lincoln town car passing by the monuments she grew up hearing about. Now in her position, she had a bigger role to uphold the vision and principles of America that no one had the guts to do every day. She went out on missions never knowing if her husband and children would think this was the last moment of saying goodbye.

Flashback.

Teagan was bent over the toilet, throwing up last night's dinner that her parents cooked at her coming home party. She was one year back from her last mission, and CJ was just getting in the habit of talking. Cole was still a baby that Christian was raising while she was away. A knock on the bathroom door came, and she sat with her eyes closed, wondering how she would tell Christian she was going back out soon, and she was pregnant. Being happily married came with struggles, and one was fighting enemies who didn't care if she had a husband and child. She put herself in certain situations Christian may not forgive or forget.

"Honey, it's me, Mom." Teagan crawled to the door and unlocked it, letting her mom come in and lock it behind her. Peering up, Teagan gave a brave smile.

"You have to go back."

Teagan nodded.

"Where?"

"I can't say."

"How long?"

"I don't know." Teagan adjusted to sit up against the counter.

"When you told me this was your plan of getting into the Navy, I was proud, but scared."

"Me too."

"You want to know what convinced me to be okay and not worry?"

"What?"

"You." She motioned at her.

"Me," Teagan said, surprised.

"Teagan, you're more of your father's temperament and presence, calm and focused. You never waver."

"I always feel like I struggle. I'm the only girl sometimes."

"Then take that thought and make it work for you. We all know what they think of women."

"So use it to my advantage?" she queried.

"Use it to guide you in life, not only missions, but your marriage and being a mother. Calm and focused," her mom reminded, running a hand down her cheek.

"Thanks."

"I'm excited for the new baby."

Teagan chuckled as her mom winked and left her to her thoughts.

Present.

"We're here, ma'am," Sean said, opening the passenger side door as Teagan got out wearing a long, black trench coat, covering a black Chanel pants suit and black heels with her hair hanging down in curls. Taking the same advice her mom told her years ago, she was calm and focused, knowing Duncan would try to rattle her.

"Thank you, Sean," Teagan said, grabbing her briefcase and purse out of the backseat.

Going through security, Teagan raised her arms up as the wand went across her shoulders, under her arms, down to the sides. She already had an appointment scheduled, and everyone knew who she was from all the media hype of her past arrest.

"Free to go," the security guard said.

"Thank you."

Teagan met up with the chief of staff standing a few feet away at Noah Anderson, an ally of The Firm, and keeping the president updated at all times. Some people came and went, but Noah was the most loyal when she needed something from the president.

"Teagan, thanks for coming," Noah said, holding his hand out for her to continue journeying.

"Thanks for setting this up."

"Well, the minute your budget gets approved, the president wants to stay in touch."

"Even though my face has been plastered all over the world?" she questioned.

"Yep." Noah chuckled with his boyish looks. Not

even hitting forty years old, he sat next to the most powerful man in the world. Noah's six-three with low cut, smooth black hair, wide shoulders, grey eyes, and full nose.

"Before we go inside, I have to tell you Duncan is here."

"I figured he'd make an appearance."

"The president wants to make sure things run smoothly."

"I have no plans of stooping to his level."

"Another thing is that afterwards, reporters will come in for photos."

"I didn't know we'd have a photo shoot today."

"The administration thought having you two together would signal all parties can work together."

"I'm not a politician, Noah."

"I agree, but you get more out of the situation and let Duncan fold under the pressure." Noah pushed the door open. Strolling in, Teagan saw the president and Duncan sitting as she smiled with her hand held out for a handshake.

"Mr. President." Teagan extended her palm, and he grasped it.

"Teagan, thank you for coming. I know it's been awhile," President Sanders remarked.

Teagan let out a low breath, turning toward Duncan as he stood to shake her hand.

"Duncan."

"Agent Stone." Duncan sat back on the individual chair as Teagan and Noah took a seat on the couch.

"I called this meeting because we need to align with the vision," President Sanders stated.

"Yes, sir."

"Did I not approve the budget?" Duncan remarked.

"As you did, it came with a little bit of a show," Teagan reminded him.

"Well, I need the American people to know where their tax money is going."

"Noah, do you want to talk?" President Sanders nudged him to dive into the conversation.

"As the president was saying, the current focus is on Maksim Petrov," Noah said. Teagan quickly looked at Duncan for any hints of him working with Maksim.

"Being on the national security committee, we've run across his file," Duncan called out.

Noah placed photos of Maksim on the table.

"What do we know so far?" Noah asked Teagan.

"He's planning something. What? I don't know. My team is working around the clock."

"If you don't have anything on him, why are we wasting money on a lost cause?" Duncan asked.

Teagan had a talent for knowing when bullshit was spraying out of someone's mouth, and Duncan was falling right into her hands.

"It's never a waste to protect American people."

"So, are we saying this man is planning an attack?" Duncan pointed at the photo of Maksim.

"I'm saying it's better to be over-cautious than under."

"Have you run across any information, Duncan, that tells us we shouldn't?" President Sanders questioned.

"Not much beside the usual."

"Really? We have a lot of information from the security council." Teagan opened her briefcase and pulled out a thick file on Maksim.

President Sanders watched as Duncan squirmed in his seat, loosening his tie.

"You must have gotten new information from the past few months. Or year."

"Must have," Teagan replied, opening the file and passing around text messages and phone call information around the room.

"These are travel dates and text messages he's been engaged in for the last few weeks," Teagan stated. Duncan's gaze never left hers as she grabbed more evidence.

"I think we need to stay on the investigation."

"We should be focused on what we know is harmful to our security, and that's China and Iran," Duncan huffed, tossing the papers back down on the table.

Teagan, Noah, and President Sanders all glanced at each other after his outburst.

"I have trust that Teagan and the team can multitask," President Sanders said.

"Don't say anything now, but it's on your shoulders following an end ride," Duncan said.

Teagan felt Duncan didn't have to be an asshole or make it seem like the work they were doing had been around for generations of presidents.

"Mr. President." Julie popped her head inside.

The president's secretary carried a piece of paper over to him to read.

"I need to take this call. Do you mind if we end our meeting early?" the president stated as he stood and extended his hand to Duncan, then to Teagan.

"I'll be here for another few hours, sir, if you need anything," Teagan said, bending down to grab the file folder with Maksim's information. Noah escorted her and Duncan out of the office. Duncan held his cell phone out, sending a text message, as Teagan watched from the side, listening to Noah explain the president's upcoming schedule.

"He's flying to Canada for two days," Noah replied.

"Huh."

"I said, the president will get to you once he's back from his visits," Noah explained. Teagan watched as Duncan's face furrowed in a harsh grimace. A few seconds went by, and he ran a sideways glance toward Teagan and Noah and hurriedly stomped away.

Noah shook his head as he continued to escort Teagan out of the White House.

"Someone's in a hurry," Noah muttered, pushing the door open on the west side as Sean stood.

"I agree with you." Teagan stared as Duncan's car pulled off soon as he entered.

"Well, I'll let you get back to your duties."

Teagan shook hands with Noah and nodded. Getting in the car, the door shut, and Sean walked around to the driver's side.

"Follow that car!"

"Yes, ma'am," Sean replied.

Teagan lifted her cell out of her purse, looking for Gregory's message thread.

Gregory: I have the video footage.

Teagan: I need you to trace something.

Sean pushed through traffic one car behind Duncan's limo.

Gregory: Who is it?

Teagan: Congressman Duncan... FN-456

Gregory: Typing it in now.

Driving through three lights, the car stopped finally in front of a coffee shop, and Duncan jumped out and rushed inside.

"Should I park, ma'am?"

"No, let's wait a minute."

Less than five minutes later, he came out with a coffee and a white package under his arm. Getting back in the car, they drove off again through main streets and arriving at the Capitol. Teagan held her cell phone up, taking pictures of Duncan hiking up the steps, drinking whatever he ordered, and holding on tight to the envelope.

Gregory: Registered to Duncan personally.

Teagan: He made another stop before heading to the Capitol.

Gregory: Was he meeting anyone?

Teagan: I don't know, but he left with an envelope.

Gregory: What's the address?

Teagan: Berry's Coffee and Bagel.

Gregory: I'll see if they have cameras and get back to you.

Teagan: Thanks, Gregory.

"We can go back to the hotel."

Closing out of the message thread, Sean left, driving at a fast speed when the whirling lights of the police came up behind them. Teagan looked through the back window, pursing her lips together, curious as to why they were getting pulled over.

"First time I've ever gotten a ticket," Sean called out.

He turned his signal light on and slowed to the right side out of Main Street.

"It shouldn't take too long," Teagan said.

A minute went by, then a knock on the window came, and a police officer leaned into the window.

"License and registration," the officer asked.

"Why was I stopped?" Sean asked.

Teagan stared at the officer as he continued talking

with Sean, holding onto her phone with the video low, filming him. Sean passed his license over.

"Speeding. What is your business in DC?" he questioned.

"What makes you think we don't live here?" Teagan brought up.

His eyes scanned to the backseat. She watched as the arrogant, cocky demeanor disappeared.

"Based on your speeding, and I'm asking the questions here."

"Of course."

"Do you have any drugs or anything I need to know?"

"No," Sean answered.

Listening to the bullshit come out of his mouth made it obvious that Duncan called in a favor.

"If we aren't getting a ticket, can we go now?" Teagan said.

She watched as his lip curled in disgust.

"Keep an eye on your speeding, and you're free to go," the officer stated, passing the license and registration back before turning back to his car.

"That was strange," Sean said.

"No, that was a warning," Teagan said, watching the police car speed by them as they headed to the hotel for the rest of the day.

* * *

A few hours later, Teagan was showered, sitting in her hotel bed on her laptop, eating the pasta she'd ordered from room service. With a Diet Coke on the nightstand, she stared at every angle of the video clip of Broderick's meeting with Malcolm and Maksim's people. Gregory sent everything as soon as he'd finished organizing and timestamping. Getting files on Saveli and Nail was just as hard on Maksim. These men had hands in high places and possibly the police force. That little stunt of getting pulled over to scare her caused a chuckle now. Earlier, it was a moment she didn't know if she'd have to throw her weight around and let him know that Duncan couldn't save him if he continued to pursue this fake speeding ticket.

The next file emailed to her contained still photos of Duncan heading into Berry's shop like a normal customer would and ordering a drink at the counter. He then went out of frame, more than likely to the bathrooms. Gregory didn't have a camera visual of that back area, so all Teagan could go with was the visual of him coming back into frame with something under his arm as he grabbed the drink from the counter.

"What are you hiding, Duncan?"

Ring

Ring

Taking her phone off the charger, she saw Christian's name pop up. Checking the time, she answered, "Hey."

"Did I catch you at a bad time?" Christian asked.

"No, just relaxing and going through some paperwork."

"The kids miss you and are ready for you to come home."

"I miss them and you."

"Did the meeting go well?" Christian always changed the subject when she got to talking about missing him. In his mind, he didn't understand why she took so many cases out of state. Being the director should come with letting other people handle those jobs.

"It did."

"What did you eat for dinner?"

"My favorite pasta and Italian bread," Teagan chortled, hearing Christian laughing on the other end of the phone.

"I won't hold you up any longer. I'll see you tomorrow," Christian said.

"Love you."

"Love you more," he responded, hanging up the phone.

Chapter Five

Three weeks later.

Sliding into the seat across from Spider, Teagan looked around the restaurant and lifted the chai latte to her lips to take a sip. Feeling the sweet nectar to her lips filled her mind and gave her a burst of energy. Since she came back to the city, she'd been home taking care of the kids and being a wife. Tatum was sick, and CJ had a few games, so she cut back on work and left Spider in charge unless it was an emergency. Now that Christian was full time as well, bringing in a nanny was an entire new job as they held interviews. Spider knew what her favorite drinks and food were just as much as Christian and made great conversations on missions.

"Thanks for ordering ahead for me," Teagan said.

The waitress walked over to their table, placing a veggie omelet, sausages, eggs, fruit, and a waffle down, along with ketchup and utensils.

"No problem. I figured you'd be ready to dive in at your favorite place."

"This is your favorite place. I just deal with the

outcome." Spider worked out and had a great physique but ate horribly, especially when it came to carbs. They'd argued many times on healthy eating. Teagan tried to get him to include more veggies, but it never worked.

"How's the family doing?" Spider questioned.

"Family is good. Christian is great."

"Did you guys find a nanny yet?" Spider poured ketchup on his hash browns.

"Not yet. Tatum just got over a cold."

"Did you give her the doll I got?"

"Yes, and she's more than spoiled thanks to you."

"My pleasure."

"Anyway, tell me how Broderick is doing?" Teagan questioned.

"They had a few gambling nights, and he's gotten footage."

Teagan cut into her omelet and took a bite, closing her eyes and moaning over the spices mixed together. Letting the steam from her tea simmer, she lifted it up and blew over the top.

"Did Gregory go through the footage?"

Spider nodded in answer. "He's still going through everything and checking over the guests in attendance."

"Has Malcolm said anything?"

"No, we keep our end of the bargain, and he'll be fine."

"You think we can bring him down?"

"Congressman Duncan? Yeah, he's going to fuck up, and we'll catch him."

Teagan leaned on the table with her hand on her head.

"Maksim is here in New York. I can feel it in my blood."

"He can't run too far without us finding out," Spider answered.

An hour into their conversation, the waitress checked in and refilled their drinks.

"Anything else I can get for you two?" Stephanie smiled, picking up the empty plates and leaving the check.

"No, everything was fine." Teagan laid her knife and fork down, wiping her mouth clean. She peered down at her phone ringing, with Gregory's name showing. She picked it up as they stood from their booth.

"Hello," Teagan said.

Spider gestured for her to walk ahead, leaving to go back to the office.

"Teagan, I wanted to update you on what I found," Gregory mentioned. Teagan headed to her security detail as Spider hopped into his car.

"Please let it be good news."

"I have Duncan's offshore account unlocked," Gregory said.

"On my way," Teagan replied, ending the call.

Thirty minutes later, Teagan and Spider walked into the conference room as Gregory and Daughtrey sat around talking. Teagan removed her jacket, placing it on the back of her chair, and sat at the head of the table.

"Let's hear the news."

Gregory held his laptop in front of him, turning it around to show Teagan and Spider.

"Joshua Kline."

"Who is this?" Spider asked.

"Remember that phone call Teagan got a few weeks ago that I couldn't trace?"

Teagan and Spider nodded. "Based on Duncan's

phone records, I was able to figure out who he's been communicating with."

"Does it lead back to this guy?" Spider queried, holding a picture of Joshua from social media.

"Any criminal records?"

"Nothing so far. I just was able to start researching before I called you."

Daughtrey tossed a crumbled paper in a ball up in the air.

"What are you thinking, Teagan?" Daughtrey wondered.

Teagan pushed the photo back, crossing her arms over her chest.

"What's the motive for Joshua and Duncan to work together?"

"Money," everyone answered at the same time.

"We can't bring this to Duncan without backup; he might go into hiding."

"The president needs to know about this update," Spider said, picking up the photo.

"I'm not so sure. We still have Maksim missing."

"I agree. Why bring down one when we can catch all the players?" Daughtrey glanced over at them.

"Malcolm and Broderick are still working at Maksim. I need to get as much evidence as possible."

"Am I the only one who's thinking of a potential attack? We knew ahead of time and did nothing," Spider fussed.

"Look, the second I bring this up, and it leaks to the press, all of our jobs are on the line," Teagan responded, motioning to the photo.

"So, we just sit and wait!" Spider threw his hands in the air, exasperated.

"That's my final decision, whether you agree or not." Teagan arched her brow at Spider.

"When are we checking in with Broderick?" Daughtrey asked.

"He should be getting us updates by tomorrow." Teagan checked her watch and stood.

Spider sighed and ran a hand down his face in frustration.

"I have CJ's football game this weekend. Spider, follow up with Gregory. We don't move on Joshua yet. Daughtrey, check in with Broderick. Keep me updated," Teagan said, leaving for the evening.

"You think she's making the wrong decision?" Daughtrey questioned.

"What if they get a hold of a bomb and something happens?" Spider whistled.

"Teagan hasn't been wrong since she came back," Gregory admitted, scratching the back of his neck.

"Let's hope she continues with that streak," Spider muttered as he pushed the door open and left for his office.

* * *

Across town later that night, Broderick stood on the main floor of Malcolm's business that he used for a gambling ring, watching for any sign of Maksim Petrov. What he didn't know was that Maksim had eyes on what was happening while he was at the warehouse meeting to finalize his plans. Soon as the money dropped into Malcolm's account, he allowed some of his property to be used, even though he kept this from Broderick and Teagan. He felt it was best to limit the amount of interaction of Maksim coming and going at his main location of funneling money.

The cigar smoke filled the room, and each person sat in unison, waiting on their boss to speak. They knew when orders were given out, they would obey without hesitation. That concept was lost on Duncan Brooks when he received a text message that since police and FBI were sniffing around, the final deposit wouldn't arrive. Maksim planned each moment to perfection. To his surprise, Duncan demanded a meeting with him.

"Speak," Maksim stated, blowing smoke in Duncan's face. A round table at Malcolm's warehouse was used at the last minute; it was in a neutral place that looked like a normal business on the outside. As Congressman, he was running on thin ice, not only in his party with getting certain bills passed, but he was also dealing with a divorce and a pill problem. He only wanted to get his five million and leave the country.

"Maksim, we both agreed that my part in this was limited," Duncan spat, rubbing his temple.

Maksim grinned, placing the cigar in the ashtray. "Mr. Congressman, have I not paid you well?" Maksim cracked his knuckles.

"You've only paid me half," Duncan answered.

"Nail, bring Mr. Congressman a drink. He's looking thirsty."

"I'm fine. I don't need anything."

"Are you refusing to drink with me? Am I not good enough for the big congressman?" Maksim joked, his men laughing along with him.

Nail leaned over the conference table, taking the glass of cognac, and poured a shot for each man. Standing, he passed the drink over to Maksim, then Duncan. Lifting it to his lips, Maksim stared into Duncan's eyes as he gulped the drink down.

"Ahhh... refreshing," Maksim said, grabbing the cigar again.

"Again, I wanted to meet because I need my other half," Duncan pleaded.

"What money?" Maksim snorted.

"I put my life on the line for you," Duncan hissed, pointing his finger at Maksim.

"Mr. Brooks, I think it's best you understand who you're speaking with."

Maksim stood from his seat, sliding his hands in his pockets, and walked over to the mirror hanging on the wall. He looked over his shoulder, winked at Duncan, and turned the switch on the wall. The window turned into a TV monitor with Duncan's soon to be ex-wife on the screen. She was standing in the kitchen, cooking.

Duncan spat out his drink, trying to jump up, but Nail held him down by the shoulders, placing a knife under his neck.

"Please, she has nothing to do with this," Duncan argued.

"You think so?"

Maksim chucked his head to the left for Nail to let Duncan go.

"Okay, I get the message," Duncan said.

"Once Joshua completes what I need, then you might get your money," Maksim told him.

"What about Teagan Stone?"

"That's your problem."

"She's onto you. I don't know how, but she has the backing of the president."

"I suggest you handle her or else she will handle you."

"Maksim."

Maksim lifted his index finger to stop him.

"You should have known things wouldn't work out for you."

Duncan rushed out of the warehouse, scrambling for his cell phone out of his pocket. Feeling like he may have bitten off more than he could handle, he dialed his wife, even though they were no longer together.

The phone rang three times with no answer.

"Pick up, goddamn it!" he growled, rubbing the back of his head. He ended the call and dialed again.

"You have reached my voicemail," Cheryl's voice recording stated.

"Fuck!" Duncan shouted, tucking the phone back in his pocket before removing his keys. He stalked to his car. Stepping off the curb, he slid the key into the door but when he heard footsteps behind him, he stuck his hand in his pocket, pretending it was a gun.

"Don't move!" he yelled.

"Congressman, it's me," Sandra spoke.

Duncan looked startled but slowly relaxed once he recognized her from TV.

"Sandra Gregg from GHS News."

"I was hoping to speak with you."

"At this time of night, eight thirty?"

"The story never sleeps," Sandra replied cockily.

"Sorry, I don't talk to reporters."

"You sure about that?" She cocked her head to the side.

"Whatever you think you know, I'll have my attorneys bury it by the morning."

"I never said I had anything, sir."

"Let it stay that way." Duncan started to slide into his car.

"The story could be me seeing suspicious activity at a warehouse."

Duncan removed his keys, jumping back out of the car.

"Are you crazy! Do you know who owns this building?" Duncan pointed.

"I do. Malcolm Holmes, a local gun and illegal gambling ringleader."

"Exactly, so tread very carefully, Miss Gregg."

"I will, and I'd say the same for you," Sandra said, walking away as Duncan got in his car again and drove off. Sandra headed to the back corner of the building where she left her car. She removed the tape recorder and pressed rewind. Listening to the playback, she smiled at possibly breaking a story with the local congressman and drug dealer. As she did this, Maksim watched from above the warehouse and smirked at more rats interfering in his game. The idea of bringing more destruction in the country gave him an excitement he loved to chase.

Chapter Six

Malcolm walked around his establishment as loud grumbles and excitement whirled around from customers winning and losing. He'd set this illegal casino to hold deals on the side with his gun business, starting out small with a few men in attendance until it grew from word of mouth. Now, criminals from all over the world showed up just to see what he offered for entertainment. A few of his men came tonight to relax and party with the strippers. Mr. Holmes stayed clean from any alcohol so he could stay focused and alert. He'd just gotten a text message that Maksim ended his meeting and left the warehouse, so he could chill slightly. He walked toward his office with Broderick, and two more bodyguards followed behind. Unlocking the door with his key, he stepped around his desk, removing his jacket and unbuttoning his shirt. Picking the phone up off the desk, he dialed to the girls' room he had built.

"This is Bambi," she said, making him grow harder in his pants. Over the past few weeks, he hadn't spent any time with her, and he knew she'd be pissed, so he tried to ease into the conversation.

"Come to my office."

"I'm busy," she answered.

"I didn't ask what you were doing."

"Malcolm," she mumbled.

"Please come to my office. I have a surprise," Malcolm responded, ending the call.

Tonya Johnson, better known as Bambi, was twenty-five years old, slim, mahogany-brown skin, five-five, full lips, high cheekbones, and a smile that lit up a room and caused every man to give her anything she desired. Currently in college to be a nurse and working part time for Malcolm as a stripper, she never expected to fall for her boss, but one night they were working late, and he offered to give her a ride home. Ever since then, she'd been his only companion. Hearing a knock on the door, he pressed the button underneath his desk, and she walked inside wearing a robe and high heels.

"Yes, you summoned me," Bambi spat, crossing her arms over her chest.

"I missed you."

"Malcolm."

"All right, come here." He reached out for her hand, and she rolled her eyes and came around his desk, allowing him to pull her onto his lap. Wrapping his arm around her waist, he squeezed her close and kissed the top of her shoulder.

"How are you?" he asked.

"Fine."

"How's school?"

"Fine."

"Really, Tonya?"

She tried to get up from his lap, but he tightened his hold.

"What do you want from me?" she questioned.

"I apologize for not staying in touch; I've been busy," Malcolm begged.

"No, you've ignored me."

Malcolm ran a hand up and down her arm.

"Work has been crazy."

"Are you still doing the deal with that Russian guy?" Bambi asked.

"I can't talk about that."

"You can't or won't?" she fussed.

"It's complicated."

"Do you know who this man is? The things he's done."

"I never said I was a saint, baby."

"You lie down with dogs, you end up getting fleas."

"I'm working with the government," Malcolm muttered.

She turned her body to sit sideways in his lap.

"What did you say?"

"Just know that I'm being protected."

"Okay." Bambi caressed his cheek.

"Okay what?"

"I'll leave it alone for now, but I refuse to put my life on the line," Bambi informed him.

Malcolm gripped the back of her neck and met her halfway for a kiss.

"Are you hungry?" Malcolm inquired, running his lips down her cheek toward the back of her neck.

"Yeah, I didn't eat much during class."

"Well, let me order you something."

"You're not working the floor tonight?"

Malcolm shook his head no.

"I have enough men. I can stay back for now."

"So, I have you all to myself tonight."

Bambi rubbed up and down his chest.

"Anything in particular you want to do?" Malcolm placed the phone back down as Bambi giggled.

"I can think of a few things." Bambi chuckled when Malcolm lifted her off his lap, planting her on top of the desk.

* * *

The weekend arrived, and Abby Kline tried once again to call and check up on her brother Joshua. The kids were in the backyard playing around as she sat with her computer, reviewing news articles and information on Maksim Petrov. After living that vague phone call with Dr. Stone, she wanted to potentially go to the police, but she was scared of what could happen to her family if it ever got out that she'd gone snooping around.

"Mommy, come play," her daughter announced, running up on her holding a doll in her hands.

"Okay, baby. Give me one minute." Abby listened as the voice message continued. She sighed, closing her eyes and feeling defeated.

"Hey, babe." Her husband bent down and kissed the back of her neck. She quickly closed her computer.

"Are you all right? Did I scare you or something?" He sat on the opposite end of the table, picking his daughter up in his lap.

"Huh?"

"What's going on? You seem distracted," Courtland wondered.

"No, I'm fine."

"Is it Josh? Babe, he's an adult," her husband stated, not knowing what was really going on with the family.

"How was work this week?" Abby changed the subject.

"Work was work. Same thing as always."

"Did you make the sale?"

He nodded in answer.

"Great, so you're home for a week, right?"

He brushed the top of his daughter's head with his palm. "No, I have to fly out in two days."

Abby stood, grabbing her daughter from her husband's lap and walking toward the swing set.

"Abby... Abby, let's not fight."

She quickly pivoted around.

"No, you're never home anymore. I feel—" She stopped, realizing she was still holding her daughter in her arms.

"Baby, go play with your brother," Abby said.

"Once this trip is done, I'll take a vacation." He closed the gap between them, wrapping his arms around her waist.

"You say that every time."

"How do you think we live in this big house and send our kids to private school?"

"Here you go with throwing your money in my face." Abby pushed him back, stomping back to the porch.

"Would you stop acting like a child!" Courtland shouted.

"Mommy! Daddy! Stop fighting!" their daughter screamed.

Abby wiped her face clear of tears and turned around, smiling.

"Honey, everything is fine. Daddy and I are just talking," Abby explained.

"Yeah, sweetheart. Keep swinging, and I'll be over there soon," he said.

"See what you made me do!" Abby hissed slowly.

"If you stop all this nonsense with your brother," Courtland argued.

She cut him off with her hand up.

"Don't talk about my brother. This has everything to do with you constantly working."

Throwing his hands in the air, he blew out an aggravated breath.

"All I'm trying to do is provide for my family, Abby."

"Which I get, but you're away more than you used to be in the beginning."

"Because as the top sales rep, they need me more."

"Whatever."

"How about we have a nice dinner tonight and send the kids to my brother's house?"

"I guess."

He pecked her lips.

"Great, I'll give him a call and make the reservations. You get the kids packed."

* * *

Sandra Gregg shut her computer down and grabbed her purse and keys. The only time she worked the weekends was during a big case, and she wanted to do more research on the warehouse Duncan was at the other night. Waving goodbye to her coworkers, she left the GHS news station. In the employee parking lot, Sandra tossed her things inside her car and slid the key into the ignition, turning on her favorite country station to the sound of Garth Brooks. She swayed her head to the music, mumbling the lyrics slowly as she pulled into traffic. This was her big breakout moment and if Maksim were brought down with her name on the article, her dream of being on the major network morning shows would catapult her to stardom. The sweltering heat in New York, and an increase in traffic, made her slow down, opening the top button of her shirt and fanning herself. Lifting her shades, she looked out the windows at the cars next to her, playing loud music. The two young men, with short, black hair, grey eyes, and olive skin tone, sitting in the BMW, looked younger than she'd date, but they were cute. One looked over at her with an evil grin on his face, pretending his finger was a gun. The car drove off before they could hear her statement.

"Asshole!" she yelled, throwing up the middle finger.

Hearing a car honking behind her, she turned into the right lane and drove on, shaking her head at the idiot drivers. Continuing on her journey, she came upon another traffic buildup five minutes later and cursed under her breath for going the long way home today. Noticing no cars moving, she looked left to right in her side mirror and saw the same car from earlier two cars behind. The passenger stared right back toward her car. Not paying too much attention, she checked the time and saw after three cars passed the four-way light on Avenue and Broadway was out.

"Just my luck." She sucked her teeth.

Letting one car go from the left, she waited, then took her turn. As she almost passed, another car drove through on the right side, almost hitting her car if she didn't speed up.

"Oh my God!" She tried getting a better handle on the steering wheel and pulled off to the side, placing her car in park and closing her eyes as her heart beat rapidly. For a split second, she opened her eyes again, seeing the BMW pass her with the passenger blowing her a kiss.

Chapter Seven

Saturday

The sun beamed down on the football field as CJ ran after his opponent while Teagan, Tatum, and Cole screamed and cheered at him. While her mind was still very much on finding Maksim and getting Duncan arrested, Teagan had to carve out of her schedule moments of being a mom, going to football games, and wearing shirts with their school mascots on the back. Tatum wore a cheerleading outfit to feel like one of the girls out on the field. Christian meanwhile slept in since he worked overtime, so she packed a cooler with snacks and tablets to keep them preoccupied on the ride over.

"Yay! Let's go, CJ!" Teagan yelled out.

Teagan helped Tatum with her bottled water and picked one up for herself. Taking her phone out of her purse, she scrolled her messages and emails for any updates.

"Mommy, can we have pizza tonight?" Cole asked.

"Not tonight, baby. I have to cook. You've had pizza already this week."

"How about tacos?" Cole counteroffered.

Teagan laughed, shaking her head.

"Another time, Cole."

"How much longer, Mommy? I want to go shopping," Tatum said.

"Baby, not much longer. Look at your brother." Teagan motioned, putting her phone back in her pocket.

"He has the ball. Go CJ!" Tatum jumped up and down, spilling her water.

The referee blew the whistle, and everyone ran to their team sections to regroup. CJ walked over to his mom, removing his helmet.

"Good job, baby." Teagan kissed the side of his cheek, wiping it off right after knowing he hated when she embarrassed him.

"Thanks, Mom. Can I go over to Kenny's house after this is over?" CJ asked, holding his hands together in prayer. Teagan hated being the bad guy, but after finding out one of her close friends was an enemy, she kept her kids from being around other families. She didn't mind the children coming to her house, but in her line of work, she couldn't trust anyone.

"Kenny can come to our house, but no more sleep-overs, baby."

CJ nodded in agreement.

"Great, let me head back out, and I'll tell him." CJ placed his helmet back on and ran to the field.

Feeling vibration, Teagan reached in her pocket and took out her phone, seeing a message from Broderick.

Teagan: I'm free.

Broderick: We got the word Maksim is here.

Teagan: How do you know?

Broderick: He contacted Duncan.

Teagan: What did Malcolm say?

Broderick: He pulled the footage from inside the warehouse.

Teagan closed the messages and dialed Broderick's number, stepping a few feet away from the kids sitting on the benches.

"Who was in the room?"

"Duncan, Maksim, Saveli, and more of his men."

"Malcolm wasn't there?"

"No, and I was pissed."

"How did that happen?"

"He had all his men at the casino."

"So he happened to just give you the footage?"

"I heard him talking with one of the strippers he's dating."

Teagan continued to stare at her kids watching the game.

"Did he say why we weren't informed about this meeting?"

"Some vague answer about running things his way."

"Bring him to the office." Teagan ended the call, walking back over to her children.

"Mommy, we won! We won!" Tatum screamed up and down.

"I see, baby. Let's grab our things so we can be ready to leave. Mommy has to make a stop before we go home," Teagan said, hating that she had to bring her kids to work, but this was time sensitive. Letting Malcolm feel like he was in charge would no longer work for her. Packing up their items, the crowd dispersed as the team enjoyed winning another game for their school. CJ ran over with Kenny behind him and his parents.

"Kenny told us you okayed for him to hang out with CJ this afternoon," Kenny's mom said.

"Yes, if you're okay with that. I can give you my phone number and my husband's," Teagan said, walking to her car.

Stacy took her phone from her purse and listened to Teagan rattle off her number.

"Kenny, be good for Mrs. Hawkins." Stacy took some of his equipment from his hands.

"I will, Mom," Kenny answered. Teagan opened the backseat and walked to the trunk to put the rest of the bags and the cooler inside.

Helping Tatum and Cole in their seats, she closed the door and hopped into the driver's side. Teagan turned the music up in the car, keeping the kids preoccupied as she sent a message to Christian on her phone.

Teagan: Babe, I need you to come get the kids.

Christian: What's going on? How's the game?

Teagan: They won, but I need to head to the office.

Christian: Teagan, really? It's Saturday.

Teagan: I know, but it's closer to my office.

Christian: You know how I feel about having them near that place.

Teagan: I'm going to have security watch them.

Christian: I'm on my way.

Teagan: Sorry.

Making it to her destination, she pulled up to the entrance, and security checked her ID before the guard gate opened.

"Mommy, where are we?" Tatum questioned.

"I needed to get something from the office, baby."

"Ooh, can I see your office?" Tatum asked.

"Not this time." Getting the green light to come

inside, she pulled forward, turning into her reserved spot. Releasing a long-held breath, she looked at the kids through the rearview mirror as they admired all the cars, vans, and military trucks.

"Mom," CJ called out.

"Honey, I need you guys to stay here with my friend Sean."

Teagan finished texting Sean to come downstairs and placed the phone in her pocket. A few seconds later, Sean came around the corner of the elevator and met her behind the car.

"Are they up there?" she asked.

"Yes, ma'am."

"Good, watch my kids. I called Christian, and he's pissed."

"Do you want me to drive them home?" Sean asked.

Biting her bottom lip, she thought about it. Christian would probably be more aggravated if he dropped them off.

"No, they're fine waiting for him. Here are the keys."

"Do they need food?" Sean questioned.

"They're not dogs, Sean. They can tell you what they need." She walked off as he smirked at her statement.

* * *

Rolling up her sleeves, Teagan strolled off to the elevator, focused on the target in her office. Sliding her key inside, she pushed the door open, glancing around the room. Broderick, Malcolm, and Spider were waiting quietly.

"Who do you think you are?" Teagan demanded, slamming her door, marching toward Malcolm, who sat in the chair in front of her desk. Spider and Broderick stood on either side of him.

"I made a mistake," Malcolm admitted.

"You made a mistake." Teagan tapped the side of her forehead.

"It won't happen again."

"Do you think we're a joke?" Teagan sat on the corner of her desk with her arms crossed.

"Listen, it won't happen again. I miscalculated," Malcolm said, looking forward at the wall of pictures.

"Mr. Holmes, this business, as you know, can be dangerous."

"What if we put a tail on him for twenty-four hours?" Broderick suggested, glaring at Malcolm.

"That won't be necessary," Malcolm responded.

Teagan shook her head, slamming her hand on the desk, eyes burning with irritation.

"You don't get to tell me or my team what is necessary."

Malcolm cleared his throat.

"How is Bambi doing?"

Malcolm's eyes rose in surprise.

"Leave her out of this," Malcolm responded.

"We got your attention now."

"He'll start a war if he finds out what I've done," Malcolm shouted.

"You won't even live long enough to see a war if you keep playing me." Teagan rose from the desk, walking around to her chair. She closed and opened her eyes a few minutes later in thought.

"Go forward with anything having to do with business, my people will know," Teagan rattled off. Malcolm interrupted, and she arched a brow.

"I want Maksim Petrov, but I'll take you down for shits and giggles if you try me again," Teagan explained, chucking her head toward the door for him to leave. Broderick left with him while Spider stayed behind.

"Think it'll work?" Spider asked.

"At this point, we have no choice."

"How was the football game?" Spider questioned, and Teagan tensed.

"Fuck!" She remembered the kids being downstairs with Sean. Grabbing her phone quickly, she dialed Christian's number.

"What's wrong?" Spider asked, following her out of the office.

"I forgot the kids downstairs." Teagan ran toward the stairs, not waiting for the elevator.

She made it to the garage, and her van was gone. Sean was talking with a coworker.

"Sean, where's the kids?" she asked.

"Your husband picked them up," Sean remarked.

Teagan relaxed, releasing a breath.

"Did he say anything?"

"Not really, just that he'll see you at home," Sean told him.

"You've never brought the kids here," Spider said.

"I know."

"I'll stay here and monitor for any updates."

"Are you sure?" Teagan replied.

Spider nodded.

"Go, you need to take a vacation anyway."

"That's been for a while. Let me get out of here," Teagan said.

Sean went over to the Lincoln town car they normally used to drive her around, opening the back passenger door. Teagan slid in and shut the door, placing her seat-belt on and trying to call Christian one more time.

* * *

Thirty minutes later, Teagan waved good night to Sean as he pulled off, sliding the key into the front door of a dark, quiet house. Shutting and locking the door, she removed her jacket and kicked off her shoes.

Walking over to CJ's room, she peeked in and saw him sleeping under the covers. She headed to Tatum and Cole's rooms. Everyone was tucked in tight as she regretted missing another night with her kids. Slowly twisting the knob of her bedroom door, she pushed it open and strolled in quietly to find Christian sitting up watching a game on TV.

"You're still up?" Teagan said.

"Yeah."

Teagan went to sit on the edge of the bed, running a hand across Christian's leg in his shorts.

"When?" Christian turned the game off, placing the remote on the corner table.

"What do you mean?"

"When is it enough? Putting my kids in harm's way may not mean anything."

"Don't go there."

"No, let's go there." Christian jumped up out of bed.

"It's my job, Christian."

"No, it's your life, and I'm tired of the bullshit."

"Baby."

"There you go trying to be manipulative."

"Really, Christian, manipulative?" Teagan rolled her

eyes and walked toward her dresser to grab her nightgown before heading to the bathroom.

"Yes, manipulative and acting like this is normal."

"I'm not in the mood to fight. It's been a long day." She picked up the toothbrush and paste, preparing for bed.

"Who are you? I don't recognize my wife and friend anymore," Christian argued.

Teagan looked at him through the mirror for a few seconds before placing the brush and paste back on the counter. She turned around and wrapped her arms around his neck.

"I promise to do better. This family is more important than anything else," Teagan pleaded.

Christian grasped her around the waist, pressing a kiss to her lips.

"I love you, Teagan."

"I love you more."

Chapter Eight

Closing the door of his Honda, Joshua fixed his work shirt, rubbing down the wrinkles. He followed two employees of the bank who held the door open for him. Trying to flirt, he slightly pinched her on the side of her waist.

"Not here, Joshua." Amy shook her finger at him.

"No one knows," Joshua said, going to the bank manager's office to work on a virus that corrupted his data. At twenty-four, Joshua was no taller than five-eight, slim, with a small belly, and well-trimmed blond hair. He wasn't the best-looking man, but he could get a girl to go out with him on a date, but never anything long term. He knocked on the door of Dave Grace, the branch manager, who waved him to enter. Joshua stood off to the side as Dave continued on the phone.

"I have the tech guy here now," Dave said, tapping a pen on the desk. Joshua scanned the room, remembering this was the second time he'd had to fix the branch manager's computer. Separate from the other employees, he predicted he was watching too much porn, and it finally died out on him.

"Let me call you back. Okay.... yeah." Dave hung up, walked around the desk, and extended a hand to Joshua.

"Sorry for making another trip out," Dave said.

"No problem. They pay me anyway," Joshua joked, placing his equipment on top of the desk.

"Well, I'll let you work. If you need anything, just call for me," Dave told Joshua, leaving his office.

Shutting the door, Joshua waited a few moments to see if anyone would walk back into the room. Checking his watch, he turned to sit down at the desk and plugged in his device monitor to see what was happening. Figuring out a reset would help, he hurriedly set in the information to the computer to mirror his own. While he waited, Joshua went through all the drawers and cabinets, checking one more time through the office window to see Dave talking with another employee across the room. The screen popped back on, Joshua typed in a code, and files popped up of accounts and addresses of customers. Whistling to himself on a good job, he copied as much information as he could and removed the device right when Dave came back to check on everything.

"Is she still working?" Dave questioned.

"All set, sir." Joshua rose, grabbing his equipment, passing a form for Dave to sign off that he completed the work.

* * *

Placing the meat lover's pizza down on the table, Joshua locked his door, walking into the kitchen of the one-bedroom apartment. Grabbing a beer from the fridge, Joshua let the music blast in his ear from his favorite band. Joshua felt good about himself at scoring a big-time money-making job. He wasn't worried about getting caught or hearing how his parents disowned him since he refused to live the way they wanted him to live. The only person he kept up with was his sister because Abby refused to be ignored whenever she came to visit. At thirty-two, Abby was older than Joshua by a few years. Growing up, their parents always instilled college and having a family which was the path she went down. Joshua was extremely intelligent and charming but lacked in social skills.

Working as a computer specialist at Tech Hines, the company had accounts with all the major businesses in the city. Being freelance was the perfect role in his eyes because he loved having enough time to hack into computers around the world and play video games, which could bring in vast amounts of money. Abby tried calling him a few times, but he never answered. He said to himself that he'd call her back later in the week. She loved being a mom; leaving the workforce and staying home was the ideal life for her since Courtland worked as a pharmacy sales representative and traveled most days.

By accident one day, she watched the news, and a picture of Maksim Petrov strolled across. She remembered going to visit Joshua at his condo and seeing a group of men walking out toward a limo. At that moment, she had no other choice but to call anonymously to try to save her brother's life. Abby didn't want him mixed up in something that would hurt her family's name.

Joshua finished off another slice of pizza, wiping his hands on his shirt. Scattered on the floor in front of him were blueprints and information for Yankee Stadium.

Maksim connected with him after seeing he was losing money gambling at Malcolm's casinos. Hearing him brag on how he was efficient in building things and computer hacking, Maksim had his men keep an eye on him for a few days before setting up a meeting and letting him know his debt was paid off. Now, Joshua and Duncan were under Maksim's hold, and he'd never let go unless it was through death.

Knock

Knock

Knock

Joshua lifted his head and checked the time on his watch. Rising up, he strolled to the door and looked through the peephole.

"Right on time," he muttered to himself, unlocking the door and pulling it open to Maksim, Saveli, and Nail. All three men, along with bodyguards, treaded into the living room. Joshua shut his door quickly, rushing to pick up his leftover clothes from last night and tossing them into his closet, reminding himself to get laundry done.

"Have a seat," Joshua said.

"I'll stand," Maksim spoke.

"Sure... uhm... okay."

"You have what we need?" Saveli questioned.

Nail stood, texting on his phone.

"Yeah, it's in my bedroom. Give me a second." Joshua walked down the hallway toward his bedroom. Not waiting for him to come back, Maksim nodded for his men to follow him. Everything was riding on his plans following through. After the American agent almost captured him and destroyed his plans, he needed to regroup and get out of the country for a little while. His cousin Nail and Saveli stayed here and kept him updated on what the police and FBI were working on since Duncan tapped into his connections. Finally, after a year of building a team, he set roots down in New York as the biggest gun and drug ring in the city.

"I have the layout and blueprints in the side pocket." Joshua motioned at the bag as he passed it over. Nail took it from his hands.

"Pay him, Saveli," Maksim said, walking out of the condo. Saveli nodded, reaching in his pocket for his phone, and logged into his text thread for their accountant.

"When are you planning this?" he called to their backs.

Maksim looked over his shoulder as he held the front door.

"I'd advise you to stay away now. I wouldn't want you to go up in smoke," Maksim sarcastically replied.

A chill ran up his arm, and a lump caught in his throat as he nodded back at Maksim, knowing he couldn't take back what he'd done. He needed to warn his sister just in case. Heading toward the window on the fourth floor, he watched as they piled into their cars. Maksim paused for a moment, glanced up toward the window, and smirked.

Chapter Nine

"Welcome to GNS, Seeking Truth with Sandra. I'm Sandra Gregg."

Sandra smiled as the director yelled cut, and she waited for makeup and hair. Tonight, she was presenting her evidence and trying to push her career to the next level; this was her moment to shine.

"We have two minutes," Winston, her co-host, told her.

With the music starting again, the red light came on as the countdown began. Sandra continued checking her makeup and clothes on the screen.

"Welcome to Seeking Truth with Sandra," she said.

"Sandra, we wanted to extend a congrats on your new show," Winston said.

"Thank you, Winston."

"What can viewers expect?"

"Glad you asked. Today, I wanted to show what our government is doing."

"The station has received a ton of comments."

"I have footage that you can see behind me of Congressman Duncan Brooks."

"Explain where you took this?" Winston asked.

"This was around nine or ten at a warehouse. Duncan was coming out alone."

"Did he explain what he was doing out there?"

"No, but I have a feeling it has something to do with Malcolm Holmes."

"The notorious drug dealer?" Winston's eyes rose in shock.

She nodded, crossing her hands in her lap.

"More details will be released soon, but I wanted the public to know where our tax money is going."

"Stay tuned for more Seeking Truth with Sandra Gregg."

The director yelled cut, and Sandra strolled to her office, removing her jacket and wiping the sweat off her nose. A knock came at her door.

"Good job on your first episode." Winston stood at the door with his hands in his pockets.

"Don't act like you care."

Sandra picked up her bottled water, taking a sip. With a twist to his lip, he stepped in closer, shutting her door. The two of them were rivals, always had been, and Sandra was underhanded with trying to make it to the top. Winston hated her but had a small crush deep down that he couldn't break.

"Where did you get the footage?"

"None of your business."

"Tell the truth, who'd you sleep with?"

"Get out of my office."

Winston leaned over on her desk with his hands planted on top.

"I bet you slept with Malcolm Holmes to get this footage."

"That's a lie!" Sandra spat.

He shrugged his shoulders.

"You get your story your way, and I make up mine."

"You're sick."

"And you're a bitch."

"There's that jealousy. Mad to see someone younger and beautiful moving up in the business," Sandra relayed.

"Don't flatter yourself." Winston turned to leave.

"Winston," Sandra called to his back.

He turned around.

"If I were you, I'd play my cards right and try to get along with me. Besides, GNS may not be here much longer." Sandra smiled with her hands on her hips.

* * *

Duncan threw a glass across the room, and it shattered on the ground.

"That bitch!" he screamed, his assistant running in to see if he was hurt.

"Sir, is everything all right?" Camilla looked at Duncan disheveled and noticed glass on the ground.

"Leave me alone."

"But sir..."

"Get out!" Duncan shouted. Camilla rushed back out, shutting the door.

Pacing back and forth, he replayed the video from GNS again, seeing a screen grab of him leaving the building. He still hadn't been able to talk with his wife since they were going through a separation.

"I need to talk to Maksim," Duncan mumbled to

himself. Running around to his desk, he picked up his cell and dialed Maksim's number.

"Mr. Congressman," he answered on the first call.

"We might have a problem."

"We or you?"

"I'm not playing around; someone saw me leaving the warehouse."

"So."

"That could be a problem for us."

"Not to me."

"If I go down..."

"Do you think it's wise to threaten me, Mr. Congressman?"

He lifted his head, shaking the water from his eyes, and the very volume of the lustral flood contented him.

"Don't call me anymore," Maksim stated, hanging up the phone.

"Wait!" Duncan pulled the phone away from his ear in disbelief.

Things were spiraling out of control, and he had no one to turn to. He decided to contact his ex for help.

"Please pick up," Duncan mumbled to himself. After three rings, the annoying voice he despised so much came through the line.

"What do you want, Duncan?" Cheryl demanded.

"Where are you?" he questioned.

"None of your business."

"Cheryl, this isn't the time to be combative."

"I'm going to hang up if you're going to have that tone with me."

"Okay... okay... sorry. I really need your help."

He was still tense and agitated; the paranoia within his mind did nothing to calm him down. Staring outside the office window, he felt like someone was watching and waiting to kill him.

"Call your parents. Better yet, the police."

"That's who I need help from."

"What are you talking about?" Cheryl pressed on.

Drifting over to the bar in the corner of his office, Duncan removed the top off the scotch bottle and took a whiff of the dark, strong, robust flavor.

"Has anything seemed off like somebody watching you?" Duncan investigated. Cheryl chuckled over the phone.

"I knew at some point your greedy ways would come back to hurt our family."

"Cheryl, I didn't do anything wrong. People I trusted betrayed me."

"Our divorce will be final soon—lose my number," Cheryl blurted out, ending the call.

"Cheryl! Cheryl! Fucking bitch!" Duncan groaned, tossing the drink back. Treading over to his desk, he pulled his key out and unlocked his secret compartment, pulling out a small bottle of cocaine.

"She'll regret this," Duncan mumbled to himself, dropping a little on the side of his wrist. With a rolled-up piece of paper, he dipped his head low and sniffed the contents up his nose. Leaning back in his chair with his eyes closed, he smiled.

* * *

The sun was setting as Teagan looked up the street. It was going on six in the afternoon, and she wanted to make it home in time to cook dinner and be with the kids before bedtime. Watching Sandra Gregg finish her conversation with a security guard out front of the GNS offices, she waited before stepping out and confronting her. Daughtrey stayed in the driver's seat, taking pictures and monitoring if anyone else was outside of the building after the video aired of Duncan Brooks. The president was pissed about the team not having a head's up and letting something like this get out to the public.

"Go time," Daughtrey said.

Pushing the door open and jogging across the street, Teagan called out her name while she strolled to her car.

"Sandra!"

Sandra peered over her shoulder.

"Agent Stone, what brings you down here?" Sandra stayed put with her grip on her keys.

"You want to tell me about the footage you have of Duncan Brooks?"

"No, I don't." Sandra started to turn and walk off.

"Sandra, you may think you're doing something to bring down bad people. But you're not."

"I know what I'm doing." Her eyes fell low, and Teagan could tell she wasn't so confident in her statement.

"You don't believe that."

"You're the last person to try to tell me how to do my job." Sandra approached, pointing her finger in her face.

"I want the footage, and I'm coming to you personally."

"Can't help you."

"I can go to your boss and get it with one phone call."

"Are you working with Duncan? Is that what this is about?" Sandra chuckled to herself.

"I'm focused on getting the truth."

"So, you're a truth teller now." Sandra sucked her teeth.

Teagan smiled coyly.

"Either you can give me the footage before the night is over, or I make one phone call and that dream job at the major network can go bye-bye," Teagan remarked, leaving Sandra speechless, watching Teagan jog back to her car.

* * *

Turning the spaghetti sauce on low, Teagan lifted the wooden spoon, enjoying the aroma of her family recipe.

"Almost ready," she said.

Tatum sat at the kitchen table coloring in her book. CJ and Cole were in the living room playing a video game. Everything was perfect in her eyes, and she looked forward to these types of days with no drama. The upcoming baseball game was something she was looking forward to, and the boys kept talking about the seats and being up close to win an actual fly ball.

"Mommy, when's dinner going to be ready?" Tatum asked.

"Soon, baby."

"What did you cook?"

Tatum put her red crayon down and came to the stove next to her mother. Teagan ran a hand over her curly hair that she'd just washed the other day and let hang for the night.

"Spaghetti, vegan patties, and for dessert, sponge cake."

Tatum clapped her hands in excitement.

"Can I set the table?"

"Sure, baby." Tatum opened the side drawer of utensils and let Tatum count out what she needed.

"Five forks, right?" Tatum asked.

"Yes, you got it right."

"Boys, dinner is almost ready," Tatum yelled from the kitchen, and Teagan chortled under her breath.

"What's going on here?" Christian stood at the archway of the kitchen, wearing jeans and a t-shirt after coming in from work.

"Dinner is almost ready, Daddy."

"Did you help Mommy with dinner, precious?" Christian strolled in further, kissing Teagan on the lips, wrapping his arms around her waist from the back.

"Yep," Tatum replied.

"Good girl," Christian said.

"How was your day?" Teagan turned in his arms, placing her hands around his neck.

"Long and boring. I did more hiring to take some of the load off me," he said.

"I'm very proud of you."

"Are you two going to kiss?" Tatum said.

"Maybe," Christian teased, releasing Teagan and tickling Tatum, lifting her in his arms as she laughed.

"Okay, Daddy, you win," Tatum laughed.

"Tatum, go wash up, and I'll set the plates," Teagan told Christian to release her as she ran out of the kitchen.

"Are you ready for the game with the kids?" Christian asked.

Mixing the noodles with the sauce, Teagan plated a large bowl and brought it to the table.

"Yeah, finally a real day off with the family."

"Good, I'm excited for the kids to be normal for once."

CJ and Cole ran in the kitchen, taking a seat at the table.

"Did you two wash your hands?" Teagan questioned, laying her apron down on the back of her seat.

"Yes, ma'am," both of them answered at the same time.

"All right, boys. Calm down and let's eat. Your mom made a lot of food."

"I sure did," she laughed, as Cole reached over to pick up the utensils in the spaghetti to feed himself.

"Cole, you're making a mess," Teagan fussed.

"A good mess though, right?" Cole jested.

"That's your son," Teagan said, and they all laughed as Tatum came back in the room and sat next to her mother. They talked about each other's day and what they would eat at the upcoming baseball game. Later on that night, everyone sank into Teagan and Christian's bedroom to watch a movie together as a family until they fell asleep.

Chapter Ten

Two days later.

Hazelnut-scented steamed latte filled the room as Teagan sipped, scanning through the video footage she was able to obtain from GNS. President Sanders pulled some strings and got the owner to release what they aired and to agree to not show any more video pertaining to Duncan Brooks or anything dealing with national security. Sandra was pissed when Teagan showed up with a lawyer from The Firm working on the behalf of DOJ. Informing her that this was a national security risk, the owner wanted nothing to do with the story any longer. Teagan felt like things were moving in a better direction, and knowing Duncan was starting to break gave her great pleasure.

"What are your thoughts?" Broderick asked, standing over her shoulder.

"It's him; the video is a little blurry, but you see a clear side view."

Broderick huffed out a breath.

"Malcolm's been a lot more forthcoming."

"He has no choice."

"What's the plan for Maksim?"

"Let's look at it from all angles." Teagan lifted the notepad and pen from her desk, drawing lines down the middle to describe her thoughts.

"We have Maksim, Duncan, and Joshua working together."

"Yeah, that we know of. Could be more people."

"No, I doubt that. Maksim's background fits the type to want to be in control."

Teagan stood, leaving the notepad on the desk. Broderick picked it up.

"He's out to do harm, and we know Duncan is in on it somehow."

"But to what extent?"

"Exactly. He's losing his reputation in the public, and his wife is divorcing him."

Broderick took notes, bobbing his head. Grabbing the other stack of files on Tech Hines Computer Services, Teagan pulled Joshua's information out, reading through the length of time he'd worked for the company.

"Joshua Kline has a sister named Abby."

"What did you find out about her?"

"She's married to a pharmaceutical sales rep, stay-at-home mom, typical housewife."

"What are you thinking? I can see it in your eyes."

Turning the file over for Broderick to see, she noticed Abby's phone records that went to her office.

"Interesting. This was the same date you received that anonymous call."

"What do you bet she was the one warning us about her brother?"

"Why would she rat her brother out?"

"Maybe trying to save him. She's older than him, and their parents seemed to cut him off."

Teagan folded her arms, staring at Broderick.

"You're thinking about paying her a visit."

"I thought about it, but that would only cause him to run. I want Maksim."

"We can put a tail on her."

"Just keep your distance," Teagan told him as he stood, gathering the information on Joshua's sister and leaving her office. Sitting back at her desk, she studied over Joshua's file, along with Duncan. Tech Hines had been around for twenty years, and Joshua started working there a few years ago. With a few complaints for being late, overall, he'd been the best computer specialist they had at the company. Grabbing her phone, she made a call over to Gregory's office.

"Broderick already told me to set up a tracker for Abby Kline," Gregory rushed out.

"Thanks, but I want you to look into Tech Hines Inc."

"Anything specific you want to look at?"

Teagan sighed and pursed her lip.

"No, I just want to make sure the company doesn't have anything to do with what Joshua is involved with."

"I can do that... Oh, I heard you got tickets for the opening game."

She smiled, dropping the papers on her desk.

"Yep, and I'm ready to take a few days off to be with my family."

"Those tickets were hard to come by. Make sure you get an autograph for me." Teagan chuckled at his comment.

"I promise to do my best but dealing with three kids in a crowded stadium is a challenge."

"That's true. Maybe I'll see if they have any last-minute tickets."

"Probably online you can see."

Logging into her email, her cell phone rang.

"Gregory, let me call you back. Christian is calling me."

"Copy that, boss. I'll email you any updates," Gregory teased, hanging up the phone.

"Hey, honey."

"I was thinking," Christian said.

"Okay ..." Teagan dragged out.

"I would like to take my wife out for lunch."

"Oh, we haven't gone on an afternoon date in a while. What's the occasion?"

"Just wanted to enjoy a little afternoon time together. You've shown me that you're cutting work down a little more."

"Yes, being the boss and delegating are my best skill sets," Teagan joked.

"Come meet me at Alamaza and show off those skills in person." Christian smiled through the phone, feeling the love of his words. She never wanted to argue or have Christian angry with her like he was a few weeks ago. It broke her to see the man she loved not have confidence in her commitment to their family. Sending a kiss through the phone, she hung up and sent an email to her team to inform them that she was leaving for lunch and to call on her cell phone if they needed her for anything.

Locking her office door, she went to the garage to have Sean drop her off at Alamaza, a local Mediterranean restaurant they'd frequented in the past.

* * *

Twenty minutes later, Sean arrived in front of Alamaza, and Teagan jumped out, telling Sean she'd call when she was ready for him to pick her up. Treading into Alamaza, she thanked the security guard for holding the door open for her and scanned the room for Christian. Seeing him in the corner near the window, she motioned to the hostess that her party was already here and seated.

"I didn't see you leave this morning." Christian tugged on her leather jacket.

"Is that a good thing or a bad thing?" Teagan hugged Christian, pecking his lips and wiping the red lipstick away.

"Good thing, babe. It would make me want to skip out on work."

Teagan gasped, fluttering her eyes.

"My husband wants to play hooky? Who is this man and where is my Christian?"

"Ha... Ha... Funny, Teagan. We both used to be spontaneous."

"That's true, before the kids came along."

"Things were simpler when it was just us."

Taking the menu in her hands, she wanted to avoid going backwards and discussing her decision to become director and take on more responsibility.

"Have you ordered yet?" she asked.

"The drinks. I got your sweet tea and a beer for me."

They scanned over the menu as their waitress approached with their drinks.

"Hello, I'm Carol, your waitress this afternoon."

"Hi, we're ready to order."

"Awesome. What would you like to start with?"

Teagan ran her finger down the menu across the lunch specials.

"Let me have the seabass and pasta," Teagan said, closing the menu and passing it to Carol. Out of the corner of her eye, she noticed a familiar face.

"I'll get the same thing and some bread please," Christian ordered, giving Carol the menu, who turned and went back to the kitchen. Teagan slowly rose out of her seat as she saw Joshua Kline leave the bank across the street. Picking up her purse, she took out her phone and snapped a picture.

"What's wrong?" Christian asked, reaching for her hand.

"Uhm... give me one second, honey."

"Where are you going?"

Teagan sprinted out of the restaurant, leaving her purse with Christian yelling out her name. She hid behind a loading truck, staring at Joshua talking on the phone. He seemed upset, with a scowl on his face.

"Talk to me," she muttered to herself.

Checking the time on her watch, she sent a text to Gregory with the photos of Joshua to see what job he had to do at the bank today. Soon as she closed out of the text thread, a car pulled up with a woman stepping out, marching over to him and yelling in his face. Wanting to get a better look, she eased down to the other end of the truck as the worker removed the loading cart.

"Sorry," Teagan said, bumping into the driver.

Her eyes rose in shock, seeing Abby Kline meeting her brother.

"I need to hear what they're saying."

Right as she started to get closer, a hand gripped her arm, turning her around.

"What the hell are you doing?" Christian fussed.

Teagan looked over her shoulder, hoping Joshua didn't see her.

"Christian, this is an emergency. Go back inside."

"I thought this was us spending time together?"

She kept glancing over, and Joshua finally noticed and made eye contact with her. His face drained in acknowledgment of who she was.

"Shit!" she barked.

Joshua ran and jumped into his car, leaving his sister standing there. Teagan waited for the cars to pass by, when Joshua pulled off fast, almost knocking her over. Christian grabbed her back by the waist, falling down on the ground.

"Who was that?"

He helped her up off the ground, running his hands across her chin, arms, and back.

"A case I'm working on." Teagan bent down to pick up her phone from the ground, noticing the screen cracked a little.

"You hurt anywhere? Do you need to go to the hospital?"

Teagan shook her head no.

"I'll be fine. I need to get back to the office," she answered, limping slightly back to the curb of the street.

"Let me drop you off then."

"I'll call Sean."

"Teagan, get in the car. You're the one who ran out without saying anything."

Staring at each other for a few seconds, Teagan ran a hand over her face, nodding her head, walked around to the other side of his Range Rover and slid in when he unlocked the door.

* * *

She scanned the faces of her team as they all sat in the conference room with a projector, showing the photos of Joshua Kline outside talking with his sister. Once Christian left from dropping her off, she promised to check with the on-staff medic if she felt any pain from earlier today. Rubbing the back of her neck, she popped two Advils to control the building migraine.

"He only worked on one computer today," Gregory stated.

"Anything suspicious left on his computer?" Spider asked.

Gregory typed on the computer, reloading documents of accounts.

"He's good, but I was able to see that he copied some high-profile accounts."

"Did the bank manager get in contact with the owners?" Teagan questioned, rubbing her temples.

"I told him to close those accounts just in case," Gregory answered.

"What do you want to do?" Spider turned toward Teagan.

"Time to end this," Teagan replied.

Everyone in the room agreed, and Teagan leaned forward with her hands crossed.

"Gregory, I want you to lock him out of everything. Spider, get whatever warrants we need."

"Should we go after his sister?" Spider wondered.

"No, that will just tip him off. Daughtrey, get the logistics together."

"And Broderick?" Spider said.

"Let him know it's time to put in his notice with

Malcolm," Teagan responded and stared around the room, focusing on each man she'd worked alongside. Going into another death situation never got old, but Teagan knew they had each other's back. The only way to survive was to not let death scare you.

Chapter Eleven

The day of the opening game finally arrived as Maksim stood amongst his men in a circle inside the warehouse. They'd been previously discussing how this large-scale job would either bring them beyond riches or complete destruction. Either way, Maksim Petrov would make a mark on the country to the world if everything stuck to the plan. The device that Joshua created sat in a bag in front of Saveli. He was in charge of making sure it was placed in the right position before detonating at the precise moment all the lights went out.

"Nail, you with me, driving toward the east side," Maksim explained.

"How many men do you have with Saveli?" Nail asked.

"Two, dressed normally. Remember we have it timed correctly at one."

"Should we take care of any leftover issues?" Saveli asked, cocking his gun back.

Maksim smirked, knowing Saveli was ready to end Duncan and Joshua's lives.

"There will be time for that later."

"I never liked that congressman," Saveli spoke, waving his hand in front of his face like Duncan smelled bad. Everyone laughed, including Maksim.

"He won't be a problem from what I've seen."

"That reporter lady," Nail brought up.

"She can be spared," Maksim said.

"What if we take her with us?" Nail made kissing sounds.

"First, we get our money, and then you do whatever you want."

"Everybody has uniforms, correct?" Maksim queried, showing photos of security uniforms on screen of the bank they'd planned to rob.

"I'd rather wear my own clothes," Nail replied, scoffing.

"Only for a little while, cousin," Maksim stated.

"Any updates from Malcolm Holmes?" Saveli brought up.

"We can let him live for now."

"To Petrov!" Nail held up his glass of rum in front of him for a toast.

All the men picked up their glasses in support of their boss and leader.

"To Petrov!" everyone yelled, finishing their drinks.

"Load up the trucks," Maksim called out, while scanning over the blueprints of the bank and the baseball stadium.

"What are you thinking?" Saveli approached, standing beside him.

"They'll never know it was us; it's perfect."

"And the spy bitch?"

Maksim waved off his comment.

"She's too stuck on other things. By the time we get the bomb set ..." Maksim made an exploding bomb motion with his mouth and hand.

"The private jet is ready, and the boat has escape routes."

"Just remember, not everyone will be leaving with us."

"I understand, boss. Kill all witnesses," Saveli said, shaking hands with Maksim and stalking out of the warehouse.

* * *

While Maksim directed his team on the next steps, Malcolm stood outside of Bambi's house holding flowers to make up for never calling again after another night of passion. Dealing with government officials and foreign mobsters had him stressed and looking over his shoulder every five minutes. When Teagan confronted him in her office, he thought that led to him being charged with a crime. Now giving over as much evidence of Maksim's whereabouts, he could try to make up with Tonya since she ignored his calls.

"Tonya, I know you're in there," Malcolm said, standing outside her apartment. She lived in a semi-decent area. It wasn't the worst but not the easiest place when you're well established like him. After a few people had been robbed or killed, trying to convince her to move was out of the question, but she refused any handouts.

"Go away, Malcolm," Tonya said on the other side of the door.

"Baby, I'm sorry," Malcolm pleaded.

"I don't care."

"Listen... I have tickets to the opening game today."

She loved baseball growing up, and Malcolm used that to his advantage when he bribed a friend who scalped his tickets.

"What row?" she asked.

"Upper deck."

"Let me see; hold them up to the door."

"Tonya."

"Malcolm, you want to come in and apologize, so start with the tickets."

Malcolm held the flowers between his arms and dug in his pockets for the tickets. Holding them up to the peephole, he heard the locks turning.

"These are for you," Malcolm said.

"Ummm... Mmhm." Tonya took the flowers out of his hands.

"I apologize for going missing on you."

"Malcolm, what are we doing?"

"What do you mean?"

"Either we're going to be together or not."

"We are together."

Malcolm strolled over to Tonya, lifting her left hand, and placed a kiss on the back of her palm.

"So, we spent an amazing night together, and I never heard from you."

"Because of business."

Tonya snatched the tickets away from him.

"Get out."

"Damnit, Tonya!"

"I'm the only one who can yell in this house."

He backed up, holding his hands up in surrender.

"Sorry, let's go to the game and enjoy a nice day out."

"Game, then you're treating me to a nice dinner at the most expensive place."

"Whatever makes you happy."

"Yeah..."

Tonya went to grab her purse and jacket from the couch. Malcolm pulled her back into his arms, holding her chin in place, pressing a long, lingering kiss.

"I'm really sorry."

"I forgive you," Tonya responded with a curl of upper lip.

Holding hands, they walked out of her apartment and down to his Mercedes Benz. Helping her inside, some of his men stood around in front of their cars.

"I thought we were going to the game," Tonya questioned, staring at Ishmael and Broderick talking to another man.

"We are."

"So, why are your men here? Are you in trouble?"

Malcolm started his car, putting his seatbelt on and adjusting his mirror.

"Baby, you know I have to be cautious at all times."

"Is there something I should know about, Malcolm?" Tonya inquired, locking her seatbelt across her waist.

"Enjoy the day, baby. I plan on spoiling you," Malcolm remarked, turning on his right signal and making a U-turn in the street. Watching out of his window, he saw everybody following him through the streets. He felt a little relief with the extra protection. Placing his hand on Tonya's thigh, he rubbed up and down.

"Thanks for the tickets," Tonya said.

"Anything for you, sweetheart," Malcolm answered.

* * *

Across town, Sandra Gregg was already at the big opening game, getting her makeup touched up. The owner didn't want her in the studio for a few days, so the program manager assigned her mundane news stories to keep her out of the way. Today's opening baseball game would keep her busy for hours since a ceremony pitch from the New York governor was planned, along with a retirement ceremony. She hated things that dealt with soft reactions from the public. No way she would make it as a bigtime journalist covering a game that was played every year with the same drug-addicted, steroid-induced, airhead players. Teagan Stone stuck to her word and got the footage pulled, but she had plans to go even deeper into The Firm and Congressman Brooks once she finished this story.

"All right, Sandra, are you ready to do a run through?" the camera guy asked. Sandra stood from the makeup chair, taking the microphone from his hands.

"How does this angel look?" Sandra questioned, posing in front of the baseball sign of New York Sparks.

"A little to the left," Mike answered.

She shuffled to the left.

"How about now?" she questioned, fluffing her hair out.

"Great, it's just a few run throughs for now." Counting down from three, two, one.

"I'm Sandra Gregg, and today we're here at the Sparks opening game." Sandra waved her hand up at the stadium sign.

"Good, but a little cheerier."

Sandra rolled her eyes.

"Here today from GNS, I'm Sandra Gregg at the Sparks opening game."

"Much better."

"Perfect, let me grab a bottle of water for a second. It's hot," Sandra complained even though she wore a pants suit like she was meeting the president of the United States.

"Take five," Mike said.

Switching to the van, she opened the cooler and took out a bottle of water. Watching the crowd of people lined up at the front line, she spotted the last person she intended to see.

What is she doing here?

Holding her hand over her eyes to block out the sun, she watched as Teagan rubbed the top of a little girl's head. A man and two boys stood next to them.

"Are you ready to film?" Mike said.

"Give me a second," Sandra stated, leaving her water and the microphone in the van, stalking over to Teagan and her family.

"Excuse me, sorry, excuse," Sandra said to some people in line.

"Watch it, lady," a young boy yelled out with his friends when she pushed him to the side.

"You bitch!" Sandra shouted; the crowd gasped in shock.

Teagan turned her head in the direction of the statement. Seeing the news reporter she'd been arguing with calling her out in public wasn't on her plans for the day.

"Excuse me," Teagan said.

"You tried to ruin my career." Sandra pointed in Teagan's face. Christian tried to block Sandra from his kids, pulling Tatum to the left side of him as the line moved toward the entrance.

"I have no idea what you're talking about, but I'm here with my children."

"You know exactly what you did. How about I tell everyone here who you really are?" Sandra taunted, tapping her foot, with hands on her hips.

"Sandra! Sandra!" Mike shouted her name.

She waved him off.

"We have a show to do." Mike pointed to the camera.

Sandra groaned, nostrils flaring, and peered at Teagan.

"This isn't over," Sandra promised.

"I look forward to the next round," Teagan teased, hearing Christian call her name when the window booth opened for them to submit their tickets.

Sandra stomped off back to the GNS news van, picking up the microphone and moving the earpiece into her ear, preparing to do another announcement.

"Ready?" Mike said.

"Just roll the camera," Sandra hissed.

Mike motioned his hands, counting down.

"Welcome to GNS News with opening day for the New York Sparks!" Sandra grinned wide, pointing at the stadium.

"We have families of all ages, ready for the opening pitch. I hope you stay tuned."

"Cut. Now let's get some footage from inside," Mike said, shifting the camera lower to hold.

For over an hour, they filmed different angles of the entrance, interviewed a few fans, and met with a few members of the management.

"When is this thing going to start?" Sandra blew out a frustrated breath, annoyed at the long wait time.

"Baseball goes for over two hours sometimes. Didn't you know this?"

"I have better things to do," Sandra spat.

"I'm going to the restroom. Watch the equipment," Mike said, leaving her alone to fuss.

While standing in the corner facing the entrance, she noticed Malcolm Holmes holding hands with a woman wearing a shirt with the Sparks logo.

"A drug dealer at a baseball game. Maybe this day can get better after all," Sandra said, looking at Malcolm in line to order some food.

"Hurry up, Mike," she mumbled to herself.

Five minutes later, Malcolm and Tonya went inside to take their seats, leaving Sandra even more pissed that she missed an opportunity to spy on him. Mike, still inside the bathroom, hadn't come out, and Sandra stomped over to the bathroom when she bumped into a guy by accident.

"Ouch! What were you going to do?" Sandra barked. Glancing up, she noticed it was the same young man who flipped her off in the car a few days ago.

"Cyka." Nail replied bitch in Russian.

Chapter Twelve

An hour earlier.

Teagan helped Tatum fix her hair while the boys went outside to get in the car. Teagan told the team to contact her if there was an emergency, but otherwise, she'd be off the radar to spend time with her family at the game. Christian was still a little extra sensitive from the situation at the restaurant. Coming home early last night and ordering food while the kids stayed with his parents helped loosen him up a little. He was back to being his old self, but she made sure to not push his buttons. Checking out her appearance in the mirror, she tightened her ponytail and touched up her makeup. Wearing a Sparks t-shirt like the family and blue jeans, she was ready to be a normal family without having to fight corruption.

"Mommy, let's go," Tatum said.

"Here I come. Did you get your purse?" Teagan queried, placing her new phone inside her black bag.

"Yes. See?" Tatum held up her little black purse that matched her mom's.

"Good job. Do you have your allowance for your snacks?"

"Yep, I saved up twenty dollars," Tatum insisted, opening her purse to show off.

"Ohh, good job, sweetie."

Tatum grabbed her mother's hand, leaving the living room together and locking the front door as Christian shut the trunk. Tatum skipped over to the car, and Christian held the back door open and helped her climb into her booster seat.

"Princess, you look beautiful."

"Thanks, Daddy."

Teagan opened the passenger door, and Christian came around to the front.

"We all set?" Christian asked the family, putting his shades on.

"Yes!" the kids answered at the same time.

"Here we go."

"The governor is throwing out the first pitch," Teagan said, turning on the radio.

"This is the biggest opening of the season, they say," he replied.

He pulled out of the driveway and turning left toward the side street. Christian ran a hand down Teagan's arm.

"Looking cute, baby," Christian remarked.

"Thank you."

"Ewe... please don't kiss," CJ said, covering his eyes with his hands.

"How do you think you three got here?" Christian joked, turning at the light to get on the freeway.

"Let's not torture the babies."

"Can we meet some of the players?" Cole asked.

"I doubt it, Cole. It's an opening game, and they're usually busy with long lines."

Tatum sang in the car, as Cole and CJ argued about changing the music as Teagan glanced at her phone, wondering if everything was going well with the team.

"Are they out on assignment?" Christian stopped at a red light.

"You know I can't talk about missions."

"I can see it in your eyes. You're here physically, but not mentally."

"Christian, don't start."

"I'm not starting, just making observations." The car went silent as Christian got off the freeway, turned left, and arrived at the Sparks stadium near the Bronx. They stepped out and opened the door toward the back to help the kids. They grabbed their hands to stick together. Teagan pulled the tickets out of her purse and handed them to Christian to let him take the lead.

"This line is long."

"We're still early, so we didn't miss anything," Christian said, pointing to the line.

"I'm hungry," Cole said.

"Once we get through the line, we can get food," Teagan replied.

"Here we go, section B," Christian said.

Teagan held onto Tatum's hand, standing next to Christian in the crowds as people screamed and yelled in excitement. The entire building was flooded with young kids, and Teagan admired how well-behaved her children were. Going out as a family was rare because the boys would end up in some type of argument. Then Tatum would throw a tantrum if she didn't get her way.

"You bitch!" Looking ahead, she didn't think anyone was calling out her name.

"Agent Stone."

Teagan stiffened in place being called Agent Stone in public.

"Excuse me," Teagan said.

"You tried to ruin my career." Sandra pointed in Teagan's face. Christian tried to block Sandra's hand and adjust the kids to the other side.

"I have no idea what you're talking about. I'm here with my children."

Growing more frustrated with Agent Stone's passive-aggressive attitude, Sandra closed the space between them.

"You know exactly what you did. How about I tell everyone here who you really are?" Sandra whispered for just Teagan to hear.

"I suggest you move along."

"Or what?"

"Sandra! Sandra!" a voice called from behind Sandra.

"You're lucky I have to work." Sandra tossed her hair over her shoulder, scowling at Teagan. Shaking her head, Teagan caught up with Christian and the kids walking in the direction of the opened ticket booth and getting their wristbands for entry.

"Can I get popcorn?" Cole said.

"Can I get a hotdog?" CJ asked.

"I want ice cream," Tatum called out.

"All right, you three. We aren't going crazy with junk food," Teagan pointed out.

"We still have to go out to dinner afterwards, so get something light," Christian backed her up.

"Okay," CJ answered.

"Babe you want to get the seats, and I'll get the food," Teagan suggested.

"Sure, be careful." Christian pecked her on the lips.

"Don't worry."

* * *

While grabbing the food for the kids, Teagan chuckled to herself at Sandra confronting her. At the same time, Nail wrapped the rope around Mike's neck in the bathroom as Saveli put the bomb in place down near the seats. Maksim was staying in contact and driving to the second location of the bank with Sergei and Vanya. Mike caught Nail putting a bomb in place underneath the counter in the bathroom, and Nail decided in a rush to kill him.

"Shush, no one is going to save you," Nail warned as Mike's legs stopped wiggling, and he pulled him into the bathroom stall. Shutting the door, he went back to setting the timer, throwing away the bookbag, and washing his hands. Coming out of the bathroom calmly, he put the out of order sign on the door and marched toward Saveli when he bumped shoulders with a woman.

"Ouch. Watch where you're going," she screamed.

Grunting, he stared into the face of the woman he knew from TV, the one Maksim had them keeping an eye on. Flipping her off during traffic, they thought she took to their threat, after posting the video of Duncan. Standing in front of her now, she was more aggravating than before.

"Cyka." Nail called her a bitch in Russian. Going in the opposite direction as her, he jogged a little faster to find Saveli.

Pushing through crowds, he ran down the stairs and caught up with Saveli coming his way.

"Hey, you left your bag!" a guy yelled out at Saveli.

"Shit!" Saveli whispered.

"Hey, man." The older guy looked like he was in his fifties. A bald head, not taller than five-eight, thin lips, and a beer belly. Heading down the steps holding the food one row over, Teagan heard the man call out to somebody and noticed Nail and Saveli walking away. Seeing those two faces as Maksim's men and the older guy trying to get their attention with a bag in his hand, caused her to drop the food.

"Sir! Don't move." Teagan held her hand out for him to stop, running over in his direction.

"Teagan, what are you doing?" Christian stood, hearing her voice.

More people walked in to find their seats.

"Christian, call the police!" Teagan yelled, making it to the older gentleman.

Christian removed his phone, knowing something was happening that wouldn't be good to have his kids involved.

"Sir, where did you get the bag?" Teagan questioned, taking her phone out of her pocket and dialing Spider's number.

"How's the game going?" Spider asked.

"Spider, we have a situation," Teagan said.

"I'm turning around now," Spider replied.

"Get everyone locked and loaded. Maksim is here."

"Shit! Are the kids safe?" Spider queried.

"They're with me. But I need all hands on deck."

"I just saw it sitting on the ground; the guy left it," Henry told Teagan.

A few security guards came over at the commotion.

"What's the problem, ma'am?" A guard wearing a red vest with the Sparks logo held his radio in his hand.

"I don't want to alarm you, but there's a bomb in this bag." Teagan hung up with Spider.

"What!" the older guy yelled and almost dropped the bag.

"Don't move! Just focus on me," Teagan said in a soothing voice.

"Hey, what are you doing?" A woman Teagan assumed was his wife came over to them.

"Margaret, go sit down. There's an emergency," Henry said.

"Ma'am, please take your seat," the security guard stated.

"The police are coming," Christian said.

"How do you know there's a bomb in the bag?" the security guard wondered.

"I work for Special Agency. The two men who walked away are a part of the biggest cartel family in the world."

"What do you need?"

"We need this place on lockdown."

"The governor is coming," the security guard remarked.

"Call and cancel, the less people the better." Teagan turned to face Christian.

"I know," Christian said.

"I promise I'll make it up to you." Teagan kissed him on the lips.

"I got the kids. You're safe," Christian demanded, holding the back of Teagan's neck and capturing her lips, tonguing her down before releasing her to go off. This could be the last time they were together, and he realized how proud he was of his wife and how she put herself on the line for others. Teagan wiped the lipstick off and grabbed another security guard to follow her as she gave direction.

"You come with me. We need to lock this down and find them." Teagan ran up the stairs.

"Teagan!" Christian called out, holding her purse.

She glanced over her shoulder and smiled, knowing he was telling her to not forget her gun. Heading back toward him, she took her purse from him, kissing each child on the cheek and telling them she loved them.

"I'll be back," Teagan said.

"Mommy, what's going on?" Tatum inquired.

"Nothing, baby. Mommy just has to work," Teagan explained, kissing Tatum once more before following the security guard.

"I want everyone in a single line checking IDs against these pictures," Teagan said.

"Can you send these pictures to my phone?" the security guard asked.

"What's your name?"

"Bobby."

"Bobby, what you're doing today isn't only for your country, but for the world."

"Yes, ma'am."

"Teagan! Teagan!" Spider yelled her name, running to her with Daughtrey and the rest of the boys.

"Catch us up," Spider said.

"We were looking on a small scale, but this son of bitch planted a bomb."

"You mean here?" Daughtrey questioned.

"Yeah." Teagan bent over, catching her breath.

"How did you find out?" Spider insisted, following in her direction.

"By accident, I spotted Nail and Saveli," she responded.

"Henry, the guy sitting over there, picked up the bag," Teagan replied.

A few people grumbled in line, wondering what was going on.

"We found something!" another security guard said.

Running in that direction, Teagan felt her cell phone vibrate.

"What do you get?" Teagan pushed through the crowd, stepping into the men's bathroom and finding Mike dead.

"As we were checking, the door was jammed, and we found his body," the guard spoke.

Unknown: Did you find my little present?

Teagan: Who is this?

Unknown: Come on now, Agent Stone. Let's not play dumb.

Teagan's brows drew into slits.

"Gregory, trace my phone," Teagan shouted.

"On it," Gregory said, running out of the bathroom.

"He's toying with us," Spider said.

"Something's not right. We need to find Joshua," Teagan muttered.

"What did you say?"

"Follow me, I want to speak with Joshua Kline."

Teagan pivoted, leaving the bathroom, and saw Sandra talking with a police officer as she walked by.

"This is all your fault," Sandra spat, throwing her hands in the air.

Jumping in the SUV, Daughtrey and Spider followed

alongside, taking the lead as they left, going in the direction of Joshua's last-known address.

"Get every location for the material needed to create those bombs."

"Are they on a timer?"

"Yeah, we have maybe an hour."

"Buckle up," Daughtrey said, pushing the gas on the car, swerving through traffic.

"Make sure the airlines have photos of Petrov's family," Teagan explained.

"Calling now," Spider said.

"Did he text back?" Daughtrey mentioned.

"No."

"He can't get away with this. What was that reporter doing there?" Daughtrey wondered.

"Filming the opening season," Teagan sighed, releasing a long-held breath.

"Abby Kline hasn't heard from her brother," Spider said, making another call.

"I hate to make this next call."

"To whom?"

"The president," Teagan said somberly, looking out of the window.

Chapter Thirteen

ame Day.

Time was running out for Joshua Kline when he saw the breaking news about a bomb at New York Sparks Stadium. He knew that was his handiwork, and he needed to get out of the country. A few days ago, he'd almost been caught but rented a hotel room for a few nights before grabbing a few more items from his apartment. When the story came on the screen, that was his cue to take the little money he had from the sale to fly to a place that didn't have extradition. Stuffing two suitcases, he looked around his apartment for any last-minute details. Opening the door of his apartment, his eyes widened in shock.

"Going somewhere, Joshua?" Teagan questioned, pointing a gun in his face.

"Please don't kill me," Joshua answered, dropping the bags.

"That depends on how much you can tell me about those bombs."

Spider and Daughtrey searched through his place as Teagan continued talking with him.

"I don't know about anything."

Teagan shot him in the foot without even blinking.

"Ahhh! You shot me," Joshua screamed, falling on the ground, holding his foot.

"Joshua, focus... look up here," Teagan said, snapping her fingers in his face.

"I need to go to the hospital. Please, you can't do this," Joshua pleaded.

"The only place you're going is to jail. That little flesh wound will be found, but the next bullet won't."

"I got some blueprints," Spider said, coming from the back.

"Now tell me again you don't know anything."

"I needed the money."

"Did you think about your family at all?"

"He promised me some money, and all I needed to do was put a bomb together."

"A bomb that can kill over twenty-thousand people!" Teagan punched him in the face.

The door opened wide, and the police stepped in.

"Take him in and book him for terrorist activities," Teagan said, pointing at Joshua.

"Wait! I'll help you."

"Too late," Teagan responded, watching the police handcuff him and drag him out of the living room.

"Look at this; they're papers with Duncan's signature at Tech Hines," Spider said.

"I bet Duncan is somehow behind Tech Hines."

Reading over the paperwork, Teagan deciphered that Duncan came in as an investor a year ago, even though Joshua had worked at the company a few years prior.

"Duncan probably was looking for a quick pay day." Teagan pointed at the amount of shares Duncan owned.

"A twenty-percent share," Daughtrey whistled.

"Let's go have a chat with Duncan."

All three left while the forensic team continued tossing the place around for more evidence.

Running back to the car and jumping in, Teagan's phone vibrated again.

Unknown: Tell me, how is Joshua doing?

Teagan logged into her thread, seeing the unknown number.

Teagan: In jail, you'll join him soon.

Unknown: Tell my friend Duncan it was nice working with him.

Teagan: You're not getting away with this.

Unknown: I already have.

Teagan: We won't stop until you're caught.

Unknown: I'd hate for your husband to find you in pieces.

Teagan: Tell it to my face.

Unknown: Have a good day, Agent Red.

* * *

Maksim sat in the armed truck wearing the fake uniform, chuckling at his text message thread. His men set up blockades along the street, while Saveli and Nail handled the baseball situation.

"America's pastime," Maksim chortled to himself.

He watched the news footage of what was going on at the stadium through social media on his phone. Maksim grinned at his plan coming together, and all the loose ends would soon be eliminated. Joshua got himself arrested, but it was nothing to have him killed in jail. No matter if Agent Stone found Duncan, anyone could be touched for the right price. Sending another text to Agent Stone was a dangerous game, but he didn't care. It was a game of cat and mouse, a challenge in his eyes ever since she came after him a few months back. Right now, he needed the men to pick up the pace before they suspected what was really going on. Checking the time, he had it synced with the traffic lights to go out as a backup plan. The flights would already have police swarming, so that was out of the question. As a backup, he had a boat paid for with a driver to take him to Miami, then Dominican Republic, and he'd fly out of the country. Maksim continued watching his men when his phone rang.

"Speak."

"We're swarmed with police," Saveli whispered.

"Where are you?"

"The place is surrounded, but we found a closet."

"You need to figure out a way to get out, or you know what to do."

Everyone made a sacrifice that instead of being caught, they'd go out by suicide. No one was to ever end up in prison. The Petrov family long-standing ritual was family first and loyalty.

"Yes, boss."

"Do what is necessary," Maksim said, ending the call.

"Maksim, we have ten more minutes before we can go," Sergei explained.

"Everybody ready?" he asked.

"Yes. How is Saveli doing?"

"Focus on your job. Saveli is handling himself," Maksim changed the subject.

Pulling out the gun from his waist, he cocked it back, making sure the safety was off. He looked at his watch.

"Soon, there will be a huge fireworks. Sergei, we've pulled it off," Maksim told him.

Sergei smiled, ready to go to the bank and take everything he'd always wanted. Maksim said there would be more than enough money that everyone could retire many times over with what was inside the bank.

"What about the Americans that helped you?

"Unfortunately, they're dead men walking."

Chapter Fourteen

Teagan slowly nudged the door open with her gun prepared. With no answer she went forward with Daughtrey and Spider behind her as they noticed Duncan's body laid on the ground with a bullet to the head. Her personal feelings aside, Teagan sighed, looking around the room. She strode closer to the body as Spider checked his pulse and shook his head.

Thinking of the amount of time they had left to find what bank was being robbed, as the bomb was being deactivated, her nerves were on high alert dealing with multiple crises at once and wanting to get her family to safety. Sauntering over to his desk, she pulled the drawers open and rummaged through filing cabinets for any evidence. Duncan was too stupid to not keep something around with his name on it. Her eyes narrowed at the locked bottom drawer. Yanking harder, it still didn't open. She looked around the desk, picked up the mail opener, and popped the lock. Inside was a thick blue envelope. She scanned it as Spider and Daughtrey called for a cleanup crew.

"What's that?" Spider pointed at the envelope.

Teagan shrugged, opening it up and seeing banking information for TransUnion on Fifth Avenue with checking account numbers highlighted. Teagan turned toward his computer and typed in the name of the bank, went to login, and it was already saved with his username. She tried to put in his last name as the password and received an error message.

"Shit!"

"What happened?" Spider stalked over to the desk.

"I need his password." Teagan tried looking in his files saved on his computer to get some sense of giveaway. With Joshua in custody and Duncan dead, only Maksim was left, and he was on the run while they locked down the airports.

The door opened for the cleanup team to arrive and take things over as they continued finding Duncan's secrets.

"We know he's money hungry, right?" Spider asked, standing with his hands crossed over his chest.

Teagan glanced up at him.

"Yeah."

"Then it wouldn't be his name or birthday. Duncan lived off being one step ahead through this entire time."

Teagan fell silent in thought of what could get them inside his account. Coming up empty, she pulled her cell out of her pocket and dialed Gregory to have him hack into the account instead.

"We're still working here, Teagan," Gregory blurted out.

"I need you to let them handle it and get to a computer."

"What's up?" Gregory yelled through the phone at someone to take over for him.

"Duncan is dead, and Maksim is gone. We're at his office trying to hack into a bank account," Teagan explained.

"Text me the information."

"TransUnion on Fifth Avenue; we're heading there now. See what you can find," Teagan requested, ending the call and dialing number one on her phone.

"Agent Red," President Sanders answered.

Teagan jumped up from the desk, grabbing the papers and heading out with Spider and Daughtrey behind.

"I need the TransUnion shut down and free rein," Teagan commanded without waiting for an answer.

"Anything else?" President Sanders replied.

"No, sir."

"And Maksim?" President Sanders asked.

"Still on the run. I have my people checking every spot."

They stepped on the elevator, heading to the lobby.

"Call me once you have an update." The president ended the call, and Teagan pressed the button for the lobby.

Five minutes later, as Teagan stepped off the elevator, the entire building was surrounded with local police, FBI, and DEA agents. Usually issues like this would be under lock with only the FBI handling the case, but with Maksim being connected, Teagan made it a priority to oversee. Marching out the doors, a strum of reporters pushed cameras and microphones in their faces. Teagan pushed through the crowd and reached for the driver's side door handle when a camera was forced in her face.

"Agent Red, is it true Duncan Brooks is dead?" Sandra smirked, holding the microphone toward Teagan.

Freezing at the question, Teagan stepped around the door, snatching the microphone from her hand.

"How do you know that?" Teagan's brow hiked in suspension.

"From a reliable source," Sandra said.

Teagan stared at Sandra, taking in her demeanor with her blond hair pulled back into a tight bun, red lipstick, and black suit.

"What color lipstick are you wearing?" Teagan questioned.

Sandra was surprised by the question, as the camera man shrugged his shoulders.

"Candy Cane Red by Ray Cosmetics. Why?" Sandra answered, shuffling from one foot to the next, her hand planted on her hip.

Teagan's mind raced back to Duncan at the training session. She closed her eyes, remembering his aggravated attitude and disheveled clothes with a red stain on his collar. Knowing it was from lipstick and the amount of knowledge Sandra possessed about everything, it was only right she fit the last piece of the puzzle. Teagan turned toward Daughtrey, motioning to grab Sandra and take her with them.

"Sandra, you're under arrest." Teagan went to open the door again.

"Wait a minute! You can't do this," Sandra screamed as flashes from the cameras and loud yelling rang out as Teagan slid in the passenger seat and dialed Gregory's number again.

"Almost got it, Teagan," Gregory called out.

"Try Sandra," Teagan responded.

She heard typing through the phone.

"How did you know that was the password?"

"Lucky guess."

As Daughtrey drove off into traffic, Teagan grabbed her seatbelt. Sandra was playing everybody, only out for herself. Fooling around with Duncan was just to get ahead, and once he cut her off for playing the video of him at the warehouse, she knew her luck of having access would dwindle.

"He has money in an offshore account, twenty million," Gregory said.

"Any trace to Maksim?"

"Bingo... Duncan received money from a Russian account. I'm willing to bet Maksim is behind the money," Gregory explained.

Speeding in traffic, Teagan kept an eye on the car behind them that held Sandra inside.

"We're almost there. Can you tell how much is in the bank right now?"

Daughtrey ran a red light as cars honked their horns. Taking a sharp right, he went down a back alley two blocks over and slowed down, scoping out the scene.

"Right there," Spider muttered from the backseat. Two bank trucks were parked in the back.

"The bank has between two hundred to five hundred million cash on hand," Gregory said. Daughtrey backed up and parked the car with the engine running, watching two men dressed in employee uniforms.

"Are the alarms off?" Teagan asked him.

"Yeah. Do you want me to trigger them and get SWAT down there for backup?" Gregory wondered.

"No. we can handle it but get me visual on the inside to my phone," Teagan demanded, ending the call. Two more black SUVs pulled up next to them, and Daughtrey pointed for them to park.

"What's the plan?" Daughtrey said.

Teagan sat in her seat and peered at the setups and the twenty-story bank building. Going in unprepared would get them all killed, but not finding Maksim could send things into a bigger tailspin.

"We're going in; get suited up."

Everyone stepped out of the car, and one of the drivers in the other SUV parked sideways, cutting off traffic. He stepped out with orange cones, signaling the road was closed. Teagan grabbed the bulletproof vest from the back and took the rifle from Spider's hand.

"Sandra's still with us," Spider said.

"Duncan was sleeping with her and feeding her information."

"Damn," Daughtrey whistled in shock.

"I remembered him having lipstick on his collar at the training segment and something she said to me a few weeks back about the budget."

Teagan lifted the headpiece out of Spider's hand, checking the range and watching movement from around the corner. Feeling her phone vibrate, she grabbed it off the seat and saw a message from Gregory.

Gregory: Check your email for the link.

Teagan: Thanks.

Chapter Fifteen

"I got a visual of inside the building. Make sure someone stays on Sandra." Teagan closed her messages and went to her email account. Clicking on the link, she got a clear picture of the front, rear, alleyway, and inside of the bank vault.

"How does it look?" Daughtrey approached with his gun ready.

"I see at least three in the vault and two at the van," Teagan replied, holding the phone up for them to see.

"I'll take it inside," Daughtrey stated, following along with Teagan.

"Great. Spider, handle the two near the van. Take two guys with you."

Everyone nodded in agreement and went their separate ways. Teagan stood against the wall, checking her gun again, motioning for backup to follow as she ducked across, behind some cars, and slipped in next to the bank building. Scanning the live camera footage, Teagan peered at the movements of the robbers, while they bagged up contents of the vault. Biting her bottom lip,

Teagan closed her eyes and counted down from five, calculating the time it'd take to get in and out without any of her team getting killed. As the director, she didn't need to go in on missions like these, but when it hit close to home, she took it upon herself to be in the field with her men to show them she was willing to go through war.

"Daughtrey, you're next to me. Tony and Eddie, focus on the rear." Pointing at the security guard to be quiet, Daughtrey picked the lock off the door using his tools. Teagan signaled for the older security guard to head out of the room to safety. Glancing around the room, they saw it was mostly empty with a few employees lying on the floor tied up. The bank was over ten thousand square feet with high ceilings, open space for seating, and cubicles separate from bank tellers. Easing down the hall quietly, Teagan held her gun up as they tread through the hallway and opened each door to see if anyone was left. Daughtrey asked Tony to get the two employees out of the building while the robbers continued packing money up in their bags.

"Let's go! We have two minutes left," a voice called out. Heart pounding, Teagan held her arm out, stopping anyone from parading further in through the commotion. Glancing up, Teagan noticed the mirror at the corner of the vault, seeing two men packing and one on the lookout in the right corner.

"One minute," the guy spoke again.

"Freeze! Put your hands up," Teagan shouted, aiming her gun. Not listening to the instructions, all three guys, wearing all black from ski masks to gloves, blasted off shots toward who they assumed was the police.

Pop! Pop!

Dropping down to the floor behind the island in the

vault, Teagan peered around the room as more bullets whizzed by her head.

"Fuck you!" a gruff voice giving out demands said. Thinking he was the one in charge, she tried to reason with him. Daughtrey hit one of the guys in the arm from close range. The guy screamed in pain and dropped his gun. Standing no more than five-nine, he charged toward Daughtrey when a third shot went through his head.

"You killed him!" Vanya shouted, grabbing a bag of money from the ground, and peered toward the other door in the room.

"Vanya, we need to go." Sergei's heart pounded at his plan falling apart in front of his eyes. Going to jail wasn't in his plans for today, and Maksim promised this was an easy spot.

Pop! Pop!

"Don't move." Teagan squinted her left eye and shot the shorter guy in the foot.

"Ahhggghhh!" Vanya almost fell on the ground, but the leader of the three pushed him in front of himself, blocking Teagan and Daughtrey.

"Not today, sugar." Sergei grinned, shoving his partner in front of them and pushing the emergency exit door that led outside. Tony and the team eased up to the suspect slowly as lay on the ground with blood dripping from every area of his body. Checking his pulse, he shook his head.

"Call for the cleanup crew," Daughtrey commanded, following Teagan.

Opening the door, Daughtrey glanced back and forth, left to right, with his gun. He saw the suspect running toward the van carrying a bag of money.

"Stop!" Teagan yelled, ready to shoot. Not complying,

he ran near the back of the van when Spider shot back at them.

"Vanya and Anthony are dead," Sergei spoke, returning fire toward the back alley and tossing the money in the back of the van.

"We need to get out of here, Sergei. They killed Ivan," his other partner Ulan said and held onto the passenger side door.

"Hold on." Sergei put the van in reverse, busting through barricades of signs and cars. He turned the car into traffic ducking bullets, not making a dent in the bulletproof windshield and side mirrors. Vanya leaned out the window and shot back as Sergei sped up, not caring if anyone got hurt as he drove through the red light. All of a sudden, the traffic light went out, forcing cars to stall and pile up. Teagan jumped in the car next, yelling to follow the van.

"They're getting away." Teagan slammed her hand on the dashboard.

Although they caught who was behind the robbery, it was still going to be a dead end. If the two in the van tried to fire back, this would end up being another front-page problem they didn't need with reporters on the front porch of her house asking questions. Teagan was certain her team was the most elite to end these situations with less bodies than the average police chase. At the same time, it could play in her favor to show what Duncan did go behind the backs of the American people.

Lifting her phone out of her pocket, she redialed Gregory's number. It rang in her ear as she pointed her index finger forward to stay on top of the robbers.

"You're on the news, Teagan," Gregory answered when the phone clicked.

"I need helicopters on the car ahead of us, Gregory."

"You want the police in on this?"

"Yeah, we have two dead and two in chase."

"Tell me the tags."

"More than likely stolen, but 4EFGJS Bronx Security Company."

Daughtrey heard typing on the other end.

"Dammit! They're getting on the highway," Daughtrey shouted.

"Gregory!" Teagan shouted, impatient.

"Arriving in ten minutes. I'm patched into the police scanner. I'll keep you updated," Gregory mentioned, ending the call. Teagan's hand felt sweaty, her throat dry from dodging gunfire and trying to keep a bomb from going off.

"Fuck!" Daughtrey avoided hitting another car as they moved out of the way. Staring out the window, Teagan saw a round of police cars lined up.

"What do you want to do?" Daughtrey questioned.

"Do what you have to."

Daughtrey nodded. "Buckle up."

Teagan reached behind her and grabbed the shotgun. Leaning out the window, she steadied her arm with the gun, squinted, and shot the tire of the black van. A loud pop caused some pieces of the tire to fly off, and the car shifted left to right. She aimed for the left tire, sending it spiraling out of control. In turn, Sergei hit the brakes to slow down. The helicopter continued riding overhead, and Teagan blew out a breath and sent another shot to the driver's side tire. Sergei turned the steering wheel, pissed at how things turned out from this job. He got the car over to the side of the embankment with Daughtrey pulling in a few feet away.

"I got Sergei," Teagan gave direction to Daughtrey.

"Eyes wide open." He eased out on the driver's side with his gun ready, monitoring every movement.

"Get out of the car with your hands up!" she called. One side of the passenger door opened.

"You guys got eyes on them?" Teagan asked Daughtrey.

"Eyes and ears."

Backup came next to her, holding the passenger door for her to come around and stride up to the vehicle.

"Keep your hands up and step out of the vehicle," she demanded. Vanya looked at Sergei, nodded, and he swiftly jumped out of the driver's side. They both fired back at Teagan and the team, until she screamed and shot him in the chest.

Daughtrey fired more shots into Sergei's body until his clip was empty.

"You good!" Daughtrey shouted, coming up to the side of the vehicle and kicking the gun away. He leaned down and checked his pulse as blood dripped on the ground.

"Clear." Teagan slid the back door of the van open. Seeing the bags of money, she lifted them and passed them over to the police.

"Get forensics to look into this."

Teagan strolled around toward Daughtrey and took Sergei's ID out of his hands.

"Related to Maksim."

"I won't be surprised if all of them are related."

She waved up toward the helicopter to leave.

"You making the call?"

Running how the conversation may go in her head,

she quickly pulled her phone out to give the confirmation they'd been waiting on.

"Hello," Christian answered.

"Hey." Teagan watched as the coroner came over to take photos of the bodies.

"Is it done?" Christian spoke on the other end of the line.

"Yes, I'm coming home."

"I guess the kids need to know that their mom won't be retiring anytime soon."

"I'm sorry."

"I know you better than you know yourself, Teagan."

"How so?" Teagan clenched her teeth.

"You want to save the world, even if you know you can't."

For years, Teagan told Christian the reason she served her country was to save the world. Even knowing it could leave her family without her would never cause her to slow down until she had CJ. Seeing all three kids in the line of drama only made her go harder.

"Where are you?" Teagan muttered, getting inside the car and closing the door.

"Driving home with the kids. We have private escorts going through traffic."

"Are the kids scared?"

"Surprisingly, they think we're like royalty right now." Teagan chuckled.

"I'll be home soon."

"Be safe."

"You too."

The door to the driver's side opened, and Daughtrey got inside and turned the radio on low as they sat waiting to head back home.

"Is everything good?"

"Yeah, local PD is handling things so we can head out."

"Good, I plan on taking a vacation for real this time."

Daughtrey turned the left signal light on and eased into traffic from behind the bank van back.

"Are you going out of the country?"

"I think so. Christian and the kids have been through enough. Time for me to go back into mom mode."

"Let me guess, France."

"What makes you think of France?"

"You look like the type of woman that loves all that French food and museums." Daughtrey winked, speeding to the off ramp.

"I do love museums and French food, but I'm thinking of London as a vacation spot."

Slowing down at the light, Daughtrey cracked his knuckles and yawned as Teagan sat back with her eyes closed in the seat.

"I admire you, Teagan."

One eye popped open.

"Huh?"

"I don't think I would've come back in the way you did. I know Broderick's an asshole, but he's always been for the team."

"Are you trying to convince me to not kick him off the team by buttering me up?"

"As long as I've known you, no one could bribe you to do anything."

"Then what are you saying?"

"Take the vacation and think about if you want to be in this forever."

"I can say the same thing to you."

"This is my life."

"Bigger things in life are more important than The Firm."

Daughtrey continued driving back to the city, tapping his fingers on the steering wheel.

"Probably but will never know," Daughtrey replied.

"The Firm lets you believe you're in control of your life. You'll learn one day."

Part II

Agent Red: Fatal Enemy

By
Ava S. King

Synopsis

Enemies come in all forms, and Teagan Stone is ready for battle, not thinking of the consequences for going to war with her ultimate rival. Can she turn back the clock or will this lead her to nally leave The Firm before it destroys her from within?

Chapter Sixteen

Camden, Nebraska small town.

Teagan stood back in the stalky, narrow grass at the uncovered buried bodies of five victims, some as young as thirteen up to twenty-three years old. Closing her eyes for a moment, she took in the chill of the Maryland weather. Having to get a call in the middle of the night from her team about a police tip about women being buried out here wasn't on her agenda for today. As she stood with her arms crossed and listening to birds chirping, police tried to block reporters from contaminating the evidence. Teagan only wanted to have a second to herself. In her mind, this could be her daughter Tatum. Having to contact the parents of these missing girls would undoubtedly hurt, but this came with the lifestyle. Even before she arrived, word spread up to Congress and the White House that a serial killer was on the loose. So before she could decline to take the case, the president made her aware that this was the reason The Firm was created. To handle certain things that local police wouldn't be able to unload promptly.

"What are your thoughts?" Teagan's eyes popped open at the sound of his voice.

"Human trafficking," they answered at the same time, clogging through the tall field of weeds that almost hit her knees. From the signs on the road at the entrance of the field, this place had been abandoned for some time—nothing for miles.

Spider could tell she was taking this case personally, and there was no use in trying to push it off on the FBI to oversee. The sun was starting to set as the crime scene photographer finished, allowing the coroner to load the body bags. Stepping closer, Teagan glanced around the area, sensing it was probably disrupted by reporters or police.

"Who was the officer that got the call?" Teagan questioned.

"The guy that's talking to the reporters right now." Spider pointed at a group of people standing off at the far end of the field.

Teagan turned her head to the right and glanced at Officer Peter Copeland smiling in front of the camera like he was the hero.

"Get those reporters out of here, and I want to know why this happened," Teagan stated, taking a minute to digest what was in front of her. The crime scene was taped off, but she'd bet the media would have photos out before she even got the girls' names to confirm with family.

"Teagan, you know as well as I do that this is going to be too much for you."

Teagan squatted down, staring at the outlines of the shallow graves; each body was laid out with their eyes closed and marks on their arms and legs from either being dragged or beaten in some form.

"I'm fine; I can handle myself." Teagan sighed, standing and removing the rubber gloves from her hands. Turning, she headed back to the car where Sean held open the door for her.

"Gather up as much information and send it to my office."

"Are we staying in town?" Spider asked.

Teagan glanced at the surrounding area, seeing the news reporters and police trying to block residents from coming near the crime scene.

"We'll see where the evidence leads us."

Closing the door behind her, Teagan removed her vibrating cell phone from her pocket, noticing Christian texting to check in on her trip.

Christian: I saw the news.

Teagan sighed, annoyed at the media already putting out the story.

Teagan: Kiss the kids for me.

Christian: How long will you be there?

Teagan: Not sure; I'll call you once I get back to the hotel.

Christian: I love you.

Teagan: I love you more.

Sliding her cell back in her jacket pocket, Teagan bit her bottom lip, thinking about the young girls and women that were found. Finding them like this only brought out the anxiety of her daughter being in a situation like those girls and not having anyone to protect them.

"Hotel, boss?" Sean asked.

"Take me to the mayor's office," Teagan answered.

Sean pressed the gas of the black, tinted, government-assigned SUV, turning out of the grassy farm area, and getting back on the main street. It was now going on three years since the Maksim case, and she was more ingrained in her role as director of The Firm. All the kids were getting older and wanting to be with their friends, but as their mom, she had to keep the socializing to a minimum. President Sanders was no longer at the helm of the government agency; the department of defense now managed it. After Duncan took his own life, President Sanders wanted to keep any individual from Congress from being able to cause another terrorist attack. So Teagan and her team reported to Pentagon headquarters while still having a single branch office in New York to work out of on a day-to-day basis. The car arrived in front of the mayor's office. Sean started to get out and open the door, but Teagan held her hand up, letting him know she was fine.

"I won't be long." Teagan looked up at the building, checking the time on her watch. Heading inside, she walked up to the reception desk.

"Hello. Can I help you?" the brunette with a short bob asked.

"I need to speak with the mayor."

"You are?" she questioned, scanning Teagan up and down.

Teagan stared at her nameplate on the desk, picking it up and repeating the name to herself.

"Audrey?"

"Yes."

"I'm Agent Stone, the person who was flown out here to solve the murder of young girls."

Audrey's mouth opened and closed, eyes blinked in surprise at her statement.

"Uhm, the mayor's available to speak now."

"I thought so."

Teagan placed the nameplate back on her desk and headed to the open door of Mayor Lloyd Henton. Knocking on the door, the mayor sat up in his seat, turning off the TV and fixing his tie.

"Am I interrupting you?" Teagan pointed toward the chair in front of his desk, and he stood, motioning to have a seat.

"You're the agent from the news." Lloyd grabbed his coat off the back of his chair, buttoning it up. He was about five feet ten with a receding hairline, black buzz cut, round belly, and a scar above his lip.

"You're the mayor."

Clearing his throat, they passed a look between each other, and Lloyd waited for Teagan to speak. Lloyd's been at the job for a year after his father retired and helped him to win the votes of the community. Lloyd was only in it to gain notoriety and sleep with women. At thirty-eight, his life growing up as the son of Bert and Amy Henton wasn't always good. He was never seen as the popular guy in school.

"I need to have full cooperation from your police department."

"That's fine; I don't see that being an issue."

"As you know, whenever outside authority comes in, some jurisdictions feel left out."

"I can assure you my office will give you the utmost support," Lloyd said, stretching his hand out for a shake.

Teagan looked at his hand and back up to his eyes, and he turned to start typing on his computer.

"Will your team need any accommodations?"

"We have a hotel for now."

Right as he started to answer, Audrey knocked on the door and stepped inside with some papers in her hand.

"Sir, the latest job numbers came through." Audrey placed the documents on his desk.

Teagan watched Audrey as she stepped near Lloyd, pointing at the pile of paperwork with her hand on the back of his chair. Studying her movements and seeing the ring on her finger, she assumed they were possibly very intimate with each other.

"How long have you been mayor, Mr. Henton?" They fell into silence as Audrey reached down, leaving the messages on top of his desk and walking out of his office.

"About a little over a year. My father retired, so I took his place."

She didn't know what to expect from him, but she could tell Llyod wasn't as confident in himself; keeping the police intact would be a bigger job if Llyod couldn't even handle keeping his secretary from giving them away. Rising out of her seat Teagan prepared to leave his office.

"I'll be in touch; if anything else comes up, please call me." Teagan left the card of the hotel she was staying at on his desk, turned, and left him to ponder what's about to happen in his city now that dead bodies of young girls are being found. Holding the door open, Teagan gets in the back passenger side as Sean steps around and climbs in on the driver's side, turning the key in the ignition and driving back to the Hilton Hotel. Her phone rings, and she notices Gregory calling.

"I'm on my way to the hotel now," Teagan said.

"We might have a problem," Gregory replied.

She groaned, throwing her head back in frustration,

not having the patience to deal with a problem so early on.

"What's the problem?"

"The police chief won't release any records to me."

"Are you sure?"

"Yeah, I've been going back and forth with him on the phone."

Letting out a frustrated breath, Teagan scratches the back of her neck, wondering if it's going to be one of those missions with the local police thinking big government agents are coming in on their territory. Limiting interference from local agencies has helped to keep leaks from getting into the press. If Teagan needed to play a little hardball, she was up to the challenge. They were learning not only about this case but also having to serve under the Pentagon and Sanders no longer as a go-to contact. The Agency will have to be strategic with how they handle themselves going forward without causing a bigger public outcry.

"Send me his name."

Chapter Seventeen

The room was filled with local drunks, petty college boys, and a few men in suits that looked like they were on the brink of tears. Teagan half expected the local police station wouldn't be so full of criminals and busy with phones ringing off the hook. Pushing through the crowd, she stood at the front counter behind an older lady speaking with the Officer about her cat getting kidnapped.

"I need someone to come by and search," the older woman suggested.

"Miss Alma, we already told you your cat died a year ago," Officer replied, rolling his eyes.

"Now, young man, I pay your salary," Alma said, waving her hand around the room.

"We'll get someone out to your house soon," the Policeman said, motioning for Teagan to step forward.

"Good," Alma responded, smiling, showing off her missing tooth in the front row.

Leaving, she bumped into Teagan and almost fell.

"Ooh, sorry, young lady."

Teagan held her up as a young man rushed in and grabbed hold of her.

"Auntie, how many times do I have to tell you about running off!"

"Leave me alone, Bert!" Alma fussed, pushing Bert's hand away.

Everyone minded their business, not paying them any attention, and Teagan was shocked at Bert's aggressive approach.

"That's it; you're going into a nursing home," Bert said.

Alma shook her head, walking off as he followed behind, yelling at her back.

"Can I help you?"

"Uh, is someone going to help her?" Teagan asked, pointing at the door Alma walked out of with Bert.

"That's Alma for you. Bert can handle her."

"His approach seems a little unorthodox."

"Again, what can I help you with?"

Sensing her patience was about to be tested, Teagan cocked her neck left, then right.

"I need to speak with the captain."

"Why?"

"Classified."

He chuckled at her response.

"Lady, I don't know who you think you are—"

Teagan held up her ID showing a government agency, cutting him off.

"I can be your friend or your worst nightmare. What would you like, Edwin?" Teagan tapped his name badge and smirked.

"Hold on, let me check if he's available."

"Make him available."

Edwin scowled, stomping to the back while Teagan

stared looked around the station at the chaos and lack of structure inside. A second later, Edwin came back and told her to follow him to the Chief's office. All the men turned their heads, staring at the woman in all black and hair pulled into a ponytail wearing a turtleneck and black jeans, and leather boots. Her plan was to go straight to the hotel and wrap up the case, eat a late lunch, and call her kids. But somehow, things never go as expected in her day. Edwin pushed the door open, and she stepped inside as the captain motioned for her to take a seat as he talked on the phone.

"Personally, I think you should go back to Washington," Chief Barrett said, hanging up the phone and leaning back in his chair, holding eye contact with her. Keeping her gaze, so there was no doubt she wasn't to be intimated. Teagan's gone to war and back, kidnapped, and tortured. A small-town Chief with an ego that's probably bigger than what he has between his pants isn't going to deter her. She crossed her hands, glanced at the photos hanging on the wall.

"Chief Barrett, I see you have a beautiful family."

"Call me Sylvester."

"Call me Teagan."

"I didn't ask for you to be here; my men can handle this case."

Teagan whistled, clasping her hands together.

"You don't believe that."

"Watch your mouth and show some respect."

"That goes two ways, Sylvester. You want us gone, and I want to find the person that did this."

"Who do you think you are!"

"You're going to get on that phone and give my men whatever they need."

"And if I don't?" His nose flared, and his brows dipped low.

"Then you'll find out who I really am and how high my name runs in Washington."

Standing, Teagan turned, heading toward the door, and pushed the photo hanging on the wall to the left by an inch to straighten it out as she left out of his office.

"Looks much better now, don't you think," she said, smiling.

* * *

Gregory sat across from Spider, Daughtry, and Teagan at the local diner three blocks from the hotel. Broderick was outside on the phone with the coroner's office as they sat huddled together eating and debriefing about the day.

"This burger is probably the best thing I've had all day," Daughtrey mentioned, taking another bite of the double cheeseburger, popping fries in his mouth. Right as they landed at the airport, it was straight to the scene without eating a proper meal. Spider reached over to steal a fry off his plate.

"Get your own man," Daughtrey scoffed, trying to move his plate out of the way.

"Boys, please."

Spider smacked the back of his head.

"Chief Barrett sent over the information." Gregory drank his Coke, wiping his mouth on the napkin.

"Did he say anything?"

"Basically, if we screw up, it's on us," Gregory grunted, taking a slice of his pizza.

"He's not happy we're here."

"You don't say." Spider sighed, running a hand across his forehead.

The waitress came back with another plate of fries and cheeseburger, setting it in front of Daughtrey.

"Here you are, sweetheart." The older woman tapped Daughtrey on the shoulder, going back to the employee kitchen.

"Your arteries are going to be clogged for a while."

"What did I miss?" Broderick spoke, coming back to the table, sitting next to Spider.

"What did they say?" Teagan asked.

"He's emailing over the findings by tomorrow."

"Stay on top of him; we can't let them hinder us from solving this crime."

"How did it go with the mayor?" Spider inquired.

"He's more open to helping us; the Chief will need a little push."

"How long do we have to be here?" Daughtrey questioned.

"Shouldn't be more than a few days, open and closed case."

"I still can't believe those girls were killed and left like that." Spider drifted off in thought.

"I can," Teagan replied; all the guys looked oddly at her.

"You know I never publicly apologized in front of the guys," Broderick started to say.

She peered at him.

"Me too. I know we talked in passing, but we got in over our head Teagan," Daughtrey explained.

"Change the subject and talk about what we know so far." Teagan took charge, getting everyone's attention. Agreeing, they listened to her breakdown what they know so far from each one laid in a specific pose with bruises on their body. Pulling out a map of the area, Teagan marked the spots where their bodies were found, along with the photos from the scene that were sent over. Hoping to give them some closure is a promise she wants to keep so they can rest in peace.

* * *

Lying in bed with the tv playing, Teagan listened to Tatum talk about her day as she rambled on about how her brothers were getting on her nerves. She wanted to laugh but decided not to interrupt her and look like she was taking their sides.

"Mommy, you have to hurry home," Tatum demanded.

"That's the plan sweetheart, is your Daddy there?"

"Hm... uhh."

"Can I talk to him?"

"Is that Mom?" Teagan heard CJ ask.

"Yes, and she wants to talk to Daddy," Tatum spat.

"Let me see the phone," CJ spoke.

"No!" she heard a rustling over the phone.

"All right, you two, get ready for bed," Christian said; Teagan lowered the volume on the TV, pulling the comforter over her waist.

"Hi."

"Hi."

"I take it; you've made it back to the hotel."

Staring at the screen of a rerun from the housewives reality show, Teagan lifted the remote and changed the channel to something that would help her sleep. Normally she'd have Christian in bed, but not having him to hold and snuggle up against, she figured a movie would help.

"We did. How was your day?"

"Long but rewarding."

"How so?"

"I signed a few clients."

"That's amazing, baby."

"Thanks and the kids had their usual activities."

"I should be home soon." She turned to her side.

"My wife is the big-time agent; I saw the news."

"They showed me on the news?"

"Yeah, showing a possible serial killer."

"I told them to not let reporters get close to the scene."

"Too late, they had your name and where you work."

"Are the kids okay?"

"A few reporters called the house, but I hung up. After the bombing situation, you're more famous, babe."

"Not something I'm looking forward to being."

"I guess I should let you get some sleep."

"No, stay on the phone. I sleep better with you next to me."

Christian chuckled on the other end of the call. It was getting later and later as her eyes grew drowsy as she listened to Christian moving around the room.

"Just be safe."

Hearing the water turn on in the bathroom, Teagan thought it was time to get off the phone, so he could relax and get some sleep since he had to get up with the kids in the morning.

"Hey."

"Yeah, honey?"

"Have a good night. I'm going to let you go."

"You sure?"

"Yes, I love you."

"I love you more."

They listened to each other breathing for a few moments, hearing the silence echo across the lingering doubts of how they'd grown as a couple. Soon, she heard the sounds of a dial tone, biting her bottom lip. She hung up the phone to fall asleep in bed, thinking of how she could get back to her family without costing any more lives. Right across town at the same time, Chief Barrett was still at the station; it was well past midnight, and he'd still felt a little on edge, so he sat back with a glass of scotch in his hands while staring at the cell phone on his desk. Deciding to make a call he knew would possibly cost him his job or worse, he needed answers because things were unraveling. Gulping down the final remnants of his alcohol, he sighed, burping, lifting his phone, and punching in star sixty-nine.

"I told you I'd be in touch," the unknown voice spoke, feeling the aggravation in their tone. Sylvester cleared his throat, hoping things went better.

"We have a problem."

"I saw the news."

"This wasn't supposed to happen."

"Too late."

"This Agent Stone is causing more problems."

"Chief Barrett, are you drinking?"

"Any idea how this is going to work without me going to jail?"

Sylvester countered with a question of his own. Feeling worn down and agitated, he needed answers because he wasn't going down alone if it came to his livelihood. Sylvester's red-rim eyes would show the exhaustion in his face; the unbuttoned top of his uniform and disheveled hair showed the age lines of a man ready to retire. Only he wasn't a clean-cut, law-abiding police officer, not in his wife's eyes. After thirty years of marriage, he'd decided to step out with a few members of the local town, but Mrs. Barrett tried to work on keeping up the appearance they were a loving couple and family. He knew if what he was doing now came to light, she'd surely divorce him and leave town.

"Don't call me, and I'll call you, Chief Barrett."

Sylvester threw the glass across the room, shattering it, causing Bert to run in to see where the noise came from.

"Chief, you okay?" Bert burst through his office, scanning around the room, down at the shattered glass.

He stepped into his office, and the chief waved him off.

"I'm fine."

"Are you sure?"

"Yeah, just keep an eye on that Agent Stone for me."

"Uh, sir, she's FBI or something."

"Bert, do what I say."

"Yes, sir," Bert replied, leaving.

"Close the door."

"Yes, sir."

Chapter Eighteen

The whimpering of a soft voice with a blindfold covering their eyes, keeping them from seeing where they were, caused a tightness in the young girl's chest. She'd just left a party at a friend's house when she was walking home and caught the eye of a handsome young guy. Finally turning nineteen, she was hopeful to see what the dating life was like but getting inside his car showed it was a big mistake.

"Shush... your crying won't help you."

"Please... let me go."

"I can't do that."

"I won't tell anyone."

He knew that was true because his intentions of taking her became an extra bonus for him. Coming off a long day with clients, he needed to let off some steam, and the young beauty crossed his path. She looked young and untouched, so he expected to make a pretty penny from selling her to the highest bidder. Grabbing the empty tray off the floor, he stood back up and left her chained to the bed as she continued crying, wearing only a white gown he'd put on her after she was cleaned.

"Get some rest; you have a big day coming up."

"Please, let me go!" She tried to yank the chain off and felt it bruising her taut skin.

"In due time."

He shut the basement door, turned the lights out, and left her alone in a dingy bed, with no other form of escape. Crying herself to sleep, Gwen only thought about her family and how she'd wished she would have stayed home the other night.

After tossing the tray away and removing his gloves, he headed into his office and turned his computer on, checking for any signs that Gwen Akerson was missing. Normally, it would take a few days before anything would come across the radar, but since the other killings, he figured they'd ramped up surveillance. He smiled to himself that nothing was posted on TV or in the newspaper about his new prize possession. Tapping the numbers on his cell phone, he listened to the voice message coming through that stated his bank account had a deposit of fifty-thousand dollars. This was the smallest fee he had received for a client since it was a last-minute pickup. He wondered if his boss was getting too cocky with the increase in merchandise, but he wouldn't deal with that right now. His focus was on getting the girl transferred over so he could get back to his day job like nothing happened.

* * *

Two days later, in the middle of the afternoon, a woman stood behind Gwen, brushing her hair in a tight ponytail after bathing the dirt away. She'd placed a new white, strappy dress on the bed and sandals for her travels today. She'd been held in the same room, chained to the bed without a TV or fresh air from a window. All Gwen could do was cry herself to sleep and dream about her parents and little brother back home, afraid they'd never see her again.

"Where am I going?" Gwen whispered.

The older woman didn't speak English; she was just as much a victim as Gwen, but her freedom was contingent on being sent back to her country to be killed. Alejandra stood on the main road, trying to make money by selling flowers when an expensive Mercedes pulled up, and the gentleman offered her a job. She'd been with him for the past two years, and she regretted her decision every day. Never being able to go out or meet anyone like herself was torture; the only decent thing her boss provided was a bed and a bathroom of her own. With around-the-clock security and cameras sitting on the property, she would never be able to escape without someone catching and killing her.

"Can you..."

Gwen wiped her nose, giving up on trying to get her to understand what she was trying to say. The lock turned, and the door opened when security waved for Alejandra to bring the girl upstairs.

"What's happening? Please, someone, tell me."

"Shut up!" A tall security guard with limp and broad shoulders, standing at five-eleven, yelled.

"I want to go home." Gwen tried to jerk out of his hold as he guided her up the stairs and down the hallway.

"You're going to a new home," he snickered, tightening his grip on her arm.

Escorting Gwen out of the basement, and down the hallway, the guard checked to make sure her blindfold was still on. Her whimpers, and tears did nothing to change his mind of the job he's getting paid to do. His boss, stepped out of the kitchen. Drinking his cup of coffee, he watched as Gwen was placed in the blue plumber van. He was dressed in his best black suit and admired his home with the living room encased in dark-grey colors, large open windows, and a massive fireplace with his name engraved. All of his accomplishments sat on top of the fireplace, and he couldn't wait for the excitement of securing more forbidden fruit.

"Boss, we're ready," another security guard spoke.

"Good, I'm ready for more fresh air."

"Are you bringing more girls?"

He turned, heading back into the kitchen to put the cup in the sink for Alejandra to clean.

"We might, but this time, you can test out what we find." He grinned, rubbing his hands together as the blond, six-feet-four guard smirked in excitement. He grabbed his coat and keys, exited the home, and jumped in the backseat of his chauffeur-driven Lincoln town car as the van pulled in behind them to follow. Checking the time on his watch, he wanted to set up a conference call with his other client, so he logged into his emails to see if any updates had come. The only way he'd lasted this long was by keeping everyone in suspense and never meeting at the same location. Falling under the radar had bene-fited, with no leaks or police knocking on his door. Stop-ping at the destination, he ended the call and stepped out of his car as the driver kept the engine running. Checking his tie while looking at the surrounding area of homes, he smiled and climbed the stairs to knock on the door. Hearing the locks, the door opened with a gun in his face and a smoke-filled room.

"Pull the van around back." the husky voice said.

He glanced over his shoulder, nodding to his security guard to drive to the back.

"Was she touched?" The short, brawny man lowered his gun and stepped to the side, allowing entrance.

The door closed, and he walked to the back, ignoring the question.

"The deal is almost done," the woman said, ending the phone call.

Pushing the door open of the one-story brick home, he stepped in as her men stood on both sides of the door with guns on their hips.

"Take a seat," she spoke.

"Cozy place."

She rolled her eyes, cupping her chin with both hands.

"I was surprised to get a call so quickly."

Unbuttoning his jacket, he crossed his leg with his hands clasped in front of him on his knee.

"I like to keep my clients happy."

She picked up a white envelope and tossed it across the desk.

"Fifty thousand."

"Thank you."

"You're not going to count, verify?"

"I know you wouldn't cross me."

"How do you know that?" Her eyes dipped low.

"You have too much to lose."

"That makes two of us."

"How is your boss?"

"Which one?"

"The one who keeps my bank account full?" He smiled smugly.

"Keeps providing what we need." She turned the monitor on the television, watching as Gwen was thrown into a bedroom as she cried out, wanting to be let go.

"When can I meet this boss?" he asked.

"Never." She walked around the desk, standing at its edge and running a hand across his shoulder.

"At some point, I'm going to want access."

"That will never happen, sorry." As she turned to walk back around to her desk, he gripped her wrist.

"Either you make it happen, or our business deal will dry up."

She looked down at his hand and jerked away with a scowl on her face.

"You don't want to threaten me; it would be bad for your business and your health."

"Only a matter of time before cops find out about your second job."

"Before or after you tell them?" she asked.

Turning the monitor off, she placed the remote down.

"Keep up this facade, but the second you get in trouble, I bet your boys will bail out on you."

She laughed at his comment.

"Doubt that."

"Why's that?"

"Being family comes with its perks."

He smirked at his reply.

"When can you get more girls?" she questioned.

"I don't know. With the killings, I can't be sure your boss won't fuck up again."

"A little carried away; it won't happen again."

"How many more?"

"At least five if possible. We have some overseas partners interested."

"So, is Gwen a personal one for him?"

"That's not your concern."

Rising out of the chair, he peered at her, watching as her pupils elevated, showing she was hiding something.

"If anything traces back to me..."

"Has anything come back on you?" She threw her hands up in the air.

"Remember to keep it that way."

"We might have something I need you to keep an eye on."

"What?"

"The chief called about visitors in town to handle investigating the deaths."

"Chief is your problem."

"Yet you're going to help because Agent Stone is asking questions."

"Still want to keep your big boss out of this, but you're requesting my help."

He leaned forward.

"From what I read, she's good at her job."

"What do you want me to do?"

"Kill her."

"That's going to cost you."

"Tell me something I didn't know."

"I have a busy day, already running behind. I'll be in touch." He pushed the envelope inside his trench coat pocket, heading toward the door.

"Remember, I need more girls asap," she called out.

Glancing over his shoulder, he acknowledged, "Yes, ma'am."

She smiled, sitting back down in her chair and turning the monitor back on.

"Your tears will dry soon," she muttered.

She knew disobeying her boss and letting Agent Stone get too close would not only destroy their career, but her life would be even more in danger. Putting up a front a few minutes ago, her throat felt constricted at the thought of being on their bad side.

Chapter Nineteen

Stepping into Gwen Akerson's family home, Teagan and Spider felt conflicted at having to deal with a family's anguish, but they needed answers on how Gwen went about the day when they spoke to her last. Watching all the police cars outside of the house, Chief Barrett let them know how the family called as soon as they realized she never came home.

"Take the lead," Teagan told Spider.

"Are you sure?"

Teagan nodded, watching as Mrs. Akerson wiped her tears away, and her husband held her in his arms. Watching as Spider went toward the couple, she scanned the room and stayed back, keeping her eyes on the entire room. A few of the police officers whispered amongst themselves about Teagan and her team coming into town and trying to take over.

"Mr. and Mrs. Akerson, I'm very sorry to bother you."

"Have you found our daughter?" Mr. Akerson questioned.

She scanned the magazines sitting on the coffee table,

taking in the homey feel that was probably full of laughter and love before Gwen was taken.

"No, ma'am. I'm Agent Hitchson and my partner Agent Stone." Spider held his badge out, pointing at Teagan.

"The chief said that you're from the FBI?" She held her hands up in prayer.

"Something like that," Spider responded.

"How can we help bring our baby home?" Mr. Akerson asked.

With a knock at their door, Officer Copeland walked inside, holding his helmet.

"Michelle, Doug, I'm so sorry about Gwen." Peter went further into the living room, bent down, and hugged Michelle, as long-time friends of the family. He brought comfort none of the other officers could do.

"Thanks for coming, Peter." Doug waved for him to have a seat on the chair opposite Spider.

"It's pretty clear we're dealing with professionals," Peter stated.

"Officer Copeland, I'd prefer we didn't give out any details on the suspects," Spider mentioned.

"I'm just keeping my friends updated," Peter replied.

"I understand, but we don't want to give false information," Spider said.

"Maybe we could give them money," Michelle blurted out.

"Situations like this don't normally revolve around money," Spider said.

"Mrs. Akerson, has Gwen had any fights or arguments with anyone lately?" Teagan asked.

Peter chewed on his bottom lip, scowling at Teagan.

He pushed out a breath, picking up the Bible lying on the end table.

"Not that I believe. Gwen's a good girl."

"What about school? Any boyfriends that might be able to help?" Spider picked up on Teagan's questioning.

"My daughter didn't have a boyfriend," Doug said.

"Can you provide a list of friends?" Spider asked.

"We gave that to the police already." Michelle sighed.

"I understand. It's just—"

"She said she already gave it to our team," Peter interrupted.

"Mr. Copeland, do you mind if we speak outside for a moment?" Teagan pointed at the front door. Peter looked annoyed at being summoned to step outside as Doug and Michelle looked on. Teagan held the door open as she waited. Closing the door, she stepped into his face.

"Mr. Copeland, I'm not going to repeat myself."

"Watch how you speak to me, lady." He looked around, making sure no one was watching the exchange.

"Agent Stone to you, and respect goes both ways."

"Fine, I need to get back in there."

Peter turned to leave, but Teagan held a hand up to block him.

"The only way you can help your friends is by cooperating with my team."

"Don't try to tell me how to do my job."

"Would you rather we leave, and more girls end up dead?"

"I know this family. Gwen wouldn't just take off," Peter explained.

"Which could be true, but until we have all of the evidence, nothing's ruled out."

Gathering that she could be correct, Peter decided

to stop fighting her to take control of the case and would step back until he saw they'd overstepped the line.

"The chief wants me to follow this case to make sure nothing is missed."

"I can assure you, nothing will be missed. My team's record will show that we always close a case." Teagan headed back inside as Peter watched on in a tempered attitude.

While Spider continued talking with the couple, Teagan went to Gwen's bedroom, opening the door. She noticed everything was neat and clean. Her bedroom held a bed, desk, with Justin Bieber posters hanging around the room. Clothes were neatly piled on her bed that looked fresh and clean. Stepping to the desk, she saw pictures of Gwen with a few friends in cheerleader outfits, posing in front of a football field. Scanning her desk, she noticed books and papers. Lifting her pen, she sifted through the documents to find anything outstanding. Mainly notes from class and homework.

"Where are you, Gwen?" she muttered to herself.

Meeting Spider back in the truck a few minutes later, he shut the door, passing her the list of friends that her parents compiled.

"What did you say to that cop?"

"Nothing I wouldn't say to anyone on our team."

Looking over at her, he smirked.

"He completely changed his attitude when he came back and was more helpful."

Teagan shrugged her shoulders, checking all three names.

"These are the same names that police already provided."

"Yeah, I think we can finish talking with them today and maybe look for a connection."

Moving through town, Teagan watched as everyone went on about their business, not feeling any disturbance from a local killer being in town.

* * *

Back at the station, a few hours later, Teagan, Spider, and Daughtrey were reading through the material they'd compiled since taking over the case. Connecting the number of missing girls over the past few weeks, she calculated a total of five, between the ages of twelve and twenty-two. Tracking the drop-offs at the barn from each person's home, there wasn't a rhyme or reason for why the girls were chosen, beyond being able to be controlled.

"You think we'll find a pattern before he strikes again?" Daughtrey asked.

"What makes you think it's a man?" Spider replies.

Teagan looked at the question.

"What did you say?"

"I said—"

She raised her hand.

"Not you. Spider."

"What? Makes you think it's a man," Spider repeated.

"That's it." Teagan jumped up and went to the white-board, picking up the black sharpie and making a list.

"What are you doing?" Daughtrey questioned as he leaned back, scratching the side of his face.

Teagan drew a line from each location where the girls were abducted to the land field.

"All were picked up and held for a few days before being dumped at the field."

Spider looked at the medical papers.

"At least a week or two," Spider said.

"So, whoever is doing this somehow gets bored or annoyed."

"We could probably put a team on the field to investigate if they come back," Daughtrey mentioned.

"What time did the coroner say they died?"

Flipping through the binder on the table, Spider repeated the time for the first three girls.

"Let's have local police sit at the location." Teagan was about to mark on the whiteboard again when a knock came at the door. The mayor walked in with Bert behind him.

"Agent Stone, I wanted to check on the progress of the case," Mayor Henton said.

"The case is coming along. We've met with the Akersons."

"Has Copeland been helpful?"

Bert stared at Teagan with his lip curved upwards, anticipating the answer. Spider and Daughtrey watched the exchange between the two.

"Copeland and I have an understanding now."

Henton reached inside his jacket and pulled out an envelope, handing it to Teagan.

"What's this?" She opened the envelope, pulling out two tickets.

"Those are tickets to the fundraiser the governor is throwing in a few weeks."

"Does he know who we are?"

"No, I had extra tickets, and I wanted to bring you as guests," Henton replied.

"Thank you," Teagan said.

Teagan passed the tickets over to Spider.

"Tell me about the governor," she said.

"He's one of those established politicians," Henton remarked.

"Officer Bert, do you mind bringing us the school records of Gwen Akerson?" Teagan asked, wanting to delve deeper into the governor's life without anyone finding out.

"That's not my job," Bert scoffed.

"Officer, either you're going to perform your duties, or you're not," Henton argued.

"Yes, sir," Bert replied.

Bert walked out of the room.

"He's a peach," Daughtrey blurted out.

"So, Governor Snyder."

"Every year, these fundraisers happen, and he invites the local leaders that have long family ties in politics," Mayor Henton recalled.

"Is he married?" Teagan glanced at the mayor.

Spider typed on his computer.

"For at least twenty years, three kids," Spider said.

"You're not thinking Snyder has anything to do with this?" Henton said.

"I keep all options open. Whoever is behind these killings has an extensive reach."

"I understand, but the governor wouldn't be behind something this dark."

"Has your assistant sent over all the documents I requested?"

She needed the list of local businesses that used to be in the surrounding areas near the farm.

"I asked her to give you whatever you needed."

"We haven't heard from her," Spider replied.

"Okay, I'll get on that. But please remember to try not to ruffle any feathers."

"Based on my background, sir, I can't promise to not push people's buttons."

Thinking over the invite as Henton left the room, Teagan wanted to make a lasting impression on the governor, better than she did the chief. It was getting later in the day, and the chief wanted to get an update from her before she went back to the hotel. Gathering up her notes, she left Spider and Daughtrey to finish gathering more evidence.

Strolling down the hallway of the station, Teagan passed Bert and Copeland talking together in the corner. They peered at her as she knocked on the chief's door. Hearing she could come in, Teagan took a long breath, released it, and smiled as she pushed the door open.

"Chief."

"Have a seat, Agent Stone."

"Thank you."

"How are things with the hotel you're staying at?"

Taken aback by his question, she paused before answering.

"Okay."

"I hear your whole team is coming along with the investigation."

"We are."

"Do you have any updates I can give the families?"

He tapped the pen across the desk, waiting for an answer.

"After speaking with the Akersons, I want to wait before doing anything that will tip off anyone."

"So you think you've found the person?" he probed further.

"No, the mayor was getting more documents sent to my team."

"As you can tell, I'm in a bind."

Seeing the stress lines over his forehead, Teagan was tempted to ask if he was being paid by somebody to answer even if it wasn't correct.

"Chief, is everything okay?"

The chief opened his desk drawer, pulled out a bottle of Pepto Bismol, poured a small amount in a cup, and drank it down.

"Stomach virus."

Seeing the sweat pooled together and eyes jumping from around the room, Teagan was skeptical it was only a virus. Since getting the call, the team had been hit with roadblocks non-stop.

"Maybe you should take some time off."

Coughing, he nodded in agreement.

"Listen, I have to do a press conference soon, and I need something."

"Call it off."

"I can't do that."

"You would be playing into their hands."

"Agent, we have dead girls in my town. I need someone to blame!" he shouted.

"That hasn't left my mind, sir."

Teagan jumped up, pointing at herself.

Pushing back from the desk, Chief Snyder stood, crossing his arms over his chest.

"Either I have something for the news by the end of the week, or I'll call to get you replaced."

"Try it now." Teagan grabbed the receiver off the phone and dialed the number at the Agency.

"Director's office," a woman said over the phone.

"Can you get the person who's in charge on the phone, please?"

"Agent Stone, is that you?" she asked.

"Yes, it's me."

"Is everything all right?"

"Chief would like to know if I could be replaced." Teagan stared into his eyes as she spoke.

"Ummm... I doubt it since you're the director of The Agency and in charge of everyone."

"Thank you, Caroline." Teagan pushed to end the call.

"Chief, your wife's out front, complaining," Bert barked, pushing his door open without waiting to be asked.

Chief muttered, "Shit, I told her not to come back up here."

"Do you mind if I use your phone? I need to check in with my family." Teagan asked. She could see he was about to decline her but decided against it.

"Yeah, just don't hog up the line," the chief replied, treading out of the room. Bert stood at the door as Teagan lifted the phone.

"It's private."

He smirked, a cocky and devilish sort of expression as he closed the door.

Dialing Gregory's number, Teagan watched through the blinds as the chief argued back and forth with his wife at the front counter. While waiting for the call to go through, Teagan rose toward the computer screen, seeing it was already open with his email and a few files, including the case.

"Gregory," he said.

"Gregory, this is Teagan."

"I was tracing this call, wondering if one of you guys had gotten into trouble."

He chuckled. Teagan chortled.

"No, but the chief had to step out for a moment, and I needed to call my family."

"What do you need?" he asked.

"Trace his computer and phone log."

"How far back?"

"At least six months."

Teagan ran her hand across the mouse, keeping an eye on the chief and Bert. Clicking on the emails that talked about the case, she mainly saw news requests and local councilmen wanting to know how things were going. Another email had popped up two minutes before she came into his office to talk.

"I'll need a little bit of time."

"Rush job," she said, clicking and opening the email.

Friend: Event tickets are sold out.

Chief: You do this every time.

Friend: Then you should do what they tell you next time.

"Gotcha, boss."

"What is—" The chief rushed back into his office with his wife beside him as Teagan quickly logged out of his email.

"I'll be home soon, honey." Teagan hung the phone up, rising out of the chief's seat.

"Who are you?" his wife asked.

Teagan extended her hand for a shake.

"Agent Stone, ma'am."

"Are you sleeping with my husband too?" she blurted out, swaying left to right.

"Ignore my wife; she likes to drink a little more at lunch than her friends," Chief groaned, nudging his wife to sit.

"I'll be in touch, Chief." Teagan reached for the knob, then a cold, still voice came from behind.

"At least try to be more discreet, Agent Stone."

Rushing down the hallway, Teagan slowly closed the door, keeping an eye on everyone in the precinct.

"You look like you've seen a ghost," Daughtrey commented nervously.

"I met the chief's wife, and something felt off about her."

"What do you mean?" Spider questioned.

Ignoring the question, Teagan ran a hand down her face.

"I spoke with Gregory, and he's going to trace the last few calls from the chief's desk."

Daughtrey and Spider both peered at the revelation.

"You think the chief is behind this?" Daughtrey whispered.

"Not sure, but I can't rule out anyone. Let's wrap up for the night and get back to the hotel."

"Camden, Nebraska has just as many secrets as Wall Street," Daughtrey mumbled.

Grabbing the brush and cleaning off the whiteboard, Teagan continued to stare at the location they found the bodies for a few extra seconds before cleaning it off.

Chapter Twenty

One week later back in DC.

Senator Steinman sat back in her office, fielding requests for the upcoming budget bill the president had planned out. She wanted to cut it by one trillion and proposed other options to try to have a bipartisan bill for the American people. She felt President Sanders only wanted to appease his base and not make the hard choices. Martha Steinman is a senator from Tennessee in office for the past ten years, working to establish her career as a hardliner on crime and pro-business. As a woman in her late fifties, married with four children, she knew what it took to be the only woman in the room. That's why going through the budget and seeing the funding for certain Defense spending caused a red flag. A knock at her door paused her reading as she called for the person to come in and have a seat.

"Senator Steinman."

He extended a hand.

"Secretary Kelton."

Waving at the chair in front of her desk, she nodded for him to sit.

"To what do I owe this visit, sir."

Smiling, Todd loosened his jacket, picking up a piece of peppermint off her desk.

"Well, I know you're working on the budget for the president."

"That's right."

"As secretary of transportation, I wanted to see if we could help each other out."

"How can I help you?"

"President Sanders won't be in office for much longer."

"Are you planning on running?"

"Something I'm considering."

"You're in his cabinet. Won't he see this as a betrayal?"

"We've never agreed on much, but this is a political move."

Todd Kelton was the snake oil type of politician; his family had a long line of political stature that he ran on. At forty years old, he was young, married with two kids, and considered one of *People Magazine*'s politicians to watch. Before taking on the transportation role, he worked on Wall Street, making millions, and decided to move into politics after seeing all of the regulations Sanders was trying to push through legislation. Running on bipartisanship to get Sanders on his side was the first step to gain his trust.

"Why should I believe you? I mean, the media says you're the one behind all of Sanders' decisions."

He chuckled at her statement.

"Sanders has no political clout left; he's run this country into the ground."

"That we can agree on. You know this budget he's proposing is outrageous."

"I heard he has funds for a certain department that's now under the Pentagon."

Martha's eyes widened in surprise.

"The Firm."

"An agency that's not to be touched. But I think we could dismantle it if done right."

"How?"

"Do I have your support?"

Martha nodded.

"Do what you do best; get them in front of the committee."

"You mean for a hearing?"

"Yes, while they're distracted. Sanders won't have time to handle everything."

"His chief of staff would point to someone in charge."

"Not if you make it where they have a last-minute distraction and set the meeting last minute."

"I don't know, Kelton."

"What are you afraid of, Martha?"

"I follow the constitution. No one is above the law."

He smirked.

"Discretion is something you'll learn very early on with me, Senator."

"Nobody in the history of the Senate committee has pulled this off."

"Until today."

"What do I have as insurance that you won't cross me like you're doing to Sanders?"

Todd gave her a knowing smile and reached his palm

out. Martha looked from his hand up to his face and back. Shaking hands, Martha wondered if she was making the right decision in what the secretary was pledging as a partnership.

"What do you want, Senator?"

"I want Speaker."

"Aiming high, I see."

"As you can see, I'm putting my name out there, and more than likely will take the fall on this if we fail."

"There's something else I need."

Martha scoffed, throwing her pen down.

"What else?"

"There's a case in Nebraska—"

"Excuse me, Senator, you have a call on line four," her secretary said.

"Thank you, Krystal. Mr. Kelton emailed me about the Nebraska case."

Todd held a hard glare across his face watching Martha take a call while he was trying to set his plans in motion.

"Okay. Thank you, Senator."

She waved goodbye to him as he left her office. Heading out of the building, Todd cracked his knuckles and adjusted his tie. Security held the door open, and Todd slid in, sitting across from another associate.

"What did she say?"

"She's on board."

"You think we can trust her?"

The limo drove out of the parking lot into traffic. He broke his gaze from looking at the people walking around.

"I can't trust you, let alone anyone else."

"Are you upset?"

"I need another one."

"What happened to the last one I gave you?"

"She's dead!" he snapped.

Sweat beads pooled at his forehead.

"Todd, you promised no more killing."

Ten minutes later, the car stopped at the Barton Restaurant near 11St. and West. Stepping out of the car, Todd looked around the area. Before he sauntered into the restaurant, he requested to be shut down.

"Mr. Secretary, your table is ready." Melinda said.

"Thank you, Melinda."

The grey-blue-eyed, blonde-haired hostess escorted him toward the private room, with his guest waiting. A few seconds later, his other passenger arrived.

"Make this quick. I shouldn't be seen with you."

"I take it our mutual colleague explained about this meeting."

"Mr. Keenan, you have five minutes of my time."

"Can I get you a drink, sir?" the hostess asked.

"No," Todd answered.

"I'll take another whiskey neat," Neal stated.

"Coming right up."

The hostess left them to continue their conversation. Todd Kelton didn't like to be summoned. His brow raised in suspicion.

"Extremely impressed you've been able to last this long."

"Is that a threat?" Todd's breathing heightened in frustration.

"Mr. Kelton, I would never put you at risk or myself that way."

"Keep it that way."

"Aren't you married with children?" Neal asked.

All eyes stared at Todd.

"None of your concern."

"Touché. But I propose a little help from you."

"What type of help?"

"The type that could be very rewarding for you and for me."

"In what way?" The hostess stepped back in the room as the waitress brought out Neal's plate filled with vegetables and steak.

"Neal works for the governor," she said.

"Does he know about me?" Todd questioned, pointing at himself.

Not wanting to waste any more time, Neal had to get an agreement signed before anyone found out what he'd planned next.

"No, I have just as much to lose as you, Secretary."

Drinking his whiskey, Neal sighed, letting the taste linger and mesh with the flavors of the steak.

"I have cargo coming in on the harbor, and I'd like to have you clear it without hassle."

"You're kidding, right?"

"Do I look like I'm kidding?"

"What type of cargo?"

"Cargo you like, Secretary Kelton."

A glint in his eyes sparkled when Neal confessed more girls were coming soon.

"How many?" Todd whispered.

"Thirty," Neal replied.

"When are they coming?" Todd licked his lips.

"Sir, remember you promised no more threats," she told him.

Loosening his tie, glancing over his shoulder, Todd waved for the waitress to come back over.

"Sir, can I get you something?" Melinda asked.

"I'll have a whiskey and steak, please," he responded, grinning at the smirk on Neal's face.

Neal raised his glass in a toast. This would be the most girls he'd brought to the country under these travels.

"You'll need to make sure nothing traces back to me."

"We're in agreement, Senator. I work for the governor, so this is between you and me."

"How much are we talking about for my cut?" she queried, hoping she could finally end working for Henton and leave the country with the money she'd saved.

"For setting up this meeting, I can do maybe twenty thousand," Todd said.

She studied him for a moment, with the audacity to only offer twenty thousand when he more than likely made close to half a million from bringing those girls.

"Let me rephrase; I want a hundred grand in my account."

Todd chuckled at her request, leaning closer and whispering, "I'm not giving you a hundred thousand dollars."

"Secretary Kelton, we both know what you like."

Twirling the butter knife on the table, Todd knew she was taking advantage of the situation and wouldn't hesitate to rat him out. He needed to get rid of her before the deal was complete and work straight through Neal going forward.

"Let me think of my options."

"Either you come up with the money, or you find someone who does."

"I can't just transfer that much money without my wife noticing."

Pulling out his ringing phone, Neal answers the call from the governor.

"Governor, is everything all right?" Neal asked.

Todd waited as Neal continued his conversation.

"Will do, sir." Neal hung up the phone.

"What does he want?" she questioned.

"About his fundraiser tomorrow."

"Are you flying back for that?" She watched as Neal gathered his wallet and left money on the table.

"Yeah, in fact, I need to leave in the next five minutes," Neal responded.

He extended his hand toward Secretary Kelton.

"Mr. Secretary, I'll be in contact about Washington Ports."

Kelton shook his hand and watched as he left the room.

"You might think I'm trying to take advantage of the situation, but I want out."

"You're out when I say you're out." Todd jumped up out of his chair, stomped out of the restaurant, and headed back to the limo as she scrambled to follow. She tried to slide in next to him, but he blocked her from entering.

"Take a cab." He slammed the door, motioning for security to drive off.

* * *

Arriving home thirty minutes later, he said goodbye for the night as he entered the mansion of his home, hearing his kids laughing and playing. Undoing his tie, he removed his jacket and went to the bar in the corner of his living room, almost tripping over the toy police car.

"Fuck!" He kicked the car against the wall.

Grabbing the bourbon off the counter, he poured the glass up to the rim and drank it down in one gulp.

Rubbing the back of his neck, Todd continued staring at his children's toys on the ground. Hearing the rumbling of his stomach, he started to go toward the kitchen when his wife and son came into the room.

"I didn't know you were home," Liz said, running into his arms, standing on her tippy toes, and wrapping her arms around his neck.

"Surprise." He pecked her lips and ruffled his son's hair.

TJ was the spitting image of him with his blonde hair and blue eyes.

"Daddy, can I go to the carnival?" TJ asked.

Todd bent down and cupped his son's chin.

"Were you good for Mommy while I was gone?"

TJ grinned, nodding his head. Todd shifted his head as his other children came into the room talking with each other. His heart beat faster seeing the chaos moving around him.

"Did you miss me?"

"Every minute," Todd replied, standing.

Chapter Twenty-One

The gun cocked back as her mind filled with every scenario that could go wrong if she didn't find out who was behind the death of two more girls—dressed in a green silk dress with thin straps and a low-cut, V-neck slit, and high heels. She checked her makeup one more time in the mirror and wondered how Christian would feel about her going undercover as someone who was going to buy girls. She smoothed her black fur coat over her dress, pulling her red lace front wig forward, seeing the hazel contact lenses and red full lips glowing under the car light. Her maturity at thirty-six was showcased as her mind games had grown beyond the first time she went undercover.

"Remember we can hear everything," Gregory mentioned.

"I shouldn't be more than an hour or two unless the conversation moves to business."

Pulling up to the exclusive party at the governor's home, the valet opened Teagan's door as Spider stepped out alongside her in his black tuxedo. Placing her hand on his arm, she smiled at the valet and watched as Sean went to park with Gregory still in the car. Daughtrey and Broderick followed in the second van and parked a block away, watching as cars came and went. Hearing the classical music from inside, Spider tightened his hold on Teagan's arm, helping her up the steps of the home. Butlers stood with both doors open in the twenty-thousand-square-foot, two-story home. Walking in, the pictures of previous governors hung on the wall, with expensive artwork alongside. Waitstaff stood with a tray of champagne glasses for them to take, and both declined, wanting to keep a clear head as they went in to meet the wealthy elite of Nebraska. Gold marble floors were inscribed with the governor's name, and a statue of his face sat near his family photo. You could tell he thought highly of himself and came from money like Mayor Henton, but he didn't use his name as a steppingstone to further his career.

"Ready for this?" Spider released the hold on Teagan's arm, scanning the room of people talking in huddles of groups.

"Try not to get into any trouble." Teagan winked, removing her fur coat and passing it to the staff. She pressed her clenched purse to her stomach. Lifting the corners of her lips, she smiled, moving into the crowd as she swished around the room, waiting for someone to take the bait as her curves swayed in her gown. After three kids, she only got more and more beautiful as she aged with constantly working out and running behind her children. Surprisingly, the kids wanted more siblings after all these years, and she explained that wasn't happening. Even with having a dog, the house was always busy with noise.

"Excuse me, do I know you?" Teagan shifted, looking

behind her at the voice calling out to her. Never knowing who she'd met throughout her time undercover, she couldn't remember the man with olive skin, short, dark hair, and six-four height.

"I don't; I'm Patricia Langston." Teagan reached her hand over for him to shake.

"You're extremely beautiful, Patricia. I'm Adam Gardner." The firm handshake and mischievous smile on his face set off high alerts that could lead her to some answers.

"Thank you."

"Are you here with anyone?" Adam brought the champagne glass to his lips.

"I have a friend here with me."

"A friend who would say something about me speaking with you."

"Depends on what the conversation is about."

Adam stepped in closer to Teagan, bent down, and whispered in her ear.

"My gut is telling me you'd like my conversation."

Teagan cocked her head to the left, grinning at Adam and licking her lips.

"What do you do for a living, Adam?" A waitstaff came over with a tray of shrimp wraps in kale.

"No, thank you," Teagan said.

"I'm an investor. What about you?" Adam placed the champagne down and took a second one from the tray.

"Same."

"Are you on Travis' payroll?" Adam questioned, glancing at Governor Snyder standing with his wife on his arm.

"No, I was invited because we have a few things in common."

"Really, like what?"

"If I tell you, I'd have to kill you." Teagan winked, starting to head over to the governor and his wife when Adam grasped her hand.

"Maybe I'm intrigued."

"I doubt what I'm into is something you'd be interested in."

"What gives you that idea?"

Staring at Travis, Teagan noticed when he tried to place his hand on his wife's lower back, and she smacked it away. Not wanting to be embarrassed, Travis cleared his throat, calling for another drink. A waitstaff made an announcement that dinner would be ready in five minutes.

"Mr. Gardner, my extra investments are sometimes off the books." Teagan remained calm, steadfast in her speaking. Erring on the side of caution, she wanted to ease him into explaining what he was into.

"Most of the people here work off the books."

"I see."

"What if we go somewhere private and talk?"

She glanced around the room, making eye contact with Spider, letting him know she was moving, and keeping an eye on everyone.

"Following your lead, Mr. Gardner."

"Call me Adam." He motioned for her to walk ahead of him as he put his champagne down and headed toward the balcony. The palace was booming with music, photographers taking pictures, and staff roaming around trying to keep things in order. Teagan estimated there were about a hundred or more guests at his home. Nodding to the women glaring at her as she sashayed outside, she chuckled at the annoyance but didn't care to address it at this moment. Tapping her thigh to make sure the gun was still within reach, Teagan turned around as Adam closed the double balcony doors behind them.

"Are you married, Patricia?"

Adam approached her with her back toward the railing.

"No, are you?"

"A man like me can't settle down. A woman wouldn't understand my needs."

"What are those needs, Mr. Gardner?"

Adam trailed his palm across her wrist, up her arm to lift her chin, making direct eye contact.

"Have dinner with me and find out."

Teagan reached up and took his hand in hers, moving it away gently.

"Only thing I'm interested in is business, Adam. I don't mix it with pleasure."

"I could change your mind; I'm known to have women groveling at my feet."

"Sounds spicy, but I love money more."

Adam chuckled. "Then we could get along fine."

"What business dealings do you have with Snyder?" Tegan ran her palm up to his chest.

"Snyder and I go way back from our college days. He's money-hungry like me."

"From looking at his home, I can see that."

"Listen, let's cut to the chase and get down to what we can do for each other, Patricia."

"I'm all ears."

"I have a few clubs I invest in and rental property."

Teagan fell back in laughter.

"You think a little club money is what I want?" Teagan started to push Adam to the side and walk off.

"Wait... I might have more ways to get money."

She closed the space between them and pursed her lips.

"Good, I hope it's something worth my time."

"Some of my friends have their hands in things outside of the legal realm."

"Dinner is being served," a waitress interrupted their conversation.

Putting space between them, Teagan stepped back, smiling at the waitress, and started to head back into the home toward the dinner party. Adam was impressed with the way her ass sat in the dress and wanted to get to the dark beauty more, but he knew divulging all his secrets early would probably put him in a bad spot with the governor and his clients. Seeing all of the guests sitting and talking with the governor at the head of the table, Teagan looked for Spider and noticed him sitting at the edge of the table. Right as she walked over, Adam grasped her hand. Teagan was startled for a moment and looked back at Adam.

"We should continue our conversation unless you're occupied with someone else."

Shaking her head no, she took him up on his offer and followed him to the empty seats near Governor Snyder. Sitting down, she placed the napkin on her leg and lifted the glass of water.

"Adam, I see you've found a friend," Snyder said, leaning over the table.

His wife Juliette rolled her eyes and continued drinking as the food was being brought out.

"This is Patricia Langston, Governor." Adam introduced me.

"Lovely to meet you, Patricia. I'm Travis Snyder." He held her palm in his hand, kissing the back of her knuckle.

"I'm his wife Juliette, but you wouldn't know that with how much of an asshole—"

"Juliette, this is not the time," Travis grunted; the grimace on her face showed she hated Travis Snyder.

"Nice to meet you, Governor. Adam has been telling me a lot about you and your beautiful wife."

Teagan studied them both, analyzing the posture and body language between the couple. If she had to bet, the marriage was just for convenience, and both of them were probably cheating on each other and only showing love in front of the cameras. Travis stood and clanked the butterknife against his glass to get everyone's attention.

"Ladies and gentlemen, thank you so much for joining us tonight.""

Spider continued taking in everybody and allowing his hidden camera on his tie to scan faces to send back to Gregory to investigate.

"As governor, your support has been wonderful and truly appreciated."

"Another campaign run!" someone shouted out.

Travis chuckled, shaking his head at the outburst from his campaign manager Neal Keenan. She had to give it to him—Travis came off very charming and outgoing.

"Well, that's something I will talk about at another time. Tonight is about celebrating our wins." Travis and the other guests raised a glass as he gave a toast.

"To us," Travis said, staring at Teagan, lifting his drink and smirking. She didn't think he could recognize her with the heavy makeup and contacts in her eyes, so she hoped by the end of the night, more secrets would be spilled.

* * *

An hour later, everybody was at the point of hungover from dinner and relaxed, so Teagan took that as an opportunity to look around. Governor Snyder was whispering in his wife's ear, Neal texted on his phone as the other guests talked back and forth.

"I need to use the restroom," she said, dropping her napkin on the table and pushing the chair back to step away.

"I can show you." Adam stood from his seat. Teagan planted her hand on his shoulder, stopping him from following. Teagan smoothly rubbed her palm across his shoulder, shaking her head no, and glanced up at Travis as he explained to turn left and down the hallway to the bathroom on the right. Carrying her purse, she swished out of the dining room, passing the portrait of Snyder shaking hands with Mayor Henton. Peering back, she checked to make sure no one else was coming as she continued toward the restroom, going past a closet left ajar. Seeing the bathroom next to another door, she placed her ear against the door to hear if anyone was inside. Gripping the door handle, she slowly turned the knob, finding it open. Glancing over her shoulder one more time, she slipped through the door, shutting it lightly. Feeling the wall, she came across a painting made of Governor Snyder. The room was dark brown with a leather loveseat, chess table, mahogany wooden desk, and world globe sitting in the corner near a trophy stand. Teagan went to the drawers, opening one by one, seeing old receipts and memos of meetings. Clicking the keyboard, the monitor popped onto the Internet Explorer, and moving the mouse over to the file folder, it was clear of any information stored.

"I'm tired of you flirting in front of me, Travis," a voice snapped.

Surprised at the voices arguing, she mumbled under her breath and tiptoed to the door, listening.

"Calm down, baby. You know I only want you," Snyder replied.

"Then tell your wife." she fussed.

Teagan's eyes peered down at the doorknob as it rotated, and the door opened slightly. She moved against the back corner of the door, out of sight.

"Come in—" Governor Snyder said.

"Travis, what are you doing?" Juliette asked, interrupting him at the door with his mistress. Teagan held her breath, hoping he didn't step further into the room and blow her cover.

"Missy needed to use the phone," Travis stated.

"She can use the one in the kitchen with the help. I mean, she does help you in some way," Juliette remarked.

"Juliette," Travis barked.

"It's okay, Travis," Missy said.

Travis' hand held the door open for another second.

"I'll show you to the kitchen, Missy," Travis told her.

"We both can, darling," Juliette responded.

Shutting the door closed, Teagan released the long-held breath and waited until the footsteps went away. Peeking through the door, she went out and slid over to the bathroom. Five minutes later, she came out of the bathroom and strolled back into the dining room. Seeing dessert placed on the table, Teagan motioned, moving her hand up her arm, letting Spider know she was ready to end the night. As soon as he stood, Teagan cleared her throat, getting everyone's attention.

"Mr. Governor, I had a lovely time, but it's past my bedtime, I'm afraid."

"You're leaving so soon." Governor Snyder held onto her palm, making circles against her knuckles gently.

"I must get to work early." Teagan slid her hand out.

"What are you doing?"

"Investments and some of the book business," she bent down and whispered in his ear.

"You should speak with my campaign manager; I could use more investments."

"Give me a call." Teagan opened her clutch, taking out a business card as Spider slid her coat around her shoulders.

"Can I walk you out?" Adam asked.

Spider and Teagan looked at each other briefly.

"I'd like that."

Adam approached, holding out his hand, and Teagan took it, walking alongside him out of the door, with Spider stalking behind. The butler held the door open as their car arrived to take them home. Teagan licked her lips as Adam stared into her eyes.

"I'd love to take you out for dinner," Adam said.

"I don't date."

Spider got in the right passenger side, shutting the door, grabbing the seatbelt.

"We can discuss the business information."

"That depends on what information you have for me." Teagan lifted her right leg about to hop in when Adam placed his hand on her lower back, stopping her.

"I know who can help you."

"Okay, how can they help me?" she questioned.

"Meet me here tomorrow at four." Adam pulled out his business card and pen, writing down an address.

Teagan spiked her left brow up in curiosity.

"If this is only about you having sex with me, Adam..."

"I promise, all business."

"We'll see." She got in the car, shutting the door, calling out for them to leave.

Spider turned his head as she reached under her dress for her gun that was holstered to her thigh. Also taking out her cell phone, Teagan contacted Broderick and Daughtrey.

"What do you think?" she asked Spider as she tossed her wig off, slid out of her heels, and changed into tights, a large t-shirt, and sneakers.

"We didn't get anything major," Gregory called out.

"Anything on your end, Broderick?"

"All license plates checked out clean," Broderick replied.

"Travis is having an affair, but nothing jumped out when I went to his office."

It started sprinkling as the car pulled up to the hotel. Holding the phone in her hand, she looked out of the window and saw Broderick pull in behind them. Ending the call, Teagan jumped out of the car and ran inside, throwing the gown and wig in the trashcan next to the elevator. Stepping on the elevator with the rest of the team, she stared at the makeup on her face through the elevator door.

Getting off on their floor, everyone marched toward their room door in thought. Removing the key from her pocket, Teagan unlocked the door and stepped in, throwing her things on the couch. Kicking off her shoes, she plopped on the bed, blowing out a breath and turning to her side. Staring at her purse for over five minutes, she got off the bed and checked for the business card Adam offered, noticing the other business card of Snyder's campaign manager. Flicking her finger against each card, Teagan sat back down on the bed and peered at the time on the clock.

"Four tomorrow," she whispered.

Chapter Twenty-Two

Turning off the shower, Neal grabbed the towel off the back of the door. Scanning the business suits in his bedroom closet, he thought about his meeting with Governor Snyder in an hour. After getting dressed and walking downstairs to his kitchen to fix his tie, Alejandra placed a cup of coffee in front of his bowl of oatmeal.

"Alejandra, I'm going to be late for dinner tonight."

"Yes, sir."

"Is our guest awake?"

"Yes, sir."

"Good."

Finishing his coffee, he grabbed the bowl of oatmeal and walked down the hall to the basement, unlocking the door. Lying on the bed, chained by her wrist, was someone he didn't expect to bring back, but she kept pushing and threatened to expose his work.

Flashback night of the party.

"I have a variety of women," Neal muttered over the phone. He stood in Governor Snyder's office on the phone.

"The girls should come clean and tested."

Neal grabbed a pen off the desk, pulling out the documents for transportation for bringing in more girls that can go unnoticed without coming back to his name.

"We have transportation confirmed."

Sending an email, Neal closed out of the computer and ended the call. The door pushed open with Missy shutting it behind her.

"Can I help you, Missy?"

"I heard you on the phone."

"I don't know what you're talking about."

"Neal, I'm not stupid." Missy stumbled to the chair, holding a bottle of wine in her hand.

She lifted it to her lips.

"Maybe you should ease up on the wine."

"Maybe you should ease up on the hookers."

"Hookers."

"Yeah, I heard you talking about buying girls."

"Does Travis know your back here?"

Dropping the bottle on the floor, Missy crawled on top of the desk, crossing her legs.

"What are you doing?"

"I know you've been watching me."

"How old are you, Missy?"

Giggling, she ran her hand down his chest.

"Old enough to know that you're doing something bad."

Grasping her wrist, he twisted it back.

"Ouch... let me go."

"Bitch, you have no idea what I'm capable of doing."

"I'm sorry."

"You're going to be."

Present.

Turning the light on in the room, Neal moved her hair out of her face, running the back of his palm across her cheek. He watched as she winced over the black eye he gave her.

"You should have kept your mouth shut."

"Please let me go home."

"You're going somewhere. Just not home."

"Travis is going to wonder where I am." Missy pushed his hand away.

"Eat."

"I'm not hungry."

"Eat or starve, it doesn't matter to me."

Putting the bowl down on the bed, Neal looked around at the scattered clothes of her dress and shoes.

"I'm moving you out of here today."

"Please, I won't say anything."

"I don't believe you." He went to the door as she threw a bowl of oatmeal against the wall.

"I'm off to work."

Jogging up the stairs, Neal grabbed his coat and keys, placed his wallet in his pants pockets, and reset the alarm, leaving his house and getting in the town car. Heading to the governor's office, Neal checked over the latest poll numbers for re-election in the next few months.

* * *

Fifteen minutes later, the security detail opened the door, letting him out of the car. He shook hands with a few coworkers outside. Seeing his secretary at her desk, she held out messages he needed to return. Unlocking his door and removing his coat, Neal stood at the window, seeing his driver talking with a few men.

"You're early."

"I have a meeting with Travis."

"Do you want coffee?"

"Yeah, with a little rum."

"This early?"

"When do you question me so much, Olivia?"

"No reason, Mr. Kenan."

Ring! Ring!

"Kenan."

"Come to my office," Snyder said.

"Yes, sir, Governor."

Neal grimaced, scratching his chin.

"Here's your coffee."

"I don't want it."

Stalking to the governor's office, he heard yelling outside of his closed door. Knocking, he pushed the door open.

"Do you have any idea how much money I'm losing?" Travis asked.

"Governor, what's the problem?"

"These numbers are the problem. I might actually have a challenger."

Snyder tossed the newspaper on the desk.

"You shouldn't stress about early numbers."

"What the hell is happening with the damn murder of those girls?"

"I'm handling it, Governor."

"I doubt that; my numbers would look better than what the polls show."

"The public doesn't feel safe with the murders."

"Where are you with that anyway?"

"The mayor has the chief of police working twenty-four-seven on the case."

"I want someone arrested for this ASAP, Neal!"

"We both do, sir."

Standing from his chair, Governor Snyder grunted and paced in front of his chair.

"I haven't heard from Missy."

"Did you have a fight?"

"Juliette caught us going into my office the other night at the party."

"Governor."

"Last thing I need is a lecture from you."

"She's probably just ignoring your calls."

"You think so?"

"She's young. Give it a day or two."

"It's not like her to ignore my calls."

"Take your wife out to dinner and try being a husband."

"Juliette's not talking to me right now either."

"We need the public to believe you're a family man."

"Yeah, family man," Snyder groaned, rubbing the back of his neck.

"Anything else?"

Governor Snyder pulled his cell phone out of his pocket, scrolling over photos of Missy and him together. Motioning his hand that he didn't need anything else.

"Great, I'll be in my office." Neal turned, leaving Governor Snyder's office and taking his phone out of his pocket to send a text message to his security at home.

Neal: Take care of our guest.

Jimmy: Same place?

Neal: See how much she's worth.

"Mr. Kenan, I have Mayor Henton on line one," his assistant said.

"Thanks, Olivia." Neal closed out of his messages and picked up the receiver from the edge of the desk.

"Mayor Henton."

"Neal, I'm surprised to hear from you."

"Well, I do work on behalf of the governor."

"Is everything okay?"

"That's why I'm calling."

"We don't have any updates on the murders."

"Hummm... Did you see the numbers for Governor Snyder re-election?"

"Not lately."

"Get this case wrapped up now, or you'll find yourself out of a job."

"Is that a threat?"

"I don't make threats, Mayor." Neal heard the end of the dial tone, holding the phone in his hand.

* * *

Adam ordered a glass of white wine as he sat in Longhorn Steakhouse, watching Patricia swish over to his table. He smiled as he stood to hug her and pull the chair out for her to sit. Taking her black shawl off her shoulders, Patricia smiled back.

"You look just as lovely as at the dinner."

"Thank you, Adam."

Their waitress came to the table holding a glass of water.

"Welcome to Longhorn. I'm Joanne," she said.

"Can we get another glass of white wine for my guest?"

"Sure, anything to eat?" Joanne asked.

"No, thank you," Patricia said.

"Are you sure? They have great buffalo burgers."

"Positive. I'm here for business, remember."

"I'll bring your wine right out." Joanne took her menu, strolling back to the kitchen. Longhorn opened two years ago in Camden to bring jobs back to the town and increase tourism.

"Something about you, Patricia."

"Adam, let me be clear. We're here to talk business."

"What about after we conclude our business?"

Gripping the glass of water, Patricia smirked, taking a sip.

"I won't be here for long."

"That breaks my heart."

"I've been known for breaking hearts and more."

"I might like that." Adam reached over the table to touch her hand.

She slid her hand away.

"My business, as I told you, deals in investments."

"Straight to business, huh?"

She tilted her head to the side.

"What do you have for me?"

Looking around the restaurant, it was mostly empty except for one or two couples engaged in conversation. Joanne came back from the kitchen, passing her glass of wine to her.

"Thank you," Patricia told me.

"I can't give you the exact details. Gotta protect myself, you know."

"Then why are we here?" she questioned.

"Some of my investments deal with importing and transporting."

"Like shipping ports?"

"Something like that."

Sitting back in her chair, Teagan stared into Adam's eyes, wondering what shipping ports had to do with the dead girls at the farm. Preparing to ask him a question, her phone interrupted.

"Sorry, I need to take this." Teagan opened her purse to grab her ringing phone.

"Do you need privacy?"

"If you don't mind."

"No problem. I have to use the little boy's room." Adam stood from his seat, buttoning his jacket and heading to the bathroom.

"Talk to me."

"Have you seen the news?" Spider asked.

"No, why?"

"We have another problem."

"What's wrong?"

"Once again, The Firm is getting the limelight we didn't want."

As she spoke with Spider, her phone clicked over with another call.

"I have another call, Spider. Hold on."

"Sure."

"Hello."

"Teagan, you need to come back home," Christian said.

"Christian? What's the matter?"

"I just received a call from our lawyer; you need to appear before the Senate," Christian said.

"The Senate."

"Everything okay?" Adam questioned, his hand on her shoulder.

"Who's that?" Christian asked.

So much going on, Teagan couldn't think straight as a migraine formed.

"Christian, let me call you back." Teagan hung up and, grabbing her purse, she jumped up, running out of the restaurant.

"Patricia! Hold up!" Adam called out, running behind her.

Jumping in the awaiting car with Spider driving, she ignored Adam.

"When can I see you again?" he yelled.

"Go!" Teagan shouted at Spider.

"The guys are packing up now."

Logging into social media, Teagan read all of the reports, removing the wipes in her purse to clean off her makeup. Tossing the wig into the backseat, she slid out of her heels and into her tennis shoes.

"Do you think this has to do with the case?"

"I can bet my last dollar it does."

"I agree; we're getting too close."

"The guys are meeting us at the airport to fly to DC."

"Has the president contacted you?"

"No, I assumed he didn't want to make it seem like he's somehow interfering."

"That makes sense."

"How long before we get to the airport?"

"About thirty minutes."

"Adam was talking about importing and transporting."

"What does that mean?"

"Your guess is as good as mine."

"This damn town has more secrets than Washington."

"At least in Washington, you know who's stabbing you in the back."

Chapter Twenty-Three

Morning in DC.

"Have a seat," President Sanders said.

"Thank you, sir."

"I have to say this doesn't get easier."

"No, it doesn't."

"How's the case going?" President Sanders questioned.

"Slow." Teagan clasped her hands together.

"Tell me the truth, are we going to make an arrest?"

"Honestly, I don't know. This seems to be more than one person."

"I agree with Agent Stone, sir," Spider commented.

"Agent Stone, your face has become the front and center of The Firm."

"I know."

"The Agency was built to weed out people who are trying to bring down our country's value."

"Yes, sir."

"Along the way, you've had to constantly fight adversaries not only foreign, but domestic."

"What are you saying, sir?"

"Maybe it's time we saw this as an opportunity to end The Firm."

This was the moment she'd been hoping for when they brought her back in to go undercover, and now she didn't know how to feel. Knocking on the door, she entered with the chief of staff and Secretary Kelton.

"Mr. President, you have another meeting," he said.

"Thanks, Teagan. Go answer the questions, this shouldn't last long," President Sanders spoke. Teagan and Spider nodded, shaking hands with President Sanders, treading out of his office, and passing Kelton.

* * *

The Firm's lawyer, flanked by Teagan and the rest of her team, marched into the room, looking around at all the reporters and senators talking amongst themselves.

"I see they decided to make this live," Spider whispered.

"Senator is looking to put on a show."

"Don't worry, she's just looking to score political points," Gary said.

"How many times have you done this, Gary?" Teagan asked.

"Too many to count." He placed his briefcase on the table, removing files.

Gregory, Daughtrey, Broderick, and Spider all sat behind Teagan as Senator Steinman called for everyone to enter and take a seat.

"What if something is classified?" Teagan asked.

"She knows certain things are classified."

"She's been on all the news circuits talking about taking us down," Daughtrey said.

"Gregory, look into her," Teagan whispered, leaning back in her seat.

He threw a thumbs up.

"We're going to begin in five minutes," Steinman said.

"Is there anything I need to know before we begin?" Gary inquired.

"You know everything we've done is by the book."

"What about the things that aren't in the book?"

"I suggest you keep it from coming up." Teagan licked her lips, sat forward, and poured a glass of water.

"Please raise your right hand," Senator Steinman told Teagan, standing in front of the cameras and congressmen over the defense budget committee and promising to tell the truth and explain in front of the world what The Firm was all about. Her attorney requested a closed meeting, but Steinman was firm on pushing her own agenda and wanted to make an example out of the team.

"Agent Stone, you are here to tell the truth."

"I am."

"Take a seat, please."

"Before we get started, I request one more time to keep the cameras out of this meeting," Gary told them.

"Request denied, Mr. Rogers," Steinman spoke.

The room went silent.

"Senator Palmer, you have the first question."

"Thank you, Senator. Agent Stone, you're married with three children, correct?"

"Yes."

"Does your family know what you do for a living?" Palmer asked.

"What relevance does this line of questioning have to do with my client?" Gary argued.

"Trying to gain clarity on Agent Stone's life."

"I agree with that question. Are you disagreeing with Mr. Rogers?" Steinman spoke up.

Holding his hand over the microphone, he whispered to Teagan, "What do you think?"

"It's fine. I know what they're doing. I'm used to interrogations."

"Go ahead, Senator."

"As I stated, Agent Stone, does your entire family know of your work?" Palmer asked.

"My family knows I work for the government."

"You're a spy, isn't that true?" The clicking of cameras and rumbling from reporters were shocking as they scrambled to get Teagan's facial reactions.

"Retired SEAL, sir."

"What about the reports of Deputy Brooks?" Steinman brought up, passing a sheet of paper over to another senator.

"Classified."

"You're under oath, Agent Stone," Steinman remarked.

"Senator, I put my life on the line, along with my men, to protect the country."

"We have no doubt you want to protect the country, but some of your techniques are questionable," Steinman said.

"I disagree."

"The files from The Firm start back from the Iraq War," Steinman said.

"What relevance, Senator?" Gary asked.

"How many people have you killed, Agent Stone?"

"My client will not answer that," Gary interrupted.

"How about we take a five-minute break," Steinman said.

An aide approached and whispered in her ear. Taking another sip of water, Teagan looked over her shoulder at her team.

"How long do we have to do this?" Teagan asked Gary.

"Depends on the next few minutes."

"Gregory, head out and see what you can come up with, Spider, stay investigating the case."

"Are you sure?" Spider replied.

"Yeah, I'm not giving up this case."

"We'll now continue if your client is ready, Mr. Rogers," Martha said.

"We're ready, Senator," Gary spoke.

"Great, Senator Gilmone, you have the next question," Martha informed.

"Thank you. Agent Stone, I understand you're overseeing a case in Nebraska." Gilmone leaned into the microphone.

"It's an ongoing case I can't talk about."

"I understand, but how do you approach these cases in general?" Gilmone inquired.

"Everything comes from the president."

The room erupted in conversation. Steinman hit the gavel to quiet the room.

"You're located out of the Pentagon, correct?"

"The main office was moved to the Pentagon, but we work out of the New York branch."

"The funding over the years has increased, but the amount of information has decreased," Gilmone implied.

"If that's your impression..." Teagan answered.

"Agent Stone, do you think this is a game? I can assure you that we take this hearing seriously."

"I would never presume you'd take this as a joke, Senator."

"Gilmone, continue," Martha insisted.

"Agent Stone, we noted that you were missing for a few years between working at The Firm."

"Is that a question?" Teagan asked.

Senator Gilmone cleared his throat. "That is a question."

"I needed a break."

"A break, or did you lose your memory?" Gilmone questioned, smirking as the cameras flashed in front of her eyes.

"Senator, I'd like to request a recess," Gary asked.

"I think today was enough, and we can end the line of questioning," Martha informed.

Teagan stood with her attorney as everyone piled out of the room, and reporters shoved cameras in her face, trying to get a scoop.

"Agent Stone! Agent Stone!"

Running toward her car, she slid in with Broderick and Daughtrey behind her and Gary getting in the front seat as the door closed.

"That old bitch is trying to bring you down," Daughtrey muttered.

"Gary, I don't want my family involved."

"I'll make some calls," Gary replied.

"How long do we have to be here?" Broderick questioned.

"Maybe a few days."

"We have a case, and then we just happen to get pulled into a senate hearing," Teagan argued.

"I agree this seems suspect, but let it play out," Gary answered as the car drove off.

"Did you get anything from that Adam guy?" Daughtrey wondered.

"Not really but look into him more and get some intel on Steinman."

* * *

An hour later, Teagan arrived back at the hotel in DC that The Firm was paying for while she went through the hearing. Walking out of the shower in a white robe, she sat on the bed and opened her laptop, scrolling through emails and messages. They weren't any closer to finding the killer, and more girls came up missing. While en route to her hotel, she got a message from Spider that a woman named Missy came up missing. She looked at the photo of the girl lying in a dumpster with her hands tied with rope and remembered she was the woman Governor Snyder was talking to at the dinner party.

"How long ago was she found?" Teagan asked.

"The coroner is still on the scene; no definite answers," Spider responded.

"They're getting sloppy."

"The governor's pissed."

"Surprised he isn't elated that his secret isn't out."

"He did a press conference talking about how she worked on his campaign."

"Ugh..." Teagan fell back on the bed, holding the phone to her ear.

"Find out everything we can about his staff."

"Should we head back to Camden?"

"Yeah, but I need to see my family first."

"How about you spend time with the family and then come meet us back down there," Spider suggested.

"You're right."

"Get some sleep, T."

"Thanks, you too."

Teagan hung up and tossed the phone on the bed, staring at the ceiling.

"Importing and transporting," she mumbled to herself.

Chapter Twenty-Four

The next morning in DC, Teagan headed to the airport to fly out to New York, letting Gary handle the hearing. Taking a cab, she jumped out, grabbed her bags, and headed through the terminal when her cell phone went off.

"Agent Stone."

"Agent Stone, this is Mayor Henton."

"Mr. Henton, what can I do for you?" Checking in at the gate, she scanned her ID and loaded her bags with the attendant.

"I wanted to call to see if any new updates have happened."

"I'm afraid I've been a little slammed with Washington."

"I did hear about some investigation and you being out there to testify."

"That's true, and my lawyer is continuing with the hearing."

"Will this hinder you finding the person?"

"No, as a matter of fact, I sent my people back to Camden."

"Great, when are you coming?"

"In a few days, I need to go to New York first."

"I just want to make sure we can give the families resolution."

"Mayor, I have to board the plane, but we'll find out who's behind the killings."

"Thank you, Agent Stone."

"See you soon."

"Boarding New York Flight 345."

* * *

Two days later, New York afternoon.

Teagan and Christian watched as the kids played with water guns, running around the backyard with their friends. They invited family and friends for a fun afternoon of a barbeque and card games. Christian went to the store and got food for the grill, and she estimated that a day or two with her family would satisfy before she headed back to Camden on the case. More girls were going missing, and the governor was getting more pissed off with talking to reporters.

"It turned out good, right?" Christian flipped the burgers over on the grill as Teagan passed him a beer.

"The kids are having fun."

Christian glanced at the laughing kids scattered around the yard. They'd recently had it expanded to include a deck for the pool, canopy sitting area, and the garden cut down. Tegan's mom picked up Tatum in her arms.

"She's getting big, Mom! Put her down," Teagan yelled.

She waved Teagan off.

"Tell me about the hearings."

"Not today, Christian. CJ, come and eat!"

"Teagan, we need to talk about this. It affects the kids."

"Don't you think I know that?"

Teagan unwrapped the potato salad, making a plate for CJ as he stomped over mad that he had to stop playing.

"What's with the long face?" she asked, adding a hamburger and fries.

"I'm not hungry, Mommy."

"You barely ate breakfast."

"Can I play a little longer?" he questioned.

"When you're done eating." She handed the plate over with a napkin, taking the gun out of his hands.

"Aghhh...." CJ blew out a breath of frustration.

She rubbed the top of his head.

"Stop fussing and eat."

"Yes, ma'am."

"Teagan, you could go to jail, do you understand that?" Christian slammed the tongs down on the grill.

Teagan rolled her eyes, looking around the backyard, closing the space between her and Christian.

"Calm down."

"You don't care, do you?"

Relaxing her shoulder, she peered into his eyes, seeing the worry and stress. Reaching up, she placed her hands on both sides of his face.

"I promise, I'm not going anywhere."

Wrapping his arm around her back, he pulled her in close, pecking her on the lips.

"Ewww, gross, Daddy," CJ said, holding his plate up for more food.

"I thought you weren't hungry?" Teagan asked.

"Hard work catching my victims."

Teagan froze at his statement.

"Teagan," Christian called her name.

"Huh.."

"You all right? You blacked out on me."

"Ummm, yeah... I'll be right back." Teagan headed into the house, but Christian gripped her hand.

"You said no work today; it's Saturday."

Smiling, she kissed him again on the lips.

"Won't be long at all."

Running inside, she went to her office, taking out Adam's business card from her bag.

Debating on calling, she thought of a plan to get him on the phone since she left him without any explanation.

Picking up the office phone, she dialed Spider instead.

"Teagan, we're a little busy."

"What's going on?"

"At the medical examiner's office getting the file on Missy."

"Any new information?"

"She had a slit throat; died within a few hours."

"The other victims were killed slowly, methodically."

"You're thinking of two different people."

"Yeah or whoever did this was in a hurry."

"When are you coming here?"

"Hopefully in the next day or two."

"Is the family's good?"

"Yes, besides Christian being worried about the senate hearing."

"Really can't blame him."

"I know. Let me call you back. I need to check in with Gary."

"See you soon."

"You too," Teagan said, ending the call. Glancing outside at the family, she typed in the president's number.

"Teagan, we never talked this much before."

"I need you to make this go away."

He sighed.

"Give me a minute, Meghan," the president said.

"Yes, Mr. President."

"You know if I interfere, that will make it even worse."

Taking a seat in her chair, Teagan said, "Mr. President, I understand what you're saying, but we might be dealing with two killers."

"Wait a minute."

"I have a feeling it's one and a copycat."

"Have you spoken with the chief about this new evidence?"

"No, I want to keep it under wraps."

"You're not thinking the chief of police is behind these killings."

"Honestly, it could be the entire town."

"Teagan, The Firm is the best in these types of situations. Are you saying the FBI should take over the case?"

"No, what I'm saying is that Senator Steinman, like Brooks, Diablo, and everyone else, is bullshitting me!" she shouted.

"Feel better?"

"I apologize, Mr. President."

"Maybe you should hand the case over and take some time with your family or go talk with someone."

"I don't need a shrink."

"Talking to a therapist can help get your thoughts together."

"Do you talk to a therapist?"

"Classified."

She chuckled at his answer.

"Thank you, Mr. President."

"I'll see what I can do about the hearing."

"Yes, sir."

Dialing Adam's number, she watched Christian run after CJ and Cole with the water gun through the window.

"Adam Gardner."

Sitting back in her seat, she introduced herself, "Mr. Gardner, this is Patricia Langston."

"Well, to what do I owe the pleasure of this phone call?"

"I wanted to apologize to you for leaving so suddenly."

"Does that mean you'll have dinner with me?" he asked.

Laughter from the kids grew close to her office door.

"When I'm back in town, but that depends on if you can give me a little more information."

"At dinner."

Gripping the phone tighter, she bit her bottom lip.

"You drive a hard bargain, sir."

"You're a beautiful one, Patricia."

"I bet you say that to every woman."

A knock at her door startled her.

"Only the ones I see potential in."

"Mommy!"

"Who's that?" he questioned.

"TV. Sorry, let me call you back." She hurriedly hung up the phone.

"Mommy, can we have some ice cream?" Tatum questioned, with Cole next to her.

"Did you both eat?" Teagan walked from around her desk, tossing the business card in the trash can.

"I did!" Tatum said.

"Sure, only one of each." Teagan gripped their hands, walking into the kitchen. For the rest of the afternoon, she enjoyed the laughter and comfort of her family all together. Later that night, after cleaning up and putting the kids to bed, she poured her favorite bath soap in the tub, grabbed a book, and relaxed with soft music while the whole house was asleep.

Chapter Twenty-Five

"Watch where you're going!" a guy in a red truck yelled. Teagan honked her horn as she drove the kids to school. Sunday dinner with Christian's parents brought back the simple times when she didn't have the world looking at her every move.

"Mom, can you sign this?" Cole asked.

"What's this?" Teagan picked up the form from his teacher.

"Field trip," Cole replied.

"You're just now giving me this, Cole?"

Teagan grabbed the pen out of his hand, signing her name.

"I forgot."

"Uhm... huh."

"Thanks, Mommy." Cole opened the door.

"Can I get a kiss?"

"No, I'm too old for that." Cole looked around at his classmates.

"Really, Cole?"

"Mom, that's for babies."

"You're my baby."

"Oh, My God!" Cole leaned in the car and kissed her fast on the cheek before anyone saw her, covering his face with the sheet of paper.

"I thought Tatum was dramatic!" Teagan blurted out.

Cole waved her off, and she laughed, pulling into traffic toward the office. She sipped on her coffee, listening to more of the hearings on the radio.

"These agencies only protect the powerful. We need transparency," Martha said

"President Sanders is not above the law," Gilmone said.

Turning the radio off, she shook her head, pulled in the garage, and held her badge out for the security guard.

"Clear, Director." The guard allowed entry.

"Thanks," Teagan replied, driving in and parking in her usual spot.

"I thought you would've taken today off." Spider met her at the elevator.

"You're here early."

"I slept here."

"You need to go home, Spider."

"I showered and ate breakfast."

"We have to have a life outside of this place." Teagan waved her hand around the elevator, hitting the button to her floor.

"This case is just pissing me off."

"Same."

"I talked with the chief again, and he's hearing it from the governor just as much as we are."

"What did the chief say?"

"Nothing really new, but he offered to put in a curfew for the town."

"It'll take more than a curfew." Teagan and Spider stepped off the elevator, heading to her office. Unlocking her door, she hung her coat on the rack and dropped her bag on the top of the desk.

"What did the president say about the hearings?"

"Nothing yet; he's trying to work on Steinman."

"She has it out for you."

Teagan sat at her desk, picking up her messages.

"Which is strange because we've never crossed paths."

She kicked her feet up on the desk.

"Most of the people are enemies of President Sanders."

"Exactly, so why don't they go after him and not me?"

"Because it's easier to cut the minions down, then the king will fall."

She held the messages up to her chin, staring at Spider.

"What do we know right now?"

"Girls are going missing, ending up dead."

"All killed at different times but located at the same place."

"The person knows the town and is familiar with the area."

"It has to be someone in public office; they trust the people."

"Either that or drugged."

"Did Gregory make any headway?"

"Not yet; he's just as torn up about these cases."

"Damn."

"Well, meet me at the shooting range. I need to let off some steam."

* * *

Hours later, Teagan arrived home with the kids, holding bags of groceries; Christian was lying across the couch when Tatum ran up and plopped down on his legs.

"When did you get here?" Teagan asked.

"About an hour ago." Christian moved Tatum, stood, and grabbed the bag out of Teagan's hand, kissing her on the lips. Throwing her purse on the couch, she followed him in the kitchen.

"How was work?"

"It was good. What about you?" he asked.

"Fine, quiet."

"Any news on the senate hearings?"

"No, but the president said he's working on trying to get it wrapped up."

"Why don't you relax, and I'll get dinner ready for tonight."

"Are you sure?"

"Yep, you've been nonstop since coming back."

"Thanks, honey. I'm going to shower and change."

"Okay, tell the kids to do their homework."

"Yes, boss," she chortled.

Running away before Christian could catch up, Teagan ran to the boys' room and knocked on the door.

"Come in!" Cole shouted.

"Honey, start on your homework."

"Okay."

"Now, Cole. Put the game away."

"Yes, ma'am."

Teagan went to the bedroom and turned on the TV as she grabbed some clothes from her drawer to change into.

"I'm voting to keep torture techniques by The Firm criminal," Martha said on the news segment.

"Are you saying the president condones torture, Senator Steinman?" the reporter asked.

"The president knows what he's doing with this program," Martha answered.

"This woman is crazy."

Shaking her head, she walked into the bathroom, turned the water on, and picked up her shower cap.

"Babe, you want tacos tonight?" Christian asked from the bedroom door.

"That's fine."

"What are you watching?"

"That crazy senator is on the news talking about the president condoning torture."

"Seriously?"

"Yeah."

She opened the cabinet to grab a clean towel when the house phone rang.

"It's probably for you." Christian headed back to the kitchen.

"I won't be long." Teagan turned the shower off, ran back in, and picked up the phone.

"Hello."

"I tried calling your cell, but no answer," President Sanders said.

"It's in my purse. I had it on silent while I was at work."

"Senator Steinman is out for blood."

"I see."

"A few things are moving on my end, so be prepared to get the word on flying out to Nebraska."

"You still want us to handle the case?"

"I refuse to let her win."

"Yes, Mr. President."

"Good. Enjoy the rest of your night, and I'll be in touch."

"You as well, Mr. President."

Chapter Twenty-Six

Flashback

The low opera music played in the background. At the same time, Audrey stood in the corner, sipping on a glass of champagne and watching as Secretary Todd Kelton talked with other congressmen at the annual mayor's meeting in Nebraska at the governor's mansion. She hated coming to these boring events because Mayor Henton always got wrapped into some type of savior complex and tried to win over his father's respect. She'd worked for the father, even sleeping with him behind his son's back, and was promised once things transitioned to his son as mayor, her position as secretary would stay the same. She made her hours, took lunch when she felt like it, and knew she wouldn't be fired because of her connection to the longtime Henton name. As a matter of fact, she met the father when she was only seventeen years old when he spoke at her high school. Gaining an internship was an opportunity for her to get out of her mother's shadow, who only used her to get what she wanted. Working at his office helped her learn the ropes of politics as his assistant. Late nights turned into more than just flirting. Audrey thought she was in love with Henton's father. When she learned he would never leave his wife, Audrey decided she was only out for herself and making money by doing what she did best— gaining the upper hand. Learning about the men who loved young girls in town, all the way up to Washington, benefited her in building a business. Now at thirty-two, she made it her priority while stalking her next client as they both kept making eye contact throughout the night. Lloyd was gullible and easy to manipulate like his father, so she whispered in his ear to find her another glass of champagne in order to get a few minutes alone.

"This is your last one for the night," Lloyd spoke, holding up the glass as he walked off.

Audrey smiled, holding two fingers crossed in the air, knowing she didn't care what he said. Dropping the smile once his back was toward her, Audrey fluffed her long hair out and pulled her sleeves lower, showing more cleavage, while strolling over to the window where Todd Kelton was laughing with Mayor Collins of Boston.

"I'm telling you, Andrew, Seattle might have a chance at the playoffs," Todd argued.

"Thanks for the confidence boost," Mayor Collins replied.

Stepping next to both men, Audrey grinned as they finished shaking hands.

"Mr. Collins, you have an urgent call," his assistant stated.

"Excuse me; I have to take this," Andrew informed me.

Todd nodded in agreement, sliding his hand in his inside jacket pocket, pulling out a cigarette case.

"I didn't know you could smoke here," Audrey said.

"You can't. I was heading outside."

"Do you mind if I join you?" Audrey asked.

"Why would a beautiful woman like you want to be around such an ugly habit," he flirted.

"Not all habits are ugly, sir."

"The ones I like are," he replied.

Letting her lead the way out front of the mansion, she walked through the crowd, dodging Llyod from finding out she was with Kelton.

"I see you're here with Henton's son." Todd lit his cigarette, blowing out smoke.

"I'm his secretary."

Todd held the silver case full of cigarettes up, offering her one.

"Thank you." She placed it between her lips, lighting it as she closed her eyes, taking in the first drag of the cigarette.

"You like working for Henton's family?"

"It has its perks."

"How old are you?"

"How old do you need me to be?"

Kelton smirked at her response.

"Something about you intrigues me."

"Good."

"I'm only here until tomorrow. Then, I fly out to Washington."

"That's fine."

"I have a hotel room."

"Following your lead, Mr. Kelton." She reached out, placing a hand on his chest.

"What about your boss?"

"He'll be fine."

* * *

Audrey slid her feet in her high heels two hours later as Secretary Kelton lay in bed, wrapped around a comforter and sheets.

"How much do you charge?" he questioned.

"For you, it was free," she said.

"You do this often."

"Do what?"

"Sleep with men in power?" he questioned.

She turned her back toward him to zip up her dress.

"The real question is why men sleep with women when they know they are married."

"What gave me away? I wasn't wearing my ring."

"I research my clients."

He chuckled to himself.

"So this is your business at night; during the day you work as a secretary?"

"Something like that."

"How many girls work for you?"

"Depends."

"On what?"

"If we're talking off the record, Mr. Kelton, I'm not in the business to end up in jail."

Kelton moved the comforter back, stood, and grabbed his pants, sliding one leg, then the other.

"I'm not a bad person."

"I hear that a lot." She leaned down, picking up her purse.

"Sometimes I like to relax with a young woman."

She smirked, knowing he was on track to being one of her clients.

"That can be arranged." Audrey cupped his chin, then turned and strolled to the door of the hotel room.

"Audrey," he called out.

Her hand gripped the door.

"I hope you understand this needs to be kept between us."

"Discretion is my middle name, Secretary Kelton."

* * *

Present.

A few days later, Audrey pulled her shades off while sitting in her car, as she watched some high school girls talking in front of a local diner with some boys. Lighting up another cigarette, she thought of a way to get one of them in her car. Checking herself out in the mirror, Audrey peered as the two girls got into their car, leaving the boys alone. Following at a close distance, Audrey checked the time on her cell, noting her lunch break was almost up. Ten minutes later, the young blond girl dropped her friend off in front of an apartment building, then drove off. The blond, green-eyed cheerleader stopped at a stop sign, music blasting. Audrey took this as an opportunity to take advantage. Speeding up, Audrey hit her car from the back, causing them both to pull over to the side of the street. Dumping her cigarette, Audrey pulled her ID out of her purse and opened the door, putting on a wide smile as she approached. Knocking on her window, the young girl stepped out of the car looking annoyed.

"I'm so sorry; I wasn't paying attention," Audrey said.

"My dad's going to be pissed," the young girl said.

"Maybe he doesn't need to know."

"What do you mean?"

"I know a car guy who can fix your car without them knowing."

"I don't know."

"Listen, you, don't have to worry. It will probably take an hour or two."

"How can I get the car there?"

"You can ride with me to the shop, and I'll have it towed."

The young girl looked over at Audrey's car.

"How far is the shop? Maybe I can call my dad."

"You want him to know what happened to his car and end up getting in more trouble?"

"I guess you're right."

"It won't take long, probably about a five-minute drive."

Audrey led the girl over to the car.

"What's your name?"

"Emily. What's yours?"

Audrey dropped her pack of cigarettes on the floor in the front passenger seat.

"Teresa, shit! Can you grab my cigarettes from the floor?"

Emily buckled her seatbelt and bent down, grabbing the case.

"This won't hurt too much," Audrey said, sticking a needle in Emily's neck.

"Ouch... What is—" Emily muttered as her eyes drew low, falling back against the window and passing out.

"Something to help you sleep."

* * *

"As we watch the hearings, we're reminded of our democracy as citizens," Charles Daniels, CGN News, reported.

"That's right, Charles. As voters, you can't imagine what goes on behind the scenes," Rachel from CGN News reported from DC.

"We are on the fifth day of hearings with Senator Steinman setting final statements," Charles said.

"As senators, we have an obligation to make sure the American people are kept informed," Martha said.

"I'd like to call a final vote," Senator Vail asked.

Picking up the gavel, Steinman called for reporters to quiet down.

"This hearing will come to a vote."

Turning the TV down, Teagan stood in her kitchen, preparing to pick up her kids from school. Teagan grabbed her keys off the holder, heading to the front door. Sean stood at the Range Rover, waiting for word.

"I'm driving myself, Sean."

"I'll follow."

"That's not necessary."

"Director, you know I can't do that."

"Fine. I can't get rid of you."

Hopping in her car, Teagan reversed out of her driveway, turning left at the light, with Sean right behind her as she headed down the street to the freeway. Turning the radio on, Teagan listened to music while driving, thinking of a vacation she finally wanted to take once the case was solved. Approaching her exit, she signaled to get over to jump off, easing in the line of cars waiting to pick up their children. Her Bluetooth rang.

"I'm with the kids, Spider."

"We had another one."

"What?"

"Yeah, I just got off the phone with chief."

"Damn."

"I know we have the hearing, but we need to get back to Nebraska soon."

Driving up further, Teagan saw her kids running toward her car.

"Send over the information." Teagan unlocked the car door, letting the kids get inside. Tatum jumped in the front seat, while CJ and Cole went to the back passenger seats.

"Mommy, can we stop for ice cream?" Tatum asked.

"We have ice cream at home. Spider, let me call you back," Teagan replied.

"Hi, Spider!" all three kids blurted out.

As Teagan ended the call, she received an alert with information on the latest victim.

"Sit back, Tatum."

Glancing at the window to see Sean still following, Teagan tried to keep it together and not get emotional about another young girl popping up dead. Making it back home, Teagan parked and turned the radio up, letting the kids out of the car.

"We have breaking news that senators voted down to get rid of The Firm."

"Tatum, you forgot your homework." Teagan grabbed her bookbag and treaded to the front door of her house. Almost tripping over CJ's shoes, she dropped Tatum's backpack at the door.

"Go change your clothes and start on your homework, please."

"Mom, can we play the game please?" CJ said.

"Once you finish your homework." Teagan kissed him on top of his head. Cole and Tatum came running into the living room, and Teagan pointed to Tatum's backpack near the door.

The front door opened, and Christian walked in holding a briefcase and the mail. Dropping them on the table, he kissed Teagan on the lips. Teagan led him to the kitchen to talk.

"I heard on the radio that they are not closing the Agency.

"Yeah, but I have to fly back to Nebraska."

"What happened?"

"Another victim."

"How old this time?"

"Not sure, but I won't be long."

"Okay. Just be careful, babe."

Chapter Twenty-Seven

Sitting at the conference table the next morning, Gregory continued scanning and researching the new photos and evidence that came through from the medical examiner. He was used to seeing dead bodies and blood, but something about a young girl's life being over so soon, he had a harder time handling these types of cases without going on a rampage. On another screen, he watched the senate vote and news reporters talking about what it could mean if the votes went another way. He logged in all of the audiotapes he listened to and scanned all of the car tags the night of the governor's dinner. A few seconds later, Daughtrey marched into the room holding a folder; Broderick held a bag of chips in his hands. Dropping the folder on the table, Daughtrey smiled, tapping on the top of the folder.

"What's this?"

"Where's Spider?" Daughtrey asked.

"Probably in his office."

"I got the toxicology report."

"And?"

"The Nebraska medical examiner missed the needle injections."

"What are you talking about?"

"I wanted to have our people look deeper into these cases."

"You think the chief was trying to cover up?" Broderick asked.

"Probably, but all the girls were injected in the same spot behind their neck to put them to sleep."

"We have to tell Teagan," Gregory said.

"That still keeps us blind to what's going on," Broderick mentioned.

As they continued talking, Gregory had Daughtrey listening to audio tapes.

"I think I can arrange that," a woman whispered into the phone.

"Wait a minute, play that back," Broderick said.

"What part?" Daughtrey said.

"Did you hear that muffled voice?"

Rewinding the tape, Gregory hit play.

"I think I can arrange that."

"It's going to take time to figure out who that voice matches."

"I wonder what she was talking about," Broderick said.

Picking up the phone, Gregory dialed Spider's office.

"He's coming down." Gregory sat back in his set, crossing his arms, taking in the photos of all the dead girls.

* * *

Turning the stove down, Teagan moved the salad bowl over to the counter and cut up tomatoes and onions.

Before she headed back to Nebraska, she made Christian's favorite fish, asparagus, salad, and strawberry shortcake. Christian came into the kitchen, wrapped his right arm around Teagan, and picked up the red bottle of wine off the cellar stand. She grabbed the wine opener from the drawer and took two glasses down from the cabinet.

"One glass before you go."

"Mhmmm..."

"Come on. It's my favorite meal, so let's celebrate with wine."

"All right, one glass. Are the kids still playing?"

"Yeah. I'll go get them to freshen up before dinner."

She tossed the salad together, plating it in a large white bowl. Teagan licked her finger, tasting the special sauce she made. Sliding on her gloves, she plated the fish and asparagus with loaves of bread. Wiping her hands clean, she tasted the piece of fish, when the phone rang. Christian gathered the kids into their seats from the backyard.

"Hello."

"Sorry to interrupt dinner."

"What's going on?"

"You should come in before we head to Nebraska."

"I just got the kids ready for dinner."

"Sorry, Teagan, but this can't wait."

"I'll be there as soon as I can." Hanging up the phone, Teagan went back into the kitchen smiling, then helped to make plates for the kids. Popping the cork on the wine bottle, he poured a glass for her and then himself.

"Ohh, can I have some wine?"

"No," Tegan and Christian said at the same time.

Both boys laughed at her.

"You're too young," CJ said.

"So! I can get what I want!" Tatum yelled.

"What did you say?" Teagan questioned.

"Huh."

"I can get what I want," Tatum said.

"You've been acting up lately, Tatum," Christian complained.

Teagan rose from her seat, thinking over those words. Picking up her cell phone, she dialed Spider's number.

"Are you on your way?"

"Not yet, but did we run all the police and city leaders through background checks?"

"I believe Gregory did," Spider muffled through the phone.

She heard him ask Gregory.

"He's running them again."

"From what we know, all the girls left with someone they trusted or felt comfortable around."

"Yeah."

"Dig deeper."

"Have you heard from the president about the outcome?"

"He's trusting we can solve this case; that's his priority."

"Hurry up, so we can."

"Is the plane ready?"

"Once you're here, we can get it loaded."

"Great, I'll be there soon."

Hanging up the phone, Teagan went down the hall to her office. She logged into her computer and checked the database of the Camden Police Department. Cole pushed her office door open, coming in with a bowl of strawberry shortcake and ice cream.

"What are you doing, Mom?"

Closing out the police files, she pulled up a chess game on the screen.

"Playing chess. Shouldn't you be eating dinner?"

"I did."

"Did you eat the asparagus?"

She patted her lap for him to sit.

"It was nasty."

He lifted a piece of cake for her to eat.

"It's healthy for you." She ate the cake, rubbing him on the back.

"You're leaving again tonight?"

"Yeah."

"I don't like your job."

"Me neither."

He grinned at her answer.

"Since you're the boss, can I be the second in command?"

"You want to become a SEAL?"

He shrugged his shoulders.

"I want to shoot guns."

"CJ, I do more than shoot guns."

"I like that part, though."

Laughing at his comment, she tapped him to get up.

"You're my son for sure."

"Can you teach me to shoot?"

"When you're eighteen."

"Shake my hand on the agreement."

"You don't trust me?"

"Mom, this is business."

"CJ, go shower for bed and give me that bowl."

Heading to put the bowl away, Teagan saw Christian sitting on the couch watching the re-airing of the senate hearing and Teagan's statement. Standing behind Christian, he grabbed her hand, kissing the back of her palm.

"You keep finding enemies."

"I guess I'm special."

"Special to me."

Teagan bent down, hugging him from behind.

"I'll see what the president says; this won't be the last attempt."

"That's what scares me."

Chapter Twenty-Eight

The next morning.

Seeing the photos from Barton Restaurant, Teagan's upper lip scrunched into a scowl, knowing the public put these people in office to protect them. This type of betrayal would be crippling on the community and state. Todd Kenton, Neal Keenan, and Audrey all looked to be in an intense conversation. All this time, a woman helped kill young girls and feed lies to the public. Women like her disgusted Teagan, and she wanted to kill all three of them without a trial.

"What else do you have?" Teagan asked Gregory as they sat in the conference room.

"That Senator Steinman wasn't only behind these bogus hearings, but I have pictures of her with Todd in her office." Gregory scrolled through the pictures on the computer.

"How fast can we get to DC?"

"The private jet can have us there in less than an hour," Daughtrey answered.

"Get Henton on the line," Teagan said.

Rubbing her temples, she clenched her eyes closed, thinking of each way to torture and kill Audrey.

"Mayor Henton," he groggily answered.

Teagan stood and leaned against the phone in the center of the table.

"Mayor Henton, this is Agent Stone."

"Agent Stone, what's going on?"

"We know who's behind the deaths."

"Have you called the chief or Governor Snyder?"

"I'll let you handle that part."

"Mayor, I'm sending to your phone some photos we've received," Gregory explained.

"Pictures of what?" he asked.

Teagan looked from Broderick to Spider.

"Your secretary Audrey." He laughed at her revelation.

"It's true, Henton."

"You must have made a mistake; Audrey would never do anything like this."

She clipped her chin at Broderick, and he turned the recording on for Henton to listen.

"I can't bring you anymore girls, Secretary," Audrey said.

"The last girl was a mistake," Kelton said.

"This puts me at a bigger risk; I need more money," Audrey replied.

"My God."

Broderick reached over and turned off the recording.

"Mr. Henton, I can't tell you how sensitive our time is to wrap this up."

"I understand."

"My team received information that the deal is going down in DC."

"We're sending you all the information that was collected."

"I'll have a statement sent out ASAP."

"Thank you, sir." Teagan ended the call.

"Next step is getting Senator Steinman to talk," Gregory mentioned.

"That shouldn't be hard."

Teagan walked toward the screen, with her back to the team, staring at the photos of the dock area with ships and cargo coming in and out.

"If we 're right, it should go down within the next forty-eight hours."

"Have you spoken with Sanders?" Broderick wondered.

"No, I'll call on our way to the Capitol."

"Suit up, boys." Spider said.

"Dead or alive?" Daughtrey asked.

Teagan turned around at the question.

"Hostile, then we take them down. Gregory, get coordinated with our people surrounding the area."

"How far of a range can we get?"

"At least six miles. Can we lock it down?"

"What about the Coast Guard?" Spider queried.

"I don't want to tip them off. Neal is counting on Kelton to have the cargo available."

"Maybe one of us can go in as security," Daughtrey said.

Rubbing her chin, Teagan thought about his suggestion.

"Gregory, can you make a fake ID ASAP?"

"Coming right up."

"Good. Daughtrey, you'll go in tonight. Broderick, you're running the transportation."

"You want me on surveillance?" Gregory asked.

"Yes, Spider and I will go in with Daughtrey and a few men," Teagan explained.

The entire team sat around the table as Spider called for more agents.

"This is Gage."

"Gage, this is Spider."

"What's going on? I don't get calls from the New York team often."

Gage Tate was a thirty-two-year-old single dad with a daughter he was raising with his parents. His wife was killed in an automobile accident years ago, and he'd taken on the role of leader of the DC Striker team. While Teagan ran the entire Agency, she hadn't worked alongside other members of The Firm until now. Going to DC, they would need more manpower; knowing Gage had the knowledge of the DC area would come in handy.

"A drop in is happening, and I need a tour guide," Spider said.

"I love tours." Gage chuckled.

"Good, this one could be rough. Are you up for that type of dance?"

"Brother, I love those rough dances."

"Will be in town soon, heading out to the plane once this call ends."

"What are we hunting for?"

"Trafficking."

"Son of a bitch!" Gage growled.

"You're a father, so you know how sensitive we have to be with this case."

"Yeah, man, who's behind this?"

"Check your phone after the call ends."

"See you soon." Gage hung up, not waiting for any more instructions.

"You think he'll be able to control himself?" Teagan asked.

"No," Spider answered, rising out of his seat.

"Perfect."

Teagan smirked, patting Spider on the back as she walked out of the room.

* * *

Forty minutes later, standing outside the private airport, dialing the president's secure line, Teagan waited outside the plane as the team loaded cargo. She hadn't spoken to Christian since last night, but she promised herself once they arrived, she'd try to let him know she had made it safely before going on her mission.

"Agent Stone."

"Mr. President." Teagan sighed, feeling nervous about what she was going to explain.

"I saw you've made strides with the Nebraska case."

"Yes, sir. Even though the bogus hearing by Steinman was trying to distract us, we've made headway."

"Who's the suspect?"

"Secretary Todd Kelton."

The call went quiet.

"Do you have proof of this?"

"Unfortunately, I do."

He mumbled low.

"Is that the highest level of corruption?"

"As far as I can tell, sir, besides Steinman being used."

"She's always been a sparring partner, but not this devilish."

"I'm not sure if she knew he was trafficking girls, but we have to keep that to ourselves."

"What can I do to help?"

"My men are loading up now. We'll be in DC in the next hour; it's going on five in the afternoon now."

"You have the support of the police and whatever else you need."

"Thank you, sir, but I'd like to keep it to as few people as possible."

"Agent Stone?"

"Yes, sir."

"Be careful."

"Always, Mr. President."

Spider jogged up the steps of the plane.

"Locked and loaded!" Daughtrey called out, pounding on the back of the plane.

Grabbing a seat, Teagan looked out of the window as Sean drove off back to the office. Blowing out a breath, she closed her eyes briefly, placing the seatbelt on as everyone clamored for a seat.

"Daughtrey, check your email," Gregory said.

"Damn, that's fast," Daughtrey replied, pulling up his email from his phone.

"No doubt." Gregory and Daughtrey fist bumped.

"Did you send Gage all the information?" Teagan questioned.

"Uploading now, boss," Gregory answered.

"We'll be taking off shortly; please turn off all devices," the stewardess demanded.

The seatbelt light came on, and everyone got comfortable as the plane lined up on the runway. A few moments after takeoff, she brought out trays of drinks and snacks for the team as they turned on their electrical devices. Gregory muttered something underneath his breath.

"Interesting," Gregory said.

"Something new," Spider commented.

"I got the financial records of the port docks."

"Let me guess; Todd Kelton is an investor," Teagan remarked.

"Before joining the Sanders administration, he co-founded Arrowlane LTD to a profit of close to five hundred million dollars." Gregory turned his computer around for Teagan to see.

"Assholes are going to probably use this as a new way to transport women."

"We have to stop them now." Spider's face screwed into a hard glare.

"Tell Gage to have his people already scoping out the location once we land. But don't engage," Teagan said.

Gregory typed on his computer as Spider sent a text message. Surveillance video footage popped up on Gregory's computer from his email, and he clicked the video, seeing vans approaching the loading dock.

"Teagan, we might have a problem."

"What?"

"I have two vans approaching the port now."

"Can you get eyes on who the company belongs to?"

"No, I just see them less than a few feet from getting inside."

"Shit! I thought we'd have a little more time to get set up."

"Should we tell Gage?" Broderick questioned.

Tapping her finger against the chair in thought, all eyes trained on her, waiting to see what direction she would give.

"Teagan."

"I'm thinking."

"They just signed in and drove through the gate," Gregory said.

"What's the name of the company?"

"Washington Port Pipeline, more than likely fake," Gregory replied.

"Tell Gage to stand back and keep surveillance. No one moves in until we get there."

"What if girls are moved?" Broderick asked.

"Then we need to have them followed, but I want all parties caught."

"Too much to keep track of, Teagan," Spider said.

"Not if we can get the president to lock down all airports, buses, and trains."

Spider's eyes rose in shock.

"Gregory, I want eyes on these vans without contacting the owners. We can't tip Kelton off."

An hour later, the team piled in the waiting cars at the airport, Teagan, Gregory, and Spider in one van, while Broderick and Daughtrey were in another.

"Remember to keep the line of communication open; nobody goes in without my go-ahead. Understood."

"Understood!" everybody said at the same time. A fleet of ten black Range Rovers lined up, driving out of the airport when three broke off, carrying Teagan and a few men from the DC office heading to make one more stop.

* * *

Senator Steinman closed down her computer for the day, feeling the ramifications from the media storm of the committee hearings. Grasping her keys and purse, Martha edged toward the door, preparing to open it when Teagan burst through.

"OMG! You scared me." Martha held a hand to her chest.

"Senator, what's the rush?" Teagan closed the door behind her.

"Wh... What are you doing here?" Martha glanced at her phone, wanting to call for help.

"You're under investigation for helping a child sex trafficker." Teagan held up a warrant.

"I have no idea what you're talking about."

Teagan marched over to her desk, turning Martha's computer back on when a password link popped up.

"What's your password?"

"Agent, you have no idea—"

"Save the speech for someone who cares. I have a cargo ship coming in with women and girls about to be sold."

"What does that have to do with me?" she asked.

"You're wasting my time!" Teagan shouted, pushing the papers off her desk.

"I don't know what you're talking about."

Jumping in her face, Teagan pointed a finger at her chest.

"Secretary Kelton is a part of a sex trafficking ring, and you helped him."

Martha's mouth opened slightly, shaking her head in disbelief.

"Do you know what you just said?"

"Charges will be brought against Secretary Kelton, the governor's campaign manager in Nebraska, and you if I don't get your help."

"The only thing I know is that he wanted me to shut down The Firm."

"Put your password in now."

Grasping her arm, Teagan shoved Martha toward her desk.

"Okay, okay."

Checking the time, it was going on six-thirty, and Spider sent a message update to hurry up.

"Here's the file." Martha moved to the side as Teagan stepped forward, reading over the documents on the screen.

"Kelton was spearheading to close The Firm and run for president?"

"He told me he was only in it for being president. I didn't know anything about women being sold," Martha said as tears pooled in her eyes.

"Gregory will need this information." Teagan searched around her computer for any other information, sending the data to Gregory to go over later.

Finally getting everything she needed, Teagan sent a text message to Spider.

Teagan: Have security come up.

Spider: On it.

"Can I go now?" Martha asked.

"Yes."

Martha stood and walked toward the door.

"But you're not going home," Teagan said behind her back as security guards opened the door.

"Wait a minute. I didn't do anything wrong."

"Ma'am, you have to come with us," a guard told her, grabbing her by the arm. She jerked away.

"Let me walk with some dignity."

Chapter Twenty-Nine

Running out of the building and jumping back in the Range Rover, Teagan lifted the bullet-proof vest and binoculars. Taking the automatic weapon from the back seat, Spider started the car, and they drove over to the dock port to meet up with Gage and his team.

"How far out are we?"

Tapping on the navigation device, Spider turned at the stoplight from the Capitol building and headed into traffic. Speeding up, Teagan checked her weapon was loaded and prepared her mindset for the next few minutes before going into battle.

"You're nervous," Spider said.

"Not Teagan." Gregory held his cell phone forward for Teagan to watch.

"He's actually there," Teagan murmured.

The screen showed Todd, Neal, and Audrey standing outside a maroon cargo ship with the name Arrowlane LTD across it.

"How many did they account for so far?" Teagan inquired.

Passing her a radio headset, Teagan checked the feedback.

"He counted at least fifteen, but there could be more since they got there late."

Driving through the underpass of the entrance, the lights were turned on as the sunset hit the dock. Parking near the other cars at the building entrance, Teagan stepped out of the car with Spider following, spotting Gage approaching with his men.

Holding out a palm for a shake, Spider went to each man to express a thank you for helping on this mission.

"Have they tried to bring the girls out yet?"

Daughtrey carried a flashlight and taser and wore a basic port uniform while allowing people to enter and leave.

"On the radar, I have heat picking up in the cargo. I think we have more than one," Gage said.

"He wouldn't be that stupid," Gregory commented.

"Sick people like this will do anything," Spider said.

Grabbing the mic, she spoke into the headset.

"Broderick, lock down the exits and entrances. We're going in now." Teagan motioned behind Gage.

"Where do you want us?" Gregory asked.

"Gage and you on the left, Spider behind me," Teagan said.

"Let's go!" Gage whistled, waving his hand in the air.

Tegan and Gage split up and went on opposite ends of the perimeter.

"Try not to give yourselves away."

Staying low, holding the gun up, Teagan wiped the sweat away as she continued walking to the end of the dock where Todd was located. Passing across to the next section, she was spotted, and a guard lifted his gun in her face, about to shoot. She held out her hand for the men to stop moving.

"Don't move," he said.

She pretended to surrender with her hands up in the air.

"Easy now, you don't want to do this."

"I need to radio this to my boss."

She lowered her left hand behind her back, letting them know on her count when to move.

"How much are they paying you?"

"Lady, keep your hands up!" he yelled as she eased in closer, cutting the distance between them. The agitation and nervousness let her know she was getting to him before he came unhinged and blew their cover. Soon as he looked to his left, she took the opportunity to pop him in the throat. He started choking, and she grabbed the gun, wrapping her arm around his throat and putting him to sleep.

"I got him," Gregory said, taking him behind the wall near the trash.

"We only have a few minutes before they notice he's gone."

Getting closer to the Arrowlane section, biting her bottom lip, Teagan looked behind, making sure the team was following.

"Ready?"

"Ready."

"On my count, one, two, three!" Teagan shouted and shot the security guards, watching Neal and Audrey duck low and try to run away.

"Grab them, Gregory." Teagan sent a shot in the head

of another guard. Gregory crossed over and went down the corridor to the right and ran to catch up to Audrey and Neal.

"Bitch!" another hired gunman cursed, dropping his gun and trying to fight Teagan. Sending a headbutt, she growled and dropped the gun, grabbing the headpiece off her face. He tossed it on the ground as she kicked him in the side of the leg, and he grunted.

"Is that all you have for me?" He smirked, wiping the blood off his lip.

"Let's go, big boy." Teagan grinned, elbowing him in the stomach and punching him in the left jaw as they continued shooting around them.

"We're here to help." she heard Spider say as the whispers and cries rose.

"Ahhhh! You bitch!" Spider looked behind him and saw Teagan being choked and the security guard on top of her.

"Shit! Gage, get them out of here," Spider said.

Gregory caught up to Audrey as she tried to jump in the car with Neal and grabbed her by the hair.

"Please don't kill me," Audrey cried out.

Teagan twisted and turned while under the guard's weight, putting all her strength into pushing him off her. Across the way, Todd slipped out while Spider moved the women into the vans to get them to safety.

"Get me out of here!" Todd called out, holding money in his hands.

"Yes, sir," the fisherman replied.

Chaos erupted all over as helicopters from the news stations flew over the area, trying to get the scoop.

"Aghhh!" Teagan screamed, lifted her leg, and bucked

her hip, throwing the guard off and triggering Teagan to get a heads up, poking him in the eye.

"Motherfucker!" he snapped.

Coughing and trying to catch her breath, Teagan grabbed the gun off the ground and knocked him over the head.

"Ugh... hmmm." she moaned, trying to catch her breath.

Spider, Gregory, and Gage walked toward her as the guard on the ground groaned to himself.

"Where's Kelton?" Teagan tilted her head and spat on the ground.

"He took off on a boat."

"Shit!"

She looked out to the water, seeing Kelton staring back at her.

"I need a boat."

"That can be arranged." Gage cocked his gun, nodding for them to follow over to the dock.

"Did all the girls get out?" Teagan ran toward the dock as Gage secured a boat.

"Yeah, Audrey and Neal are with the FBI now," Gregory said.

"They'll take credit for the arrest."

"It's better this way," Spider replied.

All three stepped on the boat, and Gage turned the ignition key as Gregory let the rope go from the dock.

"He has us beat by at least five minutes," Spider commented.

"Where do you think he's going?" Gage asked.

"He knows we're on to him; he can't get far," Teagan said.

Pushing the speed, Gage took off, trying to catch up to the boat carrying Todd.

"I see him up ahead." Gregory pointed at the boat.

"Get me close," Teagan said, removing her vest, standing close to the edge.

"What are you planning to do?"

"Whatever it takes," she responded.

"Copy that," Gage said.

"Hurry up! They're getting close." They heard Todd shouting.

"Come on, a few more feet."

"Stop! This is the police," Gage yelled over the mic.

Todd pushed his driver off the boat, took the handle of the speed boat, and sped back up.

"Shit! That idiot." Gage spat.

Teagan lifted her gun, closing one eye, and stared at Todd's back, sending a shot toward his shoulder, causing him to cry out in pain and fall out of the boat. She passed the gun over to Spider and jumped in the water, swimming to pull Todd up before he drowned.

"Aghhh... help me... please," Todd cried out.

Grabbing him around the neck, she swam over to the boat and held him up as Gregory lifted him up by his shoulders. She pushed from the bottom, climbing in next. Steering the boat to the right, he went back to the dock. Teagan pulled the zip ties from her pockets, tying Todd by the wrists and ankles.

"I'm shot, I need a doctor," Todd groaned in pain.

"You'll get a doctor. When I think you deserve one."

The helicopters hovered above, and more police cars showed up as the boat finally arrived back. Hopping out of the boat, Teagan watched as Spider and Gregory helped Todd get out, and the EMTs loaded him on the stretcher.

"Agent Stone, we have all the girls accounted for and are checking with Homeland now," a police officer said.

"Wait a minute; I'm the secretary of transportation. Do you know what you're doing?" Todd complained, trying to remove the oxygen mask.

"The president is on the line." Daughtrey jogged over to her as she listened to news reporters calling out toward them.

!."Mr. President?"

"You have him?" Sanders questioned.

"Yes, sir."

"I want him brought back to the White House," Sanders said.

"Mr. President, that might not be the wisest decision." Teagan ran a hand through her wet hair.

"What do you suggest?"

"We can't have a secretary from your cabinet show up after being captured."

"This is bad for my administration. I want him dealt with now," Sanders demanded and ended the call.

$$* * *$$

Todd Kelton received medical help and got patched up by the ambulance. Teagan directed the team to take him once he was sedated to a safe house where they could talk with him. The room was built underground by the DC agency that Gage ran with his team. She asked everyone to leave the room while she spoke with him alone. Todd was tied up by his hands to the chair with grey tape over his mouth. Running her fingers over the tray of knives,

Teagan listened as the cries got louder and louder. Smirking to herself, she picked up the army knife, turned around, and went to sit on the opposite side of the table from Kelton.

"Secretary Kelton, we finally meet."

He shook his head, crying and trying to move, but the rope was too tight, cutting off his circulation.

"I'm going to take the tape off, and you're going to answer my questions."

Standing up, she walked to him, scratching the knife against the table. She yanked the tape from his mouth.

"Ahhh!"

"Shhh... Sssh."

Teagan held the knife to her lips.

"Please, I didn't do anything."

"Mr. Kelton, please don't insult my intelligence."

"I can help you."

"Is this your way of trying to convince me to let you go?"

"I promise I can help."

"No, I doubt that, but what you've done is kill innocent girls."

"They're not girls!"

"Sick bastard." Teagan threw the knife into his shoulder, where he was shot.

"Bitch! Ughh... my shoulder."

"This is for those girls, you bastard." Teagan grabbed another knife from the tray, pulled Todd's head back, and slit his throat, dropping the blade on the ground. The doors opened, and Spider and Gregory checked Todd's pulse.

"What do you want the press release to say?" Gregory asked, picking up the knife from the floor.

"Make it a suicide; I don't care," Teagan answered, strolling out of the room and heading toward the entrance of the Agency. Seeing the cars ready to take them back, Teagan extended a hand for a shake.

"Is he dead?" Gage asked.

Holding the door open, Teagan nodded in answer.

"He won't be a problem any longer, and the president will replace his seat."

"I still can't believe he killed all those girls."

"I've seen worse, unfortunately," Teagan replied, sliding in her seat as Spider and Gregory came out a few minutes behind her, hopping in the front seats.

"See you next time, Agent Stone," Gage blurted out, tapping the hood of the Range Rover.

Chapter Thirty

The next day.

Teagan woke up in bed, stretched her arms after feeling around the bed, checking for Christian. The flight came in late after she had a meeting with the president.

Flashback.

"How many girls did he kill?" the president asked again.

Gregory, Spider, and Teagan all glanced at each other as they sat in the Oval Office. It was past midnight, and he called them on the way to the airport to speak with them about Todd Kelton. It was running all over cable news about another scandal in the Sanders administration. Teagan stood in a jogging suit and tennis shoes that the president provided for them to change into when they arrived.

"From what we know so far, it could be over a dozen."

"Damn it, Stone."

President Sanders stood in front of the window, looking out at the moon.

"What about Steinman?"

"She's going to be investigated," Teagan said.

President Sanders pulled his chair out and sat, glancing at all three soldiers.

"Send all the parents my condolences," Sanders said.

"We will, sir," Spider said.

"Anything else I need to know?" Sanders questioned.

"It was clean."

* * *

Present Day.

Rising out of bed, Teagan grabbed the remote control and turned on the TV to the local news as breaking news spoke on Secretary Kelton's suicide and would give no further commit. President Sanders sent a statement through his press secretary.

"The president would like to send his condolences to Kelton's wife and children."

Teagan stood at the counter, brushing her teeth and placing her hair in a bun before she headed to the shower. She let the water rinse away the day before. Thirty minutes later, she sauntered in the kitchen smiling at her kids, laughing and talking while eating breakfast.

"Mommy, come eat breakfast," Tatum said.

"Mmmmm... smells good."

"I helped Daddy cook," Tatum said.

Teagan grabbed a plate from the counter, placing sausage, pancakes, and eggs on her plate.

"What are you three doing up on a weekend day?"

"I have a game today," CJ said.

"I want to go to the mall," Tatum said.

"A busy day, I see." Teagan kissed Cole on the cheek.

"We can go to the mall tomorrow, Tatum. Today's about your brother," Christian said.

"Boring," Tatum muttered.

"See, Mom, I told you to have another boy," CJ joked, pouring syrup on his pancakes.

"How about we go to your game, then go to the mall with just the two of us?" Teagan suggested.

"I like that idea better," Tatum responded, smiling with her missing right corner tooth.

"How long are you home, Mom?" CJ questioned.

"Officially on vacation, honey."

"Yes!" CJ raised his hand in the air for a high five.

Cole danced in his seat as everyone laughed at him.

* * *

"Mommy, I like this color." Tatum held a pink crop top. This was the third store they'd visited, and Teagan was exhausted running behind Tatum after coming from a football game that CJ's team won. All she wanted to do was soak in a tub and sleep the rest of the day away, but Tatum had to try every store she saw. Holding four bags with mostly clothes for her daughter and one or two items she picked up for the boys, she wanted to spoil Tatum since she'd been away from her for so long.

"You're not wearing that, Tatum; try this instead." Teagan grabbed a long pink and blue jumpsuit with a sweater to match. Tatum rolled her eyes, and Teagan cocked her head to the side, passing the jumpsuit over for her to try on.

"Go ahead, try it on, and then we'll get our nails done." Teagan went to sit down on the bench as Tatum stepped into the dressing room.

"Do you need any help?" Teagan called out.

"No, I'm a big girl, Mommy."

Teagan lifted her cell phone out of her purse, checking in with Christian and the boys.

Teagan: Did you order pizza for dinner?"

Christian: Yep, along with hot wings.

Teagan: I might grab some movies.

Christian: Hurry home.

"Here I am." Tatum placed her hand on her hip.

"Oh, you look beautiful, baby." Teagan took a photo of Tatum, sending it to Christian

Teagan: Look at our baby.

Christian: Growing up too fast.

"I'll need shoes to match," Tatum informed her.

"You're just a little negotiator, aren't you?"

"I learned from you, Mommy." Tatum skipped back into the dressing room and changed. Teagan took the clothes she was holding and strolled toward the register to pay. Taking the receipt, Teagan passed the bag over to Tatum and left the store.

"Are we going to get our nails done?"

Tatum put on her seatbelt, taking her cell phone out to text with her friends.

"Who are you texting?"

"My friends."

"What friends?"

"I have friends."

"Do I know these friends?"

"Can I get colors on my nails this time?"

"No, you're not old enough for all that."

"Everyone does it, Mommy."

"Stop trying to grow up so fast."

Driving out of the parking structure, Teagan stopped at the stop sign, waiting for the cars to turn before she got into traffic.

"Can we just go home?"

Tatum huffed, throwing her phone in her purse, sitting back with her arms crossed.

"Throwing a tantrum won't get you what you want, Tatum."

"Whatever."

Teagan was getting agitated at her daughter after the long day she had spoiled her. Arriving back home, Teagan parked, turning toward Tatum as she started to open the door to get out.

"Tatum, look at me."

She didn't move.

"Do you know how much you mean to me?" Teagan questioned.

"Yes," Tatum mumbled.

"Okay, so you know I would only do what's best for you."

"I know."

"You need to realize that your dad and I only want to protect you."

"Is that why you leave a lot for work?" she asked.

"Partially, yes, but you have to understand, you can't do everything like your friends."

"I get it, Mom."

"All right, let's go in and have pizza. Your dad wants

to see your new clothes."

Teagan grabbed the bags as Tatum ran into the house, yelling for her brothers. Teagan shut the door behind her, putting the bags down on the ground. Walking up to Christian, she wrapped her arms around his waist, pecking him on the lips.

"How was shopping?" Christian inquired.

"Long."

He chuckled.

"She's stubborn like you." Christian tapped Teagan on the nose with his index finger.

"We've created a monster."

"Did you get cinnamon rolls too?"

"I did; I figured you forgot to ask when you texted, so I ordered a box with the wings."

"I could get used to this."

"To what?"

"Being a wife and mom."

"Are you saying you're retiring from The Firm?" Christian leaned his face back, staring at her.

"Considering how much we've been through over these last few years."

"Mom, come watch the movie," Cole asked.

"What did you order?"

"*The Conjuring*," Cole said.

Teagan jerked back in shock.

"He's going to be up all night with nightmares."

"That's fine; his mother will be here to read him a bedtime story."

Chuckling, she took a seat between Cole and CJ, taking some popcorn from the bowl and watching as the commercial previews came on. This was the time she enjoyed, when they could all be together and relax as a family without any worries—splurging on pizza, junk food, and movies.

"Glad you're back, babe." Christian lifted Tatum from the loveseat, letting her sit in his lap.

"Me too." Teagan winked her left eye, eating more popcorn.

Chapter Thirty-One

One week later.

Teagan stood patiently in the corner, staring at the one-way mirror. Spider and the CIA director argued against having this meeting. Getting special permission from the president to allow an unorthodox questioning of a criminal after having the senate hearings might bring more eyes on The Firm. The door opened with a guard in front and behind Audrey while chained at the wrists and legs. The news was still running the story over the massive human trafficking crime that almost went down, and to know it was a woman at the helm made Teagan's skin crawl. Teagan turned around with her arms crossed over her chest, studying Audrey's demeanor.

"Can you give us some privacy?" Teagan asked.

"We were told to stay," the guard replied.

"I think I'll be fine, don't you think, Audrey?" Teagan cocked her head to the side.

"You'll be fine."

Both guards looked at each other, then nodded,

heading out of the room. Stepping forward, Teagan pulled the chair out and sat down, crossing her legs with her hands in her lap.

"Why?" Teagan asked.

Audrey smiled.

"Is this some type of *Law and Order* interrogation?"

"No, I just want to know why."

Audrey bent forward.

"I like money," Audrey answered.

"How long have you been doing this?"

"I'd rather not do the whole abused, manipulated thing."

"Then explain to me how you ended up here?"

"Agent Stone, it's simple—I'm a businesswoman."

"Selling girls?"

Audrey shrugged her shoulders.

"You have a cigarette?" Audrey asked.

"I don't smoke."

Staring at Teagan, Audrey looked behind her at the mirror.

"How many people are behind the mirror?"

"Enough."

"I don't have a sad, soppy story."

"I think you do; something changed for you to become this way."

"Please don't psychoanalyze me."

"Do you know you're going to jail for a very long time?"

"I had a good run."

"All of those families trusted you, and this is what you do."

"What do you want?"

"Give me all the names and information of any other people involved."

"What do I get?"

"You get to live."

Audrey ran a hand through her hair, blowing out a breath and taking a few minutes to stare into Teagan's eyes, wondering if she was serious.

"Fine."

"Thank you."

Teagan rose from her seat, walked to the door, and knocked for the guards to reenter.

* * *

Camden, Nebraska

Stepping out of the car wearing her shades, Teagan brought a few men with her in case things got out of hand. Spider was across the street on the roof, zoned in on his target if they tried to take a shot. She was here to collect the final piece of the puzzle before moving on and giving all the families closure. Opening the door of the Camden police station, Bert stopped talking to Peter at the front desk as Teagan led the team of ten FBI agents inside.

"I need to see Chief Barrett."

"Why?" Bert questioned.

"Either you step aside, or we can do this the hard way."

"What is this about?" Peter asked.

"My friends here have a warrant for his arrest." Teagan pointed to the agent standing next to her.

"That's ridiculous," Bert blurted out.

"I don't have time to go back and forth with you, Bert."

"You've done enough to hurt our town. Just leave, bitch!" Bert barked.

Teagan smirked as she pushed through the door with the agents behind her.

"Call me a bitch again. I dare you," Teagan told him, cocking a left brow up.

Peter stepped between them.

"Just go do what you came to do," Peter said.

Glancing at Peter, then back at Bert, Teagan stepped around him and stalked toward Chief Barrett's office. Barging through his door, Teagan took the phone out of his hand.

"The chief will have to call you back in five to ten years." She hung up the phone.

"Hey!"

"Chief Barrett, you're under arrest."

"Are you crazy!" Chief Barrett jumped up, charging toward Teagan.

"I wouldn't do that, Chief."

An FBI agent pushed him back up against the wall.

"We know everything."

"I never touched those girls!"

"I never said anything about girls, Chief."

Chief Barrett started sweating, looking nervous.

"I want a lawyer."

"Funny, you're asking for help when I bet you didn't try to help those girls."

Part III

Agent Red (Fatal Death)

By
Ava S. King

Synopsis

Teagan Stone has walked a fine line between life and death. This time, she's come across an enemy that doesn't care if she's the most trained killer or not. They only want one thing, and that's to see Agent Red brought to her knees. In a race against time, she will have to make the ultimate decision. Will she be able to save someone close to her or put the country she gave the oath to protect before her happiness?

Chapter Thirty-Two

"Teagan, you need to stay calm. Breathe for me," Dr. Falk instructed, passing Teagan a cup of water and a napkin to wipe the tears pouring from her eyes. Everything was coming back up, and her demons that she tried to bury had shown up more and more.

"Now tell me, how are things going in your marriage?"

Teagan looked off toward the window in the office. Dr. Corinne Falk started working with Teagan a few months back to help her cope in the team. At first, she denied needing help, but her husband was adamant about having a better marriage. She needed to take care of herself and not let the The Firm become more important than her family. Teagan finally decided to commit to therapy because she wanted her kids to know their mother was healthy and present. Now at thirty-seven, the kids were older. She didn't want to miss any more time as they grew up before her eyes. Soon, they would be in high school, then college, and the house would be empty with just her and her husband.

"Fine." Teagan clenched the napkin in her hand.

Dr. Falk peered at Teagan, nodded, and wrote in her notepad. Teagan lifted the glass of water to her lips, then placed it back on the table.

"Where do you see yourself in five years, Teagan?"

Teagan shrugged her shoulders. Never in her mind did she think The Firm would bring her back in, let alone as the director, the person who puts lives at risk for national security.

"You don't know, or you refuse to answer?" Dr. Falk removed her glasses and held them in her hand.

Teagan sighed, closed her eyes, then opened them again, and balled up the napkin in her hand.

"I see myself still on the same cycle, rinse and repeat."

"Is that what you want?"

Teagan chortled.

"In this business, you don't get a choice to get out."

"I understand it's not a typical nine-to-five, but you have a choice."

Teagan wondered if the doctor knew how many people she'd killed because she was told it was best for the country.

"Dr. Falk—"

Ring!

Teagan glanced down at her cell phone ringing.

"You know I don't allow phones during the session," Dr. Falk chastised.

Dr. Falk discussed early on that Teagan was to be fully open during their sessions and to leave her phones off. Eventually, they compromised so she could keep it on vibrate, but Teagan forgot to switch it over when she walked in the office after picking up her kids from school.

"Sorry... Agent Red."

"We have a case," Spider said.

"What is it?" Teagan stood at the door with her back to the doctor.

"Teagan, we aren't finished," Dr. Falk called out. Teagan held her index finger up to pause her speaking.

"A kidnapping," Spider rushed out. Teagan reached in her pocket, grabbed her keys, and rushed out of the office. Dr. Falk jumped up, ran to the door, and called her name.

"Teagan! Mrs. Stone!" Dr. Falk yelled. Teagan ignored her demands.

"Who?" Teagan questioned and ran out of the office building.

"The last person we ever expected."

Teagan transferred the call to her Bluetooth, reversed out of the parking space, and turned into traffic as she drove back to the Agency.

"Get everyone to the office."

"I'm sending the details to your phone."

For a split second, she removed her eyes from the road and before she could make a turn... Boom!

The left driver's side was hit, swerved to the right side of the street, and barely missed the light pole.

"Pre..." Teagan mumbled as her eyes slowly drew closed as darkness surrounded her.

"Teagan! Teagan!" Spider shouted, as the blare of the horn sounded off. Someone ran a red light and careened to the side of her car. Sirens went off in the background. In a drowsy state, she tried to reach for her phone as blood slid down her cheek.

"Ma'am! Can you hear me?" a passerby called out, then reached his hand through the window to check her pulse.

"Mmmm..."

"Stay calm. Help is on the way," he reassured me.

A crowd formed around her car as witnesses watched the other driver speak with the police, while the ambulance came to the side of Teagan's car and tried to free her.

* * *

Her eyes popped open at the brightness in the room. She glanced from the loud monitors beeping to voices surrounding her.

"Mmmmm..." Teagan slowly lifted her hand to her head and felt a bandage.

"She's awake." Christian went to her in the hospital bed and grabbed her hand.

"Christian..." she mumbled. He lifted the back of her palm to his mouth and pressed a kiss.

"Shush... you're in the hospital."

"What happened?" Teagan looked at Spider, the nurses, and the doctor in the room.

"You were in a car accident."

"Accident."

Teagan tried to sit up.

"Take it easy. Relax," Christian spoke.

"Mrs. Stone, you scared us for a minute." The nurse, Kathy, checked her pupils, then her pulse.

"Where are the kids?"

"Home. Don't worry. Can you tell us what happened?" Christian inquired.

"I got a..." Teagan's eyes rose in surprise at remembering a kidnapping.

The heart monitors went off, and she tried to climb out of the bed, Christian held her down.

"Teagan, calm down. You need to relax."

"No... the president... kidnapping." Her words jumbled together.

"Teagan, it's me Spider. Everything is under control." Spider stood at the end of the bed and stared into her eyes.

"What about?" Teagan looked from the nurse to Spider. Christian knew the life they lived, but she'd already blurted out too much information.

"Everything is under control," Spider lied to keep her calm. He'd already had the team at the office gathering as much information as possible.

Finally, she stopped and relaxed back on the bed, while the nurse filled a cup with water and passed it toward her to drink.

"Thank you." Teagan took a gulp and closed her eyes momentarily to focus.

"I'll let the doctor know you're awake and get you some food brought up," the nurse said.

"Thank you," Teagan said, waiting for her to leave.

"You scared me." Christian cupped her chin.

"Did they catch who hit me?"

"A young kid," Christian replied.

"Are the kids really okay?"

"Yes, I told them you were working late." Christian pressed a kiss on her forehead. Teagan wrapped her arms around his shoulders.

That wasn't a lie because she often did work late and

after so many years, it was natural that she'd miss family dinner. When Christian got the call, he was in the middle of work and had to leave the office to check on the kids and make sure they were okay with neighbors. Christian, at times, thought the worst call he'd get would be about Teagan out on a mission. Not a car accident in the city. He was thankful for Spider when he called.

"The doctor says you'll need rest for a few days, maybe a week."

"I have a new case."

Christian looked away.

"Teagan, you're no help to anyone at this time."

"This is something I have to work on."

"Listen to the doctor before you make any decisions. Promise me." Christian caressed her cheek.

The door swung open, and Doctor Nathaniel stepped over to her bed.

"Mrs. Stone, glad you're awake." Doctor Nathaniel listened to her heartbeat.

"When can I leave?" Teagan expressed.

He sighed and glanced from her husband to Teagan.

"I'd like for you to stay for the next forty-eight hours."

Teagan shook her head.

"Doctor, you don't understand."

He raised his hand up.

"Your team already informed me of your work, as much as they could."

"So you know that time is of the essence."

"There was no major internal damage, but you need to rest. If you can promise to take it easy, you can go."

"Of course, Doctor."

"Then in the morning, you're free to go."

Teagan started to speak.

"In the morning, Mrs. Stone. You might have a major position, but you're my patient at this moment."

"Thank you, Doctor." Christian shook his hand, then the doctor walked out of the room.

"Go home and be with the kids. I don't want them to worry."

"Are you sure?"

Teagan leaned up to kiss him on the cheek.

"Yes, I'll be home tomorrow. I don't want their routine interrupted."

"All right, don't give the nurses and doctors a hard time." Christian stood and grabbed his jacket and keys off the couch.

"See you tomorrow."

Teagan picked up the remote and turned the television on with breaking news streamed across it. The chief of staff's sister is missing. Teagan's eyes rose in horror at the photos on the screen of the president's family in Italy. He's in America, while his mother and family traveled to Italy, after a trip to Paris. It was only a matter of time before Teagan would have to leave on the assignment to figure out what happened.

"At this moment, the president's family is secured," the reporter stated.

The door opened, and a nurse pushed through a cart of food. Teagan turned the TV off, sat up, and placed the remote on the bed.

"Enjoy." The nurse smiled, left the tray, and walked out of the room. Teagan lifted the lid off the plate to see only a note. Teagan's brows dipped low in confusion, as she picked the note up and flipped it open to a phone number. Teagan leaned over the bed, grabbed the phone, and placed it on her lap to dial the number.

"We've been waiting for your call."

"Who is this?"

"Glad to hear the accident didn't slow you down."

Her eyes rose in surprise.

"How do you know about that?"

"Get some rest, Agent Red. We'll be in contact soon."

The call ended, and Teagan slammed the phone down on the receiver, yanked the covers away, slid out of the bed, and tried to rush to the door when she felt pain on her side. The doctor had explained she'd be sore for a few days, maybe a week. Pushing through the pain, she opened the door and looked out at the empty nurses' station. She started to walk down the hall when the elevator opened, and the nurse that checked her vitals earlier approached.

"Mrs. Stone, you can't be out of bed."

"I need to find out who delivered my food."

"Is something wrong with it?" The nurse escorted her back to bed. Teagan scanned the empty hallway for any traces of the nurse who brought in the food.

"Do you know who else is working on this floor?" Teagan sat back down on the bed.

"Just me and Esther, but she's on break."

"What does Esther look like?"

"Tell me what this is about?" Her nurse saw the empty tray and removed it off the bed.

"Nothing, can I get some soup or something."

"What happened to the meal they brought up?" Nurse Kathy wondered.

"I... I... think it was for the wrong room." Teagan hesitated. Her head was still foggy from the car accident, then the phone call. She didn't know who to trust.

"Try to get some rest. I'll be back to check on you and bring you another meal."

Kathy patted her hand, picked up the tray, and walked out of the room.

Chapter Thirty-Three

The doors of the conference room opened, and Teagan stepped inside in jeans and a black blazer, with her hair pulled back into a ponytail. Still the presence of a bandage across her forehead showed she was still in pain.

"I didn't think you'd be back so fast." Daughtrey jumped up out of the seat and came around the table to reach out for a hug. Teagan smiled and hugged Spider next.

"Should you be out so early?" Broderick inquired, and the room went silent.

"We have more important things to worry about. Besides, I'm fine."

Early this morning, Teagan was discharged from the hospital and went home while the kids were still asleep in bed. Christian helped her to shower and demanded she take it easy before she jumped back into work. Teagan was grateful for the outpouring of support from family and friends, but the bigger issue at hand needed to be fixed.

"If it becomes too much..." Spider said.

"I'll let you know." Teagan took a seat. Spider cleared his throat and pulled up the video footage from the day of the kidnapping. The room focused in on the screen as Spider slowed the video down. It showed a blurry shot of Jacqueline Anderson walking into the dressing room to try on a dress, then the clip jumped forward with a different timestamp.

"Where did you get the footage?" Daughtrey wondered.

"My connection at CIA," Spider mentioned and paused the video.

"What do we know? It's now been more than twenty-four hours." Teagan leaned forward and clasped her hands together.

"The president wants us to go in and extract her."

"From whom?"

"We don't know."

"I received a call last night."

All eyes turned toward Teagan.

"What did they say?"

"They knew about the car crash."

"You think it was set up?" Daughtrey remarked.

"Gregory, check the number on this burner phone. I'm not sure."

Teagan removed the phone from her pocket and placed it on the table.

"As of right now, we don't have jurisdiction and if we tried to go into another country..."

"Without any direct contact or information on who is behind this, we would bring political suicide to the president." Broderick sighed and ran a hand down his face.

Gregory typed on his computer, and Teagan noticed his brows dip in confusion.

"What do you have?"

"The number not only doesn't exist, but it's pinged globally from London to Los Angeles," Gregory answered.

"They're professional." Teagan stared off.

Ring!

The office landline rang.

Gregory leaned up and hit the answer button.

"Agent Red." The raspy voice from last night came through the phone.

"This is Agent Stone." Teagan leaned forward and motioned her hand for Gregory to trace the call.

"No need to trace this call. We'll give you the exact instructions," they stated.

"What do you want?"

"President Sanders has to answer to his crimes."

"Where is Jacqueline Anderson?"

"Not too fast, Agent." They laughed on the other end of the call.

"We don't negotiate with terrorists."

"Terrorists... I'd like to think of ourselves as saviors."

Gregory pulled up on the big screen a display of numbers that redirected across the globe. Teagan stood and walked around the table, staring at the projection screen.

"The president would only work through The Firm." Teagan pointed at the highest point where the numbers came from, with the majority directed from London.

"No matter for us. He needs to meet our demands."

"How's the weather?"

"Why?"

Gregory brought up the screen for a closer look at the area she pointed and noticed several restaurants and business.

"I'd hope your claim to have Noah's sister would be true, so I'd like to know how the weather is."

"Awww... Agent Red, are you trying to trace this call?"

"I already know you're in London."

The phone went silent.

"Before we move forward, I need to speak with Jacqueline."

"I'm sending over my demands. Once we've had confirmation, you can speak with Jacqueline Anderson." Unable to get the verbal confirmation that the chief of staff's sister was alive, Teagan blew out a frustrated breath.

"Nothing." Gregory slammed his hand on the top of the table.

"We have to give the president something," Spider commented.

"Gregory, get me everything you can on the call. Daughtrey, I want you to follow up with the hospital."

"What happened at the hospital?"

"Someone passed the phone to me, but it wasn't a real nurse."

"Someone pretended to be a nurse?" Spider blurted out.

"To get Noah's sister back home safely, we need to know if she's alive. All we have is a video of her entering a dressing room."

"Are we taking a trip?"

"Once you pinpoint the exact location."

"That's going to take hours, Teagan," Broderick said.

"Traveling to Italy or London will have to be done on a need-to-know basis."

Gregory listened to the voice recording from the call to break it down in parts, while Daughtrey rewatched the videos back-to-back. Broderick held the files on Jacqueline and Noah's family.

Three hours went by, and the team was still inside the conference room breaking down the call and videos. It was going on three in the afternoon, and Teagan needed to get home for the kids and rest. She'd promised Christian she wouldn't work too long and allow Spider to handle any major cases. She checked the time on her watch and sighed.

"Keep me updated on everything, Spider."

"Get some rest, Teagan," Daughtrey suggested, while she knew deep down the anxiety of everything was creeping up again. After the last case, she'd promised a trip as a family, and now it would be put on hold while the situation with Noah's sister was handled.

Spider walked out of the conference room with her and down to her office.

"Maybe you should rest. You still have the drama from the last senate hearing in your head."

Teagan patted him on the shoulder, eased her office door open, and sat at her desk. Spider leaned on the wall and watched her move with the temperament of a leader he knew she would become from the first time they met.

"What?" Teagan turned her computer on and logged into the classified files on the chief of staff and his family.

"I think we both know the answer to this question, so I won't ask again." He pushed off from the door and stepped toward her desk. Teagan looked up into his eyes.

"I'm staying." Teagan gathered up Jacqueline's background information, social media, and pictures at the White House.

"Do the guys know about your therapy sessions?"

Teagan lived with the memories of her time fighting many battles, then her transition back into the real world of being a wife and mom. The normalcy it brought was something she couldn't tear apart. Therapy helped, but telling her team about the regrets and nightmares would only put her in a vulnerable position.

"No, and I don't plan on telling them."

"You trust me?"

Teagan sat back in her chair, crossed her arms, and nodded at Spider.

"Trust the team, we've all been in your position."

An alert on the computer popped up with a new video stream. Teagan leaned forward and opened the attachment.

"*If you want to see Jacqueline Anderson alive, you'll follow my directions.*" The video ended; Teagan replayed it again and turned the volume up. Spider angled around the desk to watch. They didn't recognize the voice, but Teagan figured it was the same person who called her in the hospital.

"I need a list of everyone who works at the hospital."

"We might not have that kind of time for that, Teagan."

"Then we make time. Right now, they're in charge. We need to make them sweat," Teagan declared. They both understood what she meant and would turn over every resource they have to bring her home safe from harm.

Ring!

"This is Teagan Stone," she answered.

"Hi, Mrs. Stone, this is Rachel from Tatum's school."

"Is she all right?" Teagan felt her heart sink with worry.

"She complained about an upset stomach, so she skipped lunch. I decided to let her go home early." Rachel's the assistant principal and understood Teagan's time from the Navy. People would think she'd always be absent from school functions, but nine times out of ten, she was there on parents' night to catch up with the daily activities of her kids.

"Thank you, Rachel. I'll be over to pick her up in a minute. Actually, I'll grab all the kids."

"I'll be here if you need anything." Rachel finished the call. Teagan reached across her desk to pick up her keys.

"Everything good with the kids?"

"Tatum's not feeling well. I don't want to worry Christian."

"Take care of the kids. I'll handle everything here."

Teagan slipped her purse on her shoulder.

"Thanks. Keep me updated, no matter how late."

"We got it from here, boss."

Teagan opened the door of her office, as Spider trailed behind. He pressed the elevator for the parking area.

"Is Sean taking you home?"

Teagan slipped her shades on.

"Yeah, Christian doesn't want me driving right now."

"I agree." Spider held the door open for her.

Teagan shook her head at how Spider treated her like she was the little sister and couldn't handle herself.

The doors closed.

* * *

Teagan held Tatum's head in her lap as the car drove out of the school parking lot with Sean driving. Once her eyes landed on Tatum, she knew her work would be limited.

"Mom, are you feeling better?" Cole glanced out the window toward his mother.

Teagan rubbed Tatum's back in circular motions.

"Why do you ask?"

"Dad said you were in an accident."

"Car accident, but I'm fine." Teagan caught Sean's stare through the rearview mirror.

"Good, I was worried."

Teagan reached over the seat and cupped his chin.

"Hey, you never have to worry about me."

"You're not invisible, Mom."

Those words made her pause in thought.

"I remember."

"Remember what, baby?"

"That time we were with those men."

Dr. Falk mentioned a few times that she thought the kids needed to speak with someone after everything they've experienced.

"Cole, you never have to worry about those men ever again."

Cole nodded in answer.

"Did you tell your mom about the ball tryouts, Cole?" Sean questioned from the front seat.

"What tryouts?"

"Not a big deal."

"Says who?"

"Mom..." Cole groaned.

The car arrived at their home.

"We'll talk about this later. Help your sister and grab

her bag." Cole climbed out of the car. Sean shut the door, came around the passenger side, and picked up Tatum.

"Sean, she can walk."

"Let her sleep," Sean spoke, and Cole followed with CJ playing on his video game. Teagan slid the key in the door and dropped her keys and purse on the couch as Cole placed Tatum's bookbag on the floor.

"Do you have homework?" Teagan turned the TV on and lifted the headphones off CJ's ears.

"Yes, ma'am."

"Okay. Go change and get your homework done. I'll start on dinner." Teagan, kissed the top of his head.

"Do you guys need anything else?" Sean placed the comforter over Tatum.

"We'll be fine. Thanks, Sean."

"All right. Get some rest, boss. See you in the morning."

"Thanks, and Sean."

He paused at the door.

"I'm grateful for your friendship."

"Always, Agent Red." Sean winked and left her home. While she studied Tatum on the couch, she slid her coat off and laid it on the back of the couch. Teagan marched into the kitchen and opened the fridge to grab a bottle of water for medicine for Tatum. Right as she sat down on the couch, the door opened. Christian strolled in with mail in his hands.

"Hey, you're home early," Christian mentioned.

"Tatum didn't feel good." Teagan popped the water bottle open.

"Where are the boys?"

"Upstairs doing their homework."

"You okay?" Christian rubbed a hand up her arm and across her shoulder to lift her chin.

"Worried about a case."

"What else is new?"

"Can you sit with her, and I'll get dinner started."

"Sure, let me check in on the boys."

"Cole had ball tryouts."

Christian stopped at the end of the stairs.

"I forgot to tell you."

"Did you?"

Christian's brows dipped low in confusion.

"What are you saying?"

"Nothing."

"Did I not just rush to the hospital to make sure my wife didn't die!" Christian argued. Teagan peered up the stairs, hoping the boys didn't hear them.

"You're right. I'm sorry."

"Seems like you're always sorry," Christian fussed, jogging up the stairs without waiting for a reply. Marriage still brought butterflies to her heart, but Teagan knew Christian wouldn't wait around for her to get out of her moods. If the case took over their lives, she needed to end the grudge soon and work in peace for everyone's sake.

Chapter Thirty-Four

Spider shook his head as he replayed the video footage another time in the office. It had been more than forty-eight hours, and time was winding down. He'd eaten, slept, and washed at the office because he knew that was something Teagan would do.

"I think I got something." Gregory held a flash drive in his hand.

"Let it be something that helps."

"Wait! You can't go back there." The door pushed open with Secret Service agents and a woman very familiar to Spider and the team.

"Secretary Harris."

Secretary of Homeland Security Gloria Harris pulled no punches and met Teagan at every level when it came to The Firm. She believed in the program to an extent as long as they worked alongside her agenda. Whenever Teagan disagreed, things took a turn and put them at odds.

"Where's Director Stone?"

"Home," Spider answered.

"I'm right here, Secretary Harris." Teagan moved around the security detail, strolled in the office, and stood next to Spider and Gregory.

"Glad you're feeling better after your car accident." Slight irritation in Gloria's voice made Teagan feel satisfied that no matter what anyone tried to do, they couldn't get rid of her stellar work that she'd proven to the president with The Firm. They hated her because she was cocky like them, but strategic in how she made her steps to get to where she was now. Never did she have to stoop down to the bitter level like Stanton or Harris to get to the top.

"Thank you, but why are you here?"

"Well, this case needs to be monitored because of the sensitive nature."

"Who authorized?"

"No one."

"I'll call you if we need you, but my team can handle everything."

"Are you sure? From what the news states, she's been gone for more than forty-eight hours," Gloria argued. Spider started to answer, but Teagan held her hand out to interrupt.

"You can't believe everything that's talked about in the media."

"Agent Stone, you're playing a dangerous game."

"Is there something we don't know?"

Gloria smirked and shifted from one foot to the next.

"No updates."

"Then I would like to get back to my case if you don't mind."

"It's your loss." Gloria stormed out of his office, with her men flanked behind her.

"What do you have, Gregory?"

"Are we going to talk about what just happened?" Gregory inquired.

"No, but I want to have someone keep an eye on her." Teagan placed her hand on her lower back.

"I had the same thought," Spider responded.

Gregory slid the flash drive in the computer and turned the volume up high.

All three listened with intense focus, leaning forward toward the computer.

The sounds were scattered noise and multiple voices until it was isolated to one sound.

"What is that?"

"Water, more or less."

"Are you saying they're near the ocean or something?" Spider mirrored Teagan's confusion.

"I don't know the exact location, but they're in Italy."

"How can you be sure?"

"Even though the tracking of the phone number pinged in multiple directions, it still showed in the same area that matches water."

Gregory clicked over to a satellite map and zoomed down to a red circle.

"Venice."

"Venice," Gregory and Spider answered at the same time.

"Get the pilot, and I'll call the president." Teagan reached in her pocket to pull out her phone. Gregory jumped up, grabbed his computer, and left the room. Spider extended his hand and dialed Daughtrey's office.

"Agent Stone," Noah answered the call. Teagan bit her bottom lip in hesitation on how much she should convey.

"Noah, is the president available?"

"Do you have news about my sister?"

"I think I should talk to the president first."

"Teagan, it's me. I know the business and how you deal with family members in these situations. I can handle anything."

"If we have any major news, I'll keep you updated."

Noah sighed, and the phone went silent for a moment.

"Mr. President, it's Agent Stone."

"Teagan."

"Sir."

"Where are we with the case?"

"My team and I are heading to Venice."

"Italy?"

"Yes, sir."

"Does Noah know if this information?"

"No, sir."

"Better to keep it that way for now."

"I agree."

"We need this to end quickly, Teagan."

"I understand the predicament your country is in right now, sir."

"I'd hoped to avoid the international circus, but that ship has sailed."

"Secretary Harris was here, Mr. President."

"What do you mean?"

"Is there something I should be aware of concerning her or the Agency?"

"The Agency is not under my rule anymore. She shouldn't have a problem with anything that happens."

"By the way she stormed out of here, it may become a problem."

"All I want to know is when Jacqueline is on our soil."

"Any hands tied on this extraction?"

"You know I can't agree or deny anything that happens."

"Say no more, sir."

"Bring her home, Agent Red."

"Yes, Mr. President." They ended the call, and Teagan waited for Spider to finish. She paced in front of his desk and tapped her finger against her cheek.

He looked at her for a second as she mumbled under her breath.

"I know that look."

"Spider."

"You're not going, Teagan."

Teagan's head swung quickly toward Spider.

"Who's name is on the director's door?"

"As your friend, I think you should stay here after the accident. I mean you still look tired."

"I can handle myself."

Nothing would get solved at that moment, so Spider dropped the conversation. A knock came at the door.

"Come in," Spider called out.

"The van is ready," Daughtrey said.

"Let me call Christian, and I'll meet you downstairs."

"You got it, boss," Spider quipped sarcastically.

Teagan dialed his cell phone.

"Hello."

"Is Tatum feeling better?"

They decided to keep her out of school for another day, even when she was able to keep food down later that night. Teagan thought it was best to give her another day of rest.

"She's watching cartoons now." Christian chuckled. Teagan smiled at his words.

"I have to go out of town."

Silence.

"When?"

"Tonight."

He sighed.

"Not for long," Teagan hurried to say.

"You can't predict that, Teagan. Have you made another appointment with Dr. Falk?"

"Christian."

"If you're telling me you're going out of town, then I need to know when you come back, my wife will be the same woman I married. We just reconnected again after everything."

"You're right. I promise I'll give her a call."

"Where are you going anyway?"

"Venice."

"In Italy!"

Teagan squeezed her eyes shut. She'd said that flights out of the country wouldn't happen, and now she's going back on her word.

"I'll have protection."

"Seems you already made the decision."

"Kiss the kids for me."

"You're leaving right now?"

"Yes, but as soon as we land, I'll call you."

"I love you, Teagan."

"I love you more, Christian. Never doubt that."

* * *

The next day, Teagan finished a FaceTime call with her family back home as she sat in the rented apartment and drank her coffee. Gregory and Daughtrey went to the embassy in Rome, while Spider and Broderick checked over the weapons they'd brought with them.

"The car is ready." Sean stepped out on the balcony. Teagan had Gregory get a place not too far from the store that Jacqueline was last seen. The streets were busy with tourists around St. Mark's Square and the Grand Canal. It would have been a nice place to bring her family. Today, she was on a mission and needed to get in the right frame of mind to capture the last moments of Jacqueline in the store. As Spider directed Sean to the store, Teagan sat quietly in thought of how the next few days would go, searching over Venice. The president wanted an answer and demanded Jacqueline's return, but if anything happened that put them in danger, he'd deny they were ever in Italy on his orders. Possible arrest or death lay at her doorstep if something went wrong. No one sensed if she still suffered from her accident, and the weight of fighting or running around would be the bridge she'd have to cross in a moment's notice. Maybe she could have had Spider lead while she stayed home to recover mentally and physically. Emotionally, Christian could see the walls Teagan held up, but she was grateful he didn't fight her even more on flying out while Tatum was under the weather.

Sean parked the truck and slid the door open. Spider and Teagan followed, looking forward and backward, with patrons moving in and out of the store. One black van approached and parked behind them, filled with men she trusted from Interpol and local police.

"We'll stay out here." Semion, their contact from

Interpol, leaned his head out of the car. Teagan nodded, and Sean held the door open. She glanced first up to the corners of the store for the security cameras. Spider removed a small device from his pocket to attach at the register for listening in on any conversations.

"Hello, I'm Arroya. Can I help you with anything?" the sales associate asked.

Teagan smiled and extended her hand.

"You have some lovely pieces here."

"Thank you. You're American." Arroya clasped her hands in front of her body.

"Yes, it's hard to get rid of the accent no matter where I go," Teagan joked.

"I love America. I hope to visit one day," Arroya said.

Teagan lifted a tag on a black dress.

"How long have you worked here, Arroya?"

"About two years. We get top-of-the-line clothing," Arroya explained grinning.

"You can keep a secret, right?" Teagan leaned in and whispered.

"Yes, of course."

Teagan glanced around the store. Spider headed around the register, placed the device, and slid to the back of the fitting room.

"I heard that someone powerful was kidnapped from here. I mean is it really safe to be here?" Teagan nervously shifted from left to right, blowing out a breath.

Arroya pushed a piece of her hair back and bit her fingernail nervously.

"Honestly, just between me and you, I was here that day."

Teagan's eyes rose in shock. She allowed Arroya the room to continue.

"What do you mean?"

"The American woman who was kidnapped. I saw her go into the back room."

"Wow, I'm surprised the police didn't keep you hidden."

Arroya shrugged her shoulders.

"I didn't see everything, just when she came into the store and went to the back."

"You're brave to even come back to work."

Teagan looked up when the door opened, and two more women came in laughing.

"Do you remember if anyone followed her that day?"

Teagan grabbed the black dress off the rack and held it up to her body.

"It was busy that day; I can't recall."

"Do you have this in cream?"

"Let me check our inventory."

"Thank you." Teagan walked alongside as Arroya scanned the tag into the computer.

She's either covering for someone or naive to the amount of trouble she could be involved with behind a kidnapping.

"Only comes up in black, gray, and red."

"The gray... I'd love to try that on."

Arroya stepped from behind the counter and went to the right side of the employee entrance. Teagan slid to the fitting room. Three of the doors were open, and the last one was closed. She glanced down at the shoes and tapped on the door.

"Spider."

He opened the door, and she slid into the room.

"Anything?"

"Check this out." Spider tapped lightly on the wall

and pushed forward to a false mirror that led down a tunnel.

"Text Sean to head out front." Teagan stepped up on the stool and climbed through the tunnel, turning the light on her phone.

"Make sure—"

Spider closed the mirror back up as though it was never moved.

Underground, they could hear cars passing. If Jacqueline was brought from the tunnel to an awaiting car, it would be a perfect kidnapping.

"The cameras only end at the front entrance of the fitting room," he said.

Teagan scanned the walls and floors for any evidence.

"How did you get away from the sales girl?"

"She's looking for a dress."

Spider paused. Finally approaching stairs, Teagan slid her phone in her pocket and climbed up slowly, easing the door open to the street that angled a few blocks from a flea market and flower shop.

Spider stood next to her.

Teagan held her hand up to block out the sun.

Spider pointed to a camera at the flea market.

"Have Gregory get the footage."

"On it." Spider headed toward the market.

Teagan stared for a few minutes, then put herself in Jacqueline's shoes when they brought her out of the tunnel. It was a dead end near the shop, so they had to go in the direction of the market if it was a crowded day.

Chapter Thirty-Five

Jacqueline sat on a chair with her face covered and her hands tied behind her back. She hadn't been able to sleep or relax since the day she was taken. Her life as a school teacher back in America was simple; she loved her life back home. This was supposed to be a fun trip with some of President Sander's family that Noah had arranged for her to attend. The one time she was away without security, her mouth and nose were covered with a cloth, and everything went dark. Once awakened, she was surrounded by silence, with people coming and going to bring her food. No one had attempted to hurt her physically.

"It's time to eat," a low raspy voice spoke.

Jacqueline sniffed the tears away.

"Remember, don't do anything crazy once I release you."

He untied her hands and placed the cold sandwich and a bottle of water in her hand.

Jacqueline quickly ate and drank, as he watched her movements.

"When we get paid, you can go."

Jacqueline wasn't naive to how the US dealt with terrorists.

"Can I talk to my family?"

He stood with both hands at his side.

"You had your one call."

"Please," Jacqueline mumbled.

"Doesn't work like that, princess." He slid a hand over her cheek. Jacqueline jerked back.

"They won't pay you."

"If they want you alive, they will." He snatched the bottle of water out of her hand, tied her back up, and locked the door. All she could do was pray her family could find her remains if something happened.

* * *

His partner sat on the couch with his feet up, typing on his computer with the TV playing.

"Did she eat?" Godfrey asked; he was the computer whiz who made the call to Teagan. Both men, in their late twenties, went against the normal society standards and worked against government entities. The idea to grab Jacqueline wasn't done lightly, and they took the job because the money sounded good enough for them to take and run.

"Yeah."

"You didn't touch her, did you, Alex?"

He smirked.

"She's not to be touched."

"Says who?"

Heels clicked against the floor and stopped at the edge of the door.

"Me." She held shades against her bottom lip.

Both men sat up straight.

"I didn't touch her." Alex rolled his sleeves up, showcasing his tattoos.

"Has she eaten?" she asked.

"I gave her a sandwich and water like you said."

"My men will have the money wired to you."

"You never told us why you wanted her kidnapped." Godfrey stared at her.

"You never asked."

She took a seat on the edge of the couch.

"I didn't find anything about you, no birth certificate, or anythimg. It's like you never existed." Godfrey looked at her in confusion.

She smiled.

"Godfrey, my dear boy, you aren't the only one good at computers."

"Then what's your real name because Blair De Leon is fake." Godfrey's voice was a little shaky.

She stood, removed her jacket, and passed her shades to her guard.

"Oskala Kingston." She reached behind her back, pulled out her gun, angled it toward Godfrey, and shot him between the eyes.

"Please don't!" Alex shouted, and Oskala held her finger up to her lips and motioned for him to be quiet.

"I promise you won't feel a thing." Oskala pulled the trigger.

"Where are we taking them?" one guard questioned.

Oskala looked at him, and he passed her a cigarette. Holding up the lighter, she took a pull.

"Burn them and grab her from the back."

Oskala Kingston waited years for her moment to get

revenge. Teagan Stone would know the pain of death before she flew out of the country. Jacqueline was a pawn in a bigger game that Oskala didn't care if she became another victim after the way they'd hindered her family's life when they took Diablo from her.

Chapter Thirty-Six

Secretary Gloria Harris held a conference at the state department on the updates on Jacqueline's disappearance. Her way of inserting herself in the case would be through back channels since the president didn't explain why Teagan and most of her team flew out in the middle of the night.

"Hello, I'd like to take this moment to say a few words. For our country, I know we all are praying for Jacqueline's safe return."

The flashes of the camera continued.

Gloria cleared her throat.

"Briefly, I want to let you know that President Sanders and this administration are doing everything possible to bring Jacqueline home safely."

"Secretary Harris, who is running point on her rescue?"

Gloria smirked on the inside and held a steady gaze. Preston, a reporter for The Daily Beat, was her inside man when she needed to look favorable in the public's eye.

"Classified, but I can say we have our best people working the case."

"You say the best, but no word if she's alive or dead," Preston followed up.

"When it comes to international friends, we have to be diligent to not give out the wrong information."

"Can you tell us if a ransom has been spoken of at all around the White House?"

"Again, Preston, classified."

"My source said Teagan Stone of The Firm has left the country."

Gloria wanted to give him a high five in that moment because it riled up the other reporters, and more hands raised.

"Not sure where you got your information. Agent Stone handles many cases."

"So, you don't deny her involvement."

While he put more focus on Teagan, it showed the credibility lacking in President Sanders' judgment to have them deal with a matter after all of the bad blood over the years.

"Don't put words in my mouth, Preston. The Firm is a trusted agency."

Teagan switched the channel and dialed the president's number.

"She's setting us up," Daughtrey hissed, watching the foot traffic outside the building.

Gregory sat in the love seat, condensing all the market footage surrounding that day.

"What do you think her endgame is?" Broderick stepped in the room.

"Same as everyone else. Appearances."

"She's using the kidnapping to her advantage." Spider held out bags of food and passed them around.

"Teagan, I need an update," Noah answered the phone in a rush.

"Is he there?"

"Be honest with me," Noah muttered.

"We don't have her, but I feel she's still alive."

He sighed.

"I guess no update is a good thing."

"Not if they saw the conference from Secretary Harris."

"The president is calling a meeting now," Noah remarked.

"I'm sorry, Noah. She's using Jacqueline to get ahead."

"It's Washington; I don't expect anything less."

"We went to the store and saw how they took her out."

"Tell me."

"It was a false wall in the room."

"Oh my God."

"I can explain more later, but I need to handle something first. Let the president know we will be in touch soon." Teagan rose off the couch with the food Spider brought and walked to the back of the apartment. Sean stood at the door.

"Is she awake?"

"She stopped screaming about two hours ago." Sean opened the bedroom door for Teagan. To find answers, she would need to get even dirtier. She brought Arroya back to the apartment and watched her sleep. Teagan would have preferred to avoid torture as much as possible. However, the only way to get Jacqueline back would be to go back into the dark place she had blocked out. There was a television with only one channel that showed repeats of a cartoon, a chair, and a blacked out window in the room. It brought to mind her time in captivity.

Arroya moaned, as her eyes fluttered open.

"Are you hungry?" Teagan held up the chicken pasta.

"Who are you?"

"I told you."

"You're an American, but I can see now you're more than a customer here to buy a dress," Arroya said in her thick Italian accent.

"Are you hungry? I brought you some food."

"I want to go home."

Teagan smiled and placed the food on the bed.

"Where is she?"

"Where is who?"

Teagan chortled and scratched her cheek.

"You aren't stupid, Arroya. I know you know why you're here."

Arroya looked at the door and back at Teagan.

"It's scary, I know, but remember, I can help you."

"I don't know anything."

"You know why I'm here."

Arroya shook her head.

"I do things that the government can't do."

"Why are you telling me this?"

"Because if you don't tell me what I want to know, I'm afraid you're never going to see your mother or grandmother again."

Teagan stood from the bed and picked up the food.

"Now are you hungry?"

Arroya hesitated for a few minutes, then reached out to grab the bag.

"I was given a note and a phone one day."

"What time?"

"When I walked out of my apartment. It was on the ground."

"No one saw it being placed."

"No."

"What about your mother or grandmother?"

"I didn't say anything to them. I just made a phone call."

"What did the note say?"

"It just held a phone number so I dialed." Arroya cut into the pasta.

"Why didn't you go to the police?"

"I thought it was a joke at first. Then, when I checked my account, I had money deposited."

"What did they say over the phone? How did they sound?"

"Basically, they asked me to keep this woman occupied and show her dresses, so I did."

"So, pile her up with clothes, then she'll be in the shop long enough for them to make a move."

Arroya wiped a tear across her cheek.

"Am I going to jail?"

"How much did they pay you?"

"A million."

After a knock, the door opened, and Sean peered in and motioned for Teagan.

"Are you going to kill me?"

"Finish your food." Teagan stepped in the hallway.

Sean closed the door.

"They found two bodies that washed up," Sean said.

"Shit." Teagan pinched her nose.

"We don't know if it's a woman or not."

"Keep a watch on her."

"You know we can't let her walk away," Sean commented.

To her dismay, she knew he was correct. That comes with being caught up in the world of danger and the work they did in The Firm. It was getting late, and she needed to get an ID on the bodies before the media got wind of anything.

"We'll handle it when we get back." Teagan stalked back into the living room and grabbed her jacket, cell, keys, and gun.

"A contact has the bodies ready for us to view." Spider explained.

"Is it a woman?"

"No, two men."

"Then why do we have to view?"

"My contact said they were found with interesting writing on their bodies."

* * *

"*Jacqueline*," Daughtrey read the words on Godfrey's torso.

"Do we have a time of death?"

"Yesterday around the afternoon," the coroner explained.

"Damn it, someone's playing with us."

"Where exactly?"

Coroner lifted the file and read off the details.

"Both men were shot and thrown in the water, no witnesses. But we picked them up near Calle del Pestrin."

"Thanks."

"We can get some guys to stake out the area." Daughtrey removed his phone and dialed Broderick.

"Be discreet until we get there," Teagan mentioned.

"Are you American detectives?"

"Something like that. But did you find any ID or phone on them?"

"Nothing besides their clothes."

"What are you thinking?" Daughtrey questioned.

Teagan rubbed her chin.

"If they're dead, that means someone bigger is in control."

"And I need to get Jacqueline out before they kill her."

"Whoever's in charge doesn't care about the money."

Daughtrey and Teagan climbed in the van, and Sean shut the door.

"We're dealing with someone smart, who's not afraid of any political ramifications."

Thoughts ran in her mind, as she looked out the window at the apartment buildings, curious if someone was watching when they arrived and left.

"The story Arroya told, do you think it adds up?" Daughtrey wondered.

"Can you stop at the market, Sean? I want to grab a few things."

"Gotcha, boss." He knew Teagan was getting frustrated and ready to head back home. If they didn't find Jacqueline soon, it would be seen as failure, and that's something she couldn't live with.

Ten minutes later, Sean arrived at the market near where the bodies were pulled out of the water. Sean climbed out of the car and opened the back door for her to step out. Teagan peered at the sign, then over to the kids playing outside on a bike. Daughtrey came around the passenger side door and started to walk alongside Teagan when a car careened around the corner, blasting toward the market.

"Get down!" Daughtrey yelled, as he reached for his gun to cover Teagan. Sean managed to block Teagan's view, as the bullets went through his chest, leg, and neck.

"Sean!" Teagan screamed. The kids cried and dropped to the ground. The black-tinted Mercedes Benz drove down the street and made a sharp turn while people scrambled for safety.

"Teagan! Teagan!" Daughtrey shouted, as he jumped up from behind the car and ran to Sean and Teagan. Sean's lifeless body lay on top of her with his eyes closed. She continued to call his name as tears fell down her cheek.

"Sean, please, wake up."

Daughtrey shifted Sean's body to the side, checked his pulse, and removed his phone from his pocket.

"Call the ambulance!" Teagan screamed at the store workers. Everyone watched as the two tried to revive him.

"Are you hit?" Daughtrey grasped her arm, and she pushed him away.

"Don't touch me!" she screamed.

A few moments later, Spider and Gregory arrived, along with the police and ambulance.

"Teagan, we need to check you out," Daughtrey said.

Her hands shook, and her eyes peered around the crowd, unable to comprehend what they were saying.

"It's Spider. Hey, focus on my voice," Spider calmly stated, wrapped his jacket around her arms, and helped to lift her from the ground.

"We need to get her back to the apartment. Too many eyes out here," Daughtrey remarked. Sean's body was loaded on the stretcher.

"Where are they taking him?" Teagan demanded, walking over to the police and the ambulance to speak from the corner.

"Teagan, he's gone," Spider softly said.

"Spider, shut up! He's not gone."

All eyes looked at her. Teagan clenched and unclenched her hands, blowing out a long-held breath.

"I need Agent Red at this moment," Spider whispered in her ear.

Teagan stopped her pacing.

Daughtrey and Gregory jumped in the car and waited.

"I want his body shipped back immediately. Notify the president, and everything should be paid for by me."

"I understand."

"No one touches him without our people watching. Make sure the family is told before the media gets the information."

"Anything else?" Spider held the door open to the backseat for Teagan to slide inside.

"Gregory."

"Pulling footage and plates," Gregory answered.

"I'm going to stay with Sean's body," Daughtrey said before she could ask.

"Kill Arroya." Teagan leaned her head back on the seat and closed her eyes.

Sean had been more than a driver and friend. He'd become like a brother to her and an uncle to her kids, and Christian became close with him, even taking him on golfing trips often. On holidays, he'd bring the kids presents, and Sean would pop up at birthday parties and spoil them more than the grandparents. He kept her abreast of the kids' after-school activities and drove them around when she wasn't available. It would be hard to explain how he would no longer be around. How would they move on as a family and team? He was a longtime military man and brother who joined the Agency and didn't mind working for a woman when it wasn't popular. Teagan knew when she retired, Sean would do the same, and they joked often that no one else could put up with her high demands and annoying attitude. Spider reached over and grabbed her hand.

"He did what he had to do."

"That's what he told me often." Teagan reflected on her conversations with Sean during long drives to work.

Chapter Thirty-Seven

Oskala's Past.

Diablo laughed with his men in the back-yard of the mansion he and his wife, Oskala, recently purchased. He could hide his lovers from his wife, while she lived in Colombia, but she'd fought with him to live together as one. Even though he held business as the Don of Kingston Cartel, no one knew of Oskala, and he'd planned to keep it that way, especially from the woman he'd met at the art show. The American beauty captured his attention, and he wanted to continue the pursuit without interruption from Oskala.

"Gentlemen, I want you to meet my beautiful wife Oskala." Diablo and Oskala went back from their youth. Their families wanted them to marry, and she'd been trained to become his wife one day. She knew all about his business as a drug lord and helped him many times when someone needed to be taken care of. What Diablo didn't know was that Oskala was deadlier than his top killers. A trained sharpshooter, with a fetish for knives, she could seduce a man within one minute and then slit his throat. The reason she was back in their home country was because Diablo thought Oskala would continue to be alone as the doting wife. They didn't have any children, and she'd never wanted to damage her body. The only things that motivated her were money, power, and her husband. Oskala lifted her hand toward the guests and smiled.

"Gentlemen, I hope my husband isn't boring you." Oskala grinned and placed her hand on his chest.

Diablo laid his hand on her lower back.

"Who did Diablo have to kill to marry you?" one of his business partners questioned.

"My husband isn't the only one who's lucky."

"Don't be fooled by that smile. She could be deadly." Diablo squeezed her waist.

"He's modest. I can be deadly but sweet at the same time." She winked at them and pulled out a cigar, and all the men clamored to light it for her.

"Thank you." She blew out the smoke and turned to walk toward the pool in only her bikini top and thong with high heels.

"Gentlemen, as you can see, I have bigger things to handle. I'd like to conclude our business."

"What you're asking is not easy, Diablo."

Diablo took a sip of his cognac.

"I want what I want."

"To get into America, you need resources and a plan."

"My money is good."

"Not about money."

Diablo waved him off.

"Either you get the trucks through Mexico or not."

"The governor won't let that happen."

Diablo smirked and stared at his wife.

"I might have another idea."

* * *

"Gloria, I understand your concerns, but my hands are tied," the governor of Mexico, Fernando Perez, spoke into the phone. The door of his home creaked open as heels clicked against the wooden floors.

"You're getting a cut, Governor Perez. Don't pretend you care about your people."

He grunted, turned around in the chair, and faced the wall of pictures.

"I run everything that goes in and out of Mexico. As of now, I plan on keeping it local." He tapped his finger on the side of his forehead.

"I'm hearing whispers of the Kingston Cartel creeping on your territory."

The governor went silent.

The door knob turned quietly, and Oskala, in a maid's uniform, held a tray with a drink, and a knife underneath.

"The Kingston Cartel can't touch me. Do you understand?" He leaned up out of the chair and cursed. Oskala laid the tray down on the desk, smiled, and stepped around to face him. His eyes ballooned wide.

"Who are you?"

"Diablo sends his regards." Oskala drew the knife across his throat and picked up the phone.

"Governor! Governor!"

"The governor is unable to take your call."

"I know this is Diablo's doing."

"If you know, then you should be scared."

"He won't get away with this."

"We'll meet, Gloria, soon." Oskala giggled.

"Who are you?"

"Someone who doesn't like it when Diablo is disrespected."

"Is the governor really dead?"

Oskala stared at his dead body.

"You can make a guess." Oskala ended the call and walked out of the room.

* * *

A few days later, Diablo sat at the table reading the paper when his butler escorted some business associates into the dining room.

"What have you done, Diablo?" He was held back by the arm of another business associate.

Diablo sat back, smiled, and peered at Oskala.

"Oscar, take a seat. Are you hungry?"

"You killed him!" Oscar shouted, throwing his hand in the air.

Diablo poured orange juice in his glass.

"Killed who?" Diablo took a sip and cut into his steak and potatoes.

"Governor Perez is dead, essentially guaranteeing your position for Mexican trucking."

"Oscar, are you scared?" Oskala spoke up, grabbed the knife, and pointed it toward him.

"The men are talking," Oscar fussed.

Oskala laughed, cut her apple in two, and took a bite.

"Sorry to hear about the governor's death. Hopefully, he didn't suffer," Diablo said.

"I know you're behind this, Diablo. Just remember it can come back to bite you."

"Is that a threat?" Oskala inquired.

"Keep Oskala on a leash, Diablo." Oscar shifted and walked out.

"She's dangerous, Diablo."

"I like them dangerous," Diablo replied and watched Oskala stand, saunter around to his chair, and sit in his lap.

"Remember, I'll always have your back, Diablo," Oskala said.

"I know."

Oskala stayed in the background as Diablo worked his connections and ran the Kingston Cartel. Years later, a raid happened at his compound, and Oskala moved back to her home and focused on the woman he was seen with in photos at certain events. She knew he wasn't completely faithful, but how could he allow himself to be taken down so easily. Now, she had to rebuild the life they had together. Oskala focused the dots on everyone that Diablo encountered, and she plotted to bring them all down, starting from the top with the woman he cheated on her with. Once she learned the ins and outs of The Firm's workflow and the US government's handling of Diablo's arrest, Oskala had a plan in motion and would let them all see how the Kingston Cartel would always be around.

Chapter Thirty-Eight

Present.

"She's sleeping." Oskala put the fork down from eating her salad and picked up her phone.

"The shooting wasn't shown on the news." Oskala's guard stood against the chair of the kitchen table. Oskala sipped on her coffee.

"We have to make a bigger move."

"What else can we do?"

"I have something lined up. Just watch and see." Oskala dialed a number.

"Action Nine News, this is Kailey."

"Hello, Kailey, I don't want my name to be used, but I have information about the Jacqueline Anderson kidnapping."

"Can I have your name?"

"No names please, or I'll call someone else with this information."

"I understand. What information do you have?"

"Two people were found dead, connected to the kidnapping of Jacqueline."

"Who are the two people?"

"All I know is that it's two men. Check with the Italian police." Oskala hurriedly hung the phone and grabbed her coffee.

"Are we moving her?"

"No. After the news gets out, she's going to come for us." Oskala picked up her gun next to her purse and held it up.

"All of our people are ready to move when you're ready."

"Keep them on standby. I have a few things to wrap up." Oskala rose, lifting her purse, gun, and shades.

"Do you need me to come with you?"

"No, I won't be long."

* * *

Oskala sat on a boat with her contact from America.

"I can't be seen with you."

"You worry too much, my friend."

"Why did you kill them?"

"They served their purpose."

Oskala sipped on her champagne.

"I can't give you any more information."

"Are you sure?" Oskala laid her hand on his chest.

"It's over, Oskala. You've made your point."

"My point is just getting started." The boat pulled back up to dock, and Oskala stood and climbed out of the boat.

"Oskala! I can't help you if you step over this line."

"Broderick, the line has been crossed when you fucked Diablo over."

Oskala switched over to the limo waiting for her to

slide in. The door shut, and the limo drove off. Her plan to infiltrate Teagan's men wasn't easy, but the secrets Broderick held fell into her lap. Diablo told her to use those tactics of a beautiful face to make men do anything she wanted, and Broderick was an easy mark. His gambling debts came back to haunt him, and the people he owed were back to collect. Oskala owned those debts. A few minutes later, they arrived at the warehouse. Oskala stood around a table of her men who were loyal to Diablo. To see a familiar face from Oscar was interesting because of how he hated her back in the past.

"Oscar, thank you for joining us."

"You made the choice easy when I looked at my bank account," Oscar responded.

"Men and their money."

"What plans do you have, Oskala?"

"The ultimate plan is to bring the Kingston Cartel back to the top."

All she heard were gasps.

"Who is in charge?"

"The only person Diablo trusted with his empire... me." Oskala removed her jacket and laid it on the back of the chair.

"No woman should lead the cartel." Oscar leaned up against the table.

"Oscar, times have changed. You have to wake up to what is right in front of you."

Oskala angled around the table to stand behind Oscar.

"You're being a fool."

Oskala planted her hands on his shoulder.

"What I'm doing is taking the business to another level you fools could never have imagined."

"Diablo wouldn't want you in charge."

"Diablo put his entire life in my hands and taught me everything. I can lead."

"So why are we here then?" another mafia boss stated.

"I need your resources to bring Kingston back to where we want to be."

"What percentage are you negotiating?" Oscar wondered.

"Give us access to your men, and you'll receive five percent of the first kilo."

"Twenty," Oscar blurted, and Oskala narrowed her eyes.

"Oscar, you're in a position to bring in a lot of money from this deal."

"If we give up so much, and you end up taking the cartel to a bigger level, that's more eyes from the police. We deserve compensation." He pointed in the air.

"Ten percent and let me say, you don't want me as an enemy," Oskala announced.

Everyone went silent.

Oskala picked up her jacket.

"You know what I am capable of, gentlemen. Don't disappoint me."

Chapter Thirty-Nine

President Sanders sat in the Oval Office and listened to his staff break down the situation with Jacqueline in Italy. The Kingston Cartel was behind the kidnapping, they'd discovered. His last campaign almost ended when Diablo's name was brought back into the media. There was a point when the media posted outside Noah's family home and searched through his family background to associate them with an international crime ring.

"Do we have exact eyes on her?" President Sanders leaned back in his chair. Noah stood stoic near the side door that led to his office.

"Nothing yet," the deputy chief of staff said.

"How did we miss this! I want a full investigation." President Sanders glowered at his team of military staff and FBI.

"Diablo was watched at all times; there is no evidence of outside communication." FBI coordinator Ryan Magnum showed him the photos of Diablo under custody at the time after the first run in with Teagan.

"We continue to be behind these incidents, and it makes me wonder if we have a leak in the White House." President Sanders glanced around at his team. Everything of that day played across the media from news stations to internet posts about the abduction. President Sanders's administration had more to accomplish before his term ended. He felt if he couldn't keep safe the people who worked closest to him, it would show in the public opinion he wasn't living up to the position of being the president of the United States. The confidence he displayed often in front of the camera was slowly fading away as the days went on without a word from the team.

"Which means we need to think of alternatives."

"Secretary Harris." Secretary of Homeland Security Gloria Harris extended a hand to the president, removed her coat, and placed it on the back of the couch.

"Mr. President, I looked from all angles."

"Are you saying to put my sister in harm's way?" Noah called out. Gloria looked over her shoulder at Noah and slid one hand in her pocket.

"Hopefully, I'm not speaking out of turn. But as the chief of staff, you're too close to the recovery mission."

"That's my sister," Noah scoffed, pointing at his chest.

"Noah," President Sanders spoke and glanced at him. Gloria cleared her throat.

"I know you have your team out there, but we need a heavy presence to show that we don't take the kidnapping of the chief of staff's family lightly." Gloria motioned her hand at Noah.

"What are you proposing?"

"Military intervention."

President Sanders shook his head, stood, and turned to the window in his office.

"I can't do that."

"Either we make a statement now, or we lose our power." Gloria crossed her arms over her chest.

Noah understood the president's hesitation, even though he wouldn't want to put the world at war. But to know he didn't try everything to bring her home caused a sharp pain in his chest.

"We wait until we hear from Teagan. I trust her decision."

"That would be a major mistake, Mr. President."

"I hear you, Gloria, but we need to give them more time."

"The people who have her don't care about some agent you've depended on in the past. We need to fight with fire." Gloria raised her voice.

"Give me the room." The president waved for them to leave. Gloria turned to leave the room, and he stopped her.

"You stay."

Noah stared at Gloria, then walked to his office.

The president closed his eyes in thought.

"If there's something you know, I suggest you tell me."

"Excuse me, Mr. President."

"What do you know about Jacqueline's kidnapping?"

"Nothing."

"If we hear you're behind anything..."

"Sir, I'm loyal to our country and to this administration," Gloria said.

"Teagan is in charge of Jacqueline's case. Either you work with her, or you're against us."

"Sure thing, Mr. President." Gloria slid her hands in her pockets and left. Noah came back into the room and stood next to the president's desk.

"She knows something."

"About Jacqueline?" Noah pressed.

"We've had too many people screw us behind our backs. Keep an eye on her."

"The call never came, and so we were waiting on confirmation from Teagan."

"Give them time. She's on to something."

"After Sean's death, we don't know how this will play out for us."

"Have the arrangements been made for his funeral?"

"In the planning stages now."

"Make sure you have a note and flowers sent from me."

"Are you going to give a speech on the incident with Sean?"

"Taylor gave a briefing earlier on and sent our condolences."

"We're going to get Jacqueline back, Noah."

"I know."

"If you need to take some time, I understand."

"Until she's back on our home soil, I won't be able to rest at home."

Knock! Knock!

"They're ready for you, sir." Taylor poked her head in the office. The president buttoned his suit and walked out of the office to the press briefing room.

* * *

"Please have a seat," the president spoke to reporters.

"The president will take a few questions, but he won't be able to stay long," the press secretary stated.

"Mr. President, do we know who's behind what has happened in Italy?" The reporter held his hand up.

"At this time, we can't release that information."

"Some people say this is about your connections to The Firm."

"Paul, I won't get into any rumors."

Another reporter raised their hand.

"What is the latest status of Jacqueline's release?"

"Mary, we're doing everything to work with our partners to make sure Jacqueline is home safe."

"With all due respect, Mr. President, you've already lost a man. How can the American people trust you to bring Jacqueline home safely?"

The president shifted from one side to the next, clearing his throat.

"Mary, what I would say to you and the American people is that we have the best military in the world and agents we trust to do their jobs. We've lost a great man, but he would want us to continue and bringing her home."

"The president has another call. We'll have him come back." Taylor ended the press briefing, and all of the press threw out questions as he left.

Chapter Forty

Teagan closed the door to her car and stared at the camera pointed at the shop Jacqueline frequented the day she was taken. As the time ticked, she knew it was now or never to make a move and bring her home safely. After the president spoke, and outlets received a tip that two bodies were found connected to her disappearance, Teagan figured they'd escalated. She checked her holster and vest and walked to the back of the building. Daughtrey came up behind her with a tool kit in his hand. After the night of the ambush, Gregory was able to get more intel that was shocking and surprising about Diablo.

"Watch out."

Teagan looked behind her as the people went about their business and didn't notice or say anything about two people lurking around an apartment building.

"Got it." Daughtrey unlocked the back door of the building, and Teagan followed him.

"Stay behind me," Teagan said.

"What made you pick this place?"

"I got a feeling."

A cat ran through the hallway.

"Shit!" Daughtrey cursed.

Teagan noticed an older couple coming out of an apartment.

Boom!

A large blast outside caused frantic tenants to run out of their apartments and run for safety.

"Teagan!" Daughtrey shouted when someone bumped into him and split them up.

"Outside!" Teagan scrambled through the crowd and came back outside. Police and fire trucks surrounded the area and helped to calm the crowd down. Teagan pushed through the crowd to see a car on fire in front of the same spot Sean was shot.

"Stay back!" a policeman yelled.

Teagan started to raise her ID, but Daughtrey caught her arm.

"Not here," Daughtrey said.

"It's them, Daughtrey." Teagan yanked out of his hold.

"We can't make it known, Teagan."

Teagan glanced around the crowd and noticed two men leaning against a car laughing as people cried and needed support.

Teagan whispered in his ear.

"Check your view on the left." Teagan kept her eyes forward.

"You want to take it?"

"Don't make a scene but split up and follow."

"Keep your location on."

"Check in five minutes."

Teagan moved through the crowd and kept an eye on

the police. Then the two men jumped in the car. Teagan motioned for a taxi, hopped in the back, and told him to follow the car in front of them. She texted Daughtrey.

Tegan: We're behind the car.

Daughtrey: Texting Spider and the team.

Teagan: Keep the police away.

The car weaved through traffic and stopped at the light.

"How much further?" the taxi driver questioned.

"Cut the meter. I'll pay you for the rest of the day."

Daughtrey: Spider's heading out now.

The black Audi stopped at a restaurant not far from where the explosion occurred. Teagan looked behind her, and traffic slowed down. She removed money out of her pocket and passed it to him and hopped out of the car.

"Stay close," Teagan said to the taxi driver, strolling to the side of the building out of sight of the men as they talked with another group of men. One looked older with gray hair, a beard, and a protruding belly.

Ring!

"Where are you?" Spider inquired.

"At the restaurant not far from them."

"I see you. Don't move until we get there."

"Daughtrey's on the other side."

"We need to keep a tail on them. The van just pulled up."

"Here I come." Teagan hung up, covered her face with her hand, and climbed in the van driven by Spider. Gregory and Broderick were in the back.

"It's them."

"How do you know?"

"Too easy of a setup."

"I mean it could be a trap for you," Broderick countered. The car came around the corner, and Daughtrey jumped in when he pulled off.

"What did you see?" Teagan ignored Broderick.

"I counted four men. I couldn't add the tracker, but I paid the waiter to put a tap on his clothing," Daughtrey explained.

"Stay over here and wait," Teagan said.

"Look, they're getting back in the car." Spider pointed, starting the van again.

"Stay a car or two back."

Spider nodded and sped up to not get blocked behind a food truck. Teagan's only motivation was to get answers and find out who was behind the entire situation.

"We have a track with visuals of four men from the heat signal," Gregory remarked.

The car arrived at the apartment building. Spider turned to the corner and parked, then everyone jumped out.

"Daughtrey's with me, and Spider and Broderick, you stay back on visuals," Teagan explained.

Spider removed equipment from the car and handed an extra gun to Daughtrey, along with a headpiece and goggles.

"Wait until it gets darker."

"Everyone stay alert. This might not be the end of things."

"We're doing this for Sean." Daughtrey hugged Gregory and Spider.

"You stay close to Daughtrey." Spider clapped Teagan on the back.

"Spider, I'm focused," Teagan answered.

"They went up to what looked like the sixth floor," Gregory answered, motioning at his computer visual.

"I can't wait any longer." Teagan started to walk over to the building.

"Teagan!" Spider shouted, and she ignored him. Daughtrey followed her to catch up.

"She's acting reckless again!" Broderick barked.

"Let her go. We need to get in place," Spider ordered.

Chapter Forty-One

After Spider dropped the equipment in the car, he grabbed his cell and sent a message to Teagan. He was on standby, as was Daughtrey, and the rest of the team went forward with the plan. Jacqueline was safe, but nothing would stop Teagan from capturing each person that set out to hurt her people. All of this became too much for him, and he understood if Teagan wanted to quit after what happened, to focus on her family. Sean's family heard the news of his death and were on their way to the White House to meet with the president. His body was getting flown home. At first, the Italian government wasn't open to providing support, but President Sanders expressed his concerns on how it would look. It would become an international disaster if they were denied any support when the death happened on their soil.

Their private plane was ready to go once they arrived, but Teagan might not leave until she executed the entire cartel. To know Diablo had a wife gave her a disgusting feeling. Sean's life was lost over betrayal. All about revenge to force Teagan out in the open.

"They have five more minutes before they arrive." Broderick peered at the camera footage provided by the goggles Daughtrey wore. Once they breached the barrier of the building and turned the camera footage off, anything traced back would be linked to dummy footage of the same events the prior night.

"If Oskala gets away, we're screwed." Spider stared at the message thread from some of the team at the hospital.

"How did we miss her?" Broderick rubbed his chin in thought.

"Not sure, but she's made it her mission to make Teagan suffer."

"Do you think Teagan was deeply involved with Diablo?" Broderick glanced at Spider.

All of them had done undercover work and had gotten involved in situations where they needed to pretend to fall for someone, but Teagan stayed under for much longer. Broderick thought it could have been one of the reasons she left the Agency—to escape the questions and looks from every time people brought up the case. Spider always could read Teagan, but even he had doubts when it came to her and Diablo.

"I trust her."

"Not the question I asked."

"It's the only answer you'll get from me. What are they doing now?"

Spider stood off to the side of the car and waited to get word if they needed backup. Average citizens went on about their lives, unaware a kidnapping by a terrorist group was only a few feet away.

"They made it inside." Broderick held the camera up to Spider.

"Teagan, can you hear me?" Spider spoke in the earpiece.

A few minutes of silence came over the headset.

"I'm here."

"All clear out here."

"I suggest you tell Spider I need your undivided attention," a soft but commanding voice demanded.

* * *

Daughtrey glanced from Teagan back to Oskala and her men that stood with guns raised toward their heads. Teagan thought it was too easy at first but knew her commitment to find Jacqueline came at a sacrifice. If this would be her last moment, she was prepared to take out as many of Kingston's men as possible. Oskala motioned for her soldier to grab their guns, and Daughtrey puled the trigger and shot him in the head. Oskala smiled at the death of her men. She wasn't like Diablo who held feelings for anyone working for them. Diablo kept her hidden from the outside world because she was unpredictable and would do anything to get the cartel in the news. Teagan put her hand on Daughtrey's shoulder.

"Oskala, we can talk about this."

Oskala lowered her gun, stepped in Teagan's face, and stared into her eyes.

"I see what Diablo saw in you. Very beautiful."

"You can still live."

"Oh. I've heard about the American negotiations." Oskala winked her left eye at her soldiers, raised her hand, and knocked Daughtrey on the head with the butt of her gun.

"Arghhh!" Daughtrey dropped down to his knees.

"Don't do this, Oskala. Take me instead," Teagan argued.

"Where is my husband?"

"I don't know."

"You know everything, Agent... Red." Oskala paused and tilted her head to the side.

"Diablo is a high-priority witness for the government."

"Where is my husband, Agent Red?" Oskala pointed the gun into Daughtrey's head.

"We don't know!" Teagan shouted.

Boom!

Smoke filled the room from the blast and Spider marched in with more men beside him as Teagan reached out and knocked Oskala's hand away from Daughtrey. Oskala punched Teagan in the face and ran down the hall of the apartment. Teagan choked on the smoke and bent down to help Daughtrey to stand.

"Daughtrey, hold on." Teagan helped him on the couch and took off down the hall.

"Teagan, wait!" Spider shouted.

"Go! I'm fine." Daughtrey ripped his shirt off and tied it around his wound. Teagan jogged through the hallway and down the stairs. She reached Oskala and tried to grab her arm. Oskala turned and smacked her across the face.

"You ruined my life!" Oskala shouted, grabbed Teagan by the hair, and hit her in the stomach. Teagan bent over in pain and coughed, elbowing Oskala in the stomach. Oskala released her hold and ran out of the building.

"Fuck!" Teagan stood and held the side of her stomach. She waved through the smoke, picked up her pace, and left. She saw Oskala run toward a car, jump in, and shoot back at Teagan. To avoid the shot, Teagan ran back to the door and hid until the car pulled off.

"Gregory! Gregory, I need visuals!" Teagan shouted in her headpiece.

A car pulled around back, and Teagan hesitated to get in the car until she saw Spider roll the window down.

"Come on!" Spider yelled, and Teagan took off running toward the car.

"Where's Daughtrey?" Teagan asked, opening a bottle of water.

"Broderick has him."

"Only a car ahead of you," Gregory answered through the headpiece.

"I see them," Spider responded.

"We need to get them alone."

"She's not too far off."

"Where is she staying?" Teagan asked Gregory.

"She's registered at a hotel near the market."

"That was the plan all along," Teagan muttered.

"Take the turn up here and beat them before she gets there," Gregory announced.

"You sure she's going to stop off?" Spider quipped.

"She's a creature of habit."

Chapter Forty-Two

Oskala stood with a grin on her face and the gun in her hand, motioning for Teagan to place her gun on the floor and step back. Teagan told Spider to stay outside, and she would handle her alone, but the look in her eye reflected that it would get ugly between them.

"You look like his type."

"What do you want, Oskala?"

"Your blood."

"Diablo knew what he wanted."

"You Americans lied and arrested him." Oskala gripped the bottle of tequila, poured some in her glass, and gulped it down, before refilling a second shot.

"My people have the building surrounded."

"Fuck you!" Oskala took a sip. Teagan took that moment to run around the side of the wall, and Oskala sent a shot a few feet away.

"Bitch! Diablo never loved you," Oskala screamed.

Teagan remembered her gun was left on the floor.

"Come out, come out, wherever you are." Oskala laughed.

Teagan removed her vest and holster and threw them to distract her. Oskala came around the corner, and Teagan grabbed her arm with the gun, pushed it upwards, and punched her in the nose.

"Arghh!" Oskala screamed.

Teagan started to wrap her arm around Oskala's neck but was pushed back against the wall.

"Ughhh!" Teagan groaned, and Oskala used her head to pop Teagan in the eye.

"You're going to die today, Teagan Stone," Oskala seethed, bashing her in the head. Teagan stared at the gun in the right corner near her foot.

"Diablo used you; he told me," Teagan taunted.

Oskala's eyes rose in shock.

"Fuck you, bitch!" Oskala launched forward, and Teagan lifted her foot and kicked Oskala back, jumping toward the gun before Oskala could recover, and shot her in the chest.

"Ahhh!" Oskala gasped, blood pouring through her clothes and from her mouth.

Teagan breathed heavily, watching Oskala's slide to the ground, her eyes slowly rolling back.

"Diablo can pick them for sure," Tegan muttered, limped out of the room, and saw Spider and Gregory ready to charge in to help her.

"Call the police; a dead body is left."

* * *

"Soon, we will be landing in New York. Please fasten your seatbelts," the stewardess announced.

"Thank you." Teagan lifted the bottle of water to her lips. She glanced down at her arm wrapped in a bandage.

"I got word that her body was taken to the morgue." Spider ended his call.

"Good, she needed to be put to rest."

"I can't believe we're almost back home," Broderick said, and Teagan stared at him.

"Broderick," Teagan called out.

"Yeah?"

"Did you ever meet Diablo's wife?" Teagan questioned.

Spider glanced at him.

"I had no clue."

"I figured."

The plane landed, and Teagan stood and grabbed her bags, following down the stairs to the black SUVs waiting for the team.

"Take a week off," Teagan told the team.

"What about you?"

"With this, I'll probably take a month off," Teagan joked, watching them load bags in the trunk.

Teagan slid her seatbelt on and laid her head back on the seat.

"Agent Stone, I'm Jason, one of your new details."

"Have you met my family?"

"Yes, ma'am."

"Call me Teagan."

"I'd prefer Agent Stone."

"He preferred to call me boss." Teagan chuckled to herself.

"I'm sorry?"

"Nothing."

The van pulled out of the airport with Spider riding

with her, and Gregory tagged along with Daughtrey and Broderick. After dropping Spider off, Jason arrived at Teagan's home and parked. She picked up her bag. For the rest of the night, Teagan checked on her family, ate dinner, and sat in her office after she showered and arranged for Sean to receive an honor for the work he'd done with the Agency. The news reports repeated the video of Sean's body when it arrived home.

Ring!

"Teagan Stone."

"Agent Stone?"

Teagan sat up in her chair in a soft, timid voice.

"This is her."

"Sorry to call you so late. My brother told me to wait."

"Jacqueline?"

"Yes, sorry, this is Jacqueline Anderson."

"You're fine, Jacqueline."

"I just wanted to call and personally thank you again for saving me."

"No need to thank me. I was doing my job." Teagan recalled Jacqueline in the apartment chained to a chair, blindfolded. Nonstop chaos when they busted in the apartment.

Jacqueline sniffed.

"I don't know how I can ever thank you. I thought I would never see my family again."

"Focus on your family."

"I know you lost one of your team members out there."

"Unfortunately, we did, but we all signed up for this work."

"I still have nightmares."

Teagan didn't know how to respond.

"Noah suggested a therapist."

"He's right."

"Maybe. I just have the feeling of anxiety not knowing if this will happen again."

"You can't think like that, Jacqueline."

"I won't hold you any longer but again, thank you, Teagan."

"Get some rest and remember your brother would risk it all for you again."

Chapter Forty-Three

A week later.

Sean's family held the burial at a family plot, and Teagan decided to bring the kids to pay their respects. Christian held Tatum's hand as she cried in his arms. CJ and Cole wiped their eyes, and Teagan watched the flowers being laid on top of his casket. A few of his family members gave speeches, and the president stood next to the family. A small amount of press was allowed to accompany him. Teagan still held guilt, even though his family gave their gratitude for everything she did trying to save Sean.

"You're ready to go." Christian glanced at the casket being laid in the ground.

"Yeah, we should get the kids home." Teagan and her family headed to their car.

"Teagan."

Teagan paused and motioned for Christian to go ahead to the car when the president approached.

"Mr. President."

"How are you feeling?"

"Feeling ready for work."

"You know it's fine to take some time off."

"Everyone keeps telling me that."

"Oskala's no longer an issue."

"We've interrupted what she was planning with the Kingston Cartel."

"She's been after me for a while."

"Gloria tried to push her agenda."

The president walked alongside Teagan to her car.

"The only thing that matters is that Jacqueline is home safe."

"I saw your press briefing the other day."

"It won't end until they try to find something on the Agency."

"Definitely shown." Teagan stopped in front of her car.

"Thank you again, Teagan. Noah is overjoyed and grateful."

"I did my job, Mr. President," Teagan said.

"A job we know that's not easy."

"You should know." Teagan smirked.

The president reached out for a hug, and Teagan opened the passenger door and climbed in as security walked the president back to the beast.

* * *

Later that day, Teagan punched the weight bag in the training room of the Agency, then removed her gloves and walked to the gun range to pick up her weapon. She wiped the sweat off her brow and picked up goggles. Teagan sent off shots and pushed the button to see the target sheet. All the bullets went into the head, Then the door opened, permitting Spider.

"How long have you been hiding down here?"

"Soon as the funeral was over."

"His family wanted to see you at the house."

"It would have been too hard."

"Saw you with the president."

"He just told me about Gloria having an agenda, and I already knew that."

"All politicians have an agenda," Spider replied.

"We have to get better with the people we have on our team."

"How so?"

"Keep a tighter eye on everyone. Oskala was too familiar with our moves."

"What are you saying?"

"Another leak probably, but I can't be sure."

"You sound paranoid."

"I might be paranoid, but with my past, I wouldn't put it past anyone."

"Including me?"

Teagan reloaded her gun and shot at the target.

"Everyone."

Teagan holstered her weapon, removed her goggles, and they stepped on the elevator to head to their office.

Teagan grabbed a change of clothes out of her bag and hopped in the shower.

A few minutes later, she sat at her desk and opened the file on the case. She pulled photos of each person from Oskala, Godfrey, Alex, Arroya, Sean, and Jacqueline. Teagan studied the details and locations of the shop and the distance to travel to the apartment where Alex and Godfrey were found.

Timelines ran over and over in her head, including every step from the moment she got the call of her kidnapping at the store. For a second, she thought of tracking all the calls from the Agency going out.

Ring!

"Hello."

"Are you coming home soon?"

"What time is it?" Teagan raised her wrist up and checked the time.

"Going on eight."

"I didn't know it was that late."

"The kids finished dinner."

"Logging out now. Be home soon."

"See you soon, babe."

"Love you."

"Love you more, Teagan."

Teagan closed the folder and threw it in her bag, turned the light off in her office and strolled to the elevator to leave for the day. A half hour later, Teagan read a book to Tatum, kissed her on the forehead, and tucked her under the comforter. She checked on Cole and CJ, then strolled in her bedroom and saw Christian up with sports on the TV.

"Hey."

"Did you eat?" Christian asked.

"Not hungry." Teagan kicked off her shoes and dropped her bag on the floor.

"You get Tatum to sleep."

"She was waiting for me. I read her a story." Teagan lay on the bed, slid next to him, and wrapped her arm around his waist. Christian rubbed her back.

"Sean's funeral was nice."

"It was."

"What did the president need to talk to you about?"

"He wanted to check in and see how everything is going with me."

Christian pressed a kiss to her forehead.

"CJ has his game coming up."

"Are you going to be able to come?"

"I'll be in the front row."

"I'll make t-shirts." Christian chuckled.

"What's going on with your work?"

"Work is busy, but the family is my priority. I hate to see you going through the loss of your friend."

"I have an appointment with Dr. Falk."

"Is she helping?"

"She's helping me."

"The new detail."

"Are the kids comfortable with them?"

"Yeah, not sure they'll get close like they did with Sean."

Teagan moved out of his arms and sat against the headboard. Christian turned to face her.

"Today was long. Try to sleep, and we can have breakfast after we drop the kids off at school."

"Like a date?" Teagan teased, rubbing the top of his head.

Christian chuckled, leaned forward, and kissed her on the lips.

"It's a date."

Chapter Forty-Four

D r. Falk talked to her secretary at the desk as Teagan opened the door and pulled the umbrella down. She signed in, and Dr. Falk waved her back. Teagan went into her office and left the coat on the end of the chair.

"Would you like water, tea, or anything?"

"Water is fine."

Teagan crossed her legs and sighed.

Dr. Falk grabbed a bottle of water from the fridge in the corner and handed it over to Teagan. She slipped the lid off and took a sip. Dr. Falk took a seat in her chair, picked up her notepad, and waited for Teagan to talk.

"Whenever you're ready."

"I just buried one of my friends."

"Sorry to hear that."

"Funny, I thought I would be the one to go first in my group."

"How is your team handling everything?"

"Everyone is walking around in a daze."

"How are you and Christian?"

"Good. He's given me space."

Dr. Falk waited for her to continue.

"You think you two need to reconnect without the kids?"

"We are. He wants to take me to a cabin to get away."

"That sounds like something that would be good for the two of you."

"Sean would tell me all the time to go easy on Christian." Teagan chortled.

"Sean thought highly of you two."

"He was like a brother, and my kids are having a hard time with him gone."

"Sean wouldn't want you to fall into a dark place again."

"Do you think I'm a bad person?"

"Do you think you're a bad person?"

"Sometimes. The decisions I've made..."

"And you think Sean's death is the karma for some of those decisions," Dr. Falk inquired.

Teagan clasped her hands together in her lap.

"Deep down, I know I shouldn't feel like that, but if I would have stayed home and let someone else take the lead, maybe Sean would still be alive."

Dr. Falk dropped the pen on top of the pad.

"Teagan, the feelings won't disappear overnight. I want you to start writing in your journal. When someone passes away, it doesn't mean you'll stop the grieving process overnight."

"I used to tell myself I could handle the conversation with my children about grief, but look at me. At my age, I can barely process it myself."

"You're not alone, and you're not invisible from pain."

"But I should be able to protect my people."

Dr. Falk grabbed the box of tissues and passed it over to her.

"Sean did his job."

"I... I... Sean died protecting me." Teagan broke down in tears. Dr. Falk went to sit across from her and grasped her hand in comfort.

"It's okay to cry. Just know you're not betraying anyone when you let the pain release, Teagan."

"Thank you." Teagan cleared her throat.

"How about you go home and spend time with your family. We did enough for today."

Teagan nodded, grabbed her coat and umbrella, and stood to leave.

* * *

Hours later, Teagan watched as the kids played card games in the living room while she cooked baked chicken, rice, and veggies with chocolate cake for dessert.

Knock!

Teagan turned down the stove, walked to the living room, and saw Christian shake hands with Spider, Daughtrey, and the rest of the guys.

"We have company." Tatum jumped up, ran to Spider, and hugged him around his waist.

"What are you doing here?"

"Just left a bar and wanted to check in with you." Spider pinched Tatum on the cheek.

Teagan glanced at Christian.

"We made plenty of food. You guys can pull up a chair," Christian said. Teagan smiled and kissed him on the lips.

"Thank you."

Christian rubbed her back.

"Anything for you."

"So, who's in the lead?" Daughtrey spoke, sitting down next to CJ and picking up some cards.

"Me!" Tatum shouted and plopped down on the floor.

"How did you know we needed this?"

"I know my boss." Spider nudged Teagan's shoulder.

"Tatum, watch Daughtrey. That one can be sneaky," Teagan teased, heading back to the kitchen to finish cooking.

Chapter Forty-Five

A month later.

After Tatum helped Christian and Teagan pack up the car, she climbed in the back passenger seat and buckled her seatbelt. CJ had his first basketball game, and the entire family was going to cheer him on, including Teagan, who decided to spend the day with her kids. With everything that happened, her conversations with Dr. Falk helped her to see that she needed more balance and to not take on the guilt lingering in her heart.

"Everybody ready?" Christian looked in the backseat at all the kids. Tatum and Cole wore headphones and watched movies. CJ held his cell phone in his hand and texted his teammates.

"Ready!" everyone answered.

"You good?" Christian watched Teagan zip up her purse and place it on the floor under her feet.

"I'm good, Christian." Teagan leaned over the seat and kissed him.

"Did you get the shirts?" Christian wondered.

"In the trunk... I got everybody's shirt."

"I like this."

"What?" Teagan interlocked their hands.

"You are more laidback, hanging with the family and ditching work."

"Well, I've learned to let the people that work alongside me do their jobs."

Christian lifted her hand and kissed the back of her palm, then backed out of the driveway. He turned the radio up slightly, and Teagan stared out the window. She noticed her new detail behind them at a distance as they drove toward the yellow light and stopped. Once Oskala was eliminated, in the aftermath of Sean's death, Spider interviewed a new person to be her driver and bodyguard for her family. At first, she was in a rush for a change, but she let it happen after a talk with Christian. The kids seemed to be okay with someone new coming into their lives.

Twenty minutes later, they arrived and parked. Christian helped Tatum and Teagan out of the car as CJ grabbed his bag and ran inside.

"Slow down, Cole!" Christian yelled.

"He's your son," Teagan joked, grabbing Tatum's hand and escorting her to the bleachers.

Christian pulled out the shirts and passed one to everyone. Teagan helped Cole and Tatum put their shirts on, then slipped one on and grabbed the phone to start recording. The team was announced, and all the kids ran out in a line and shook hands with the opponents.

"Mommy, I want something to drink." Tatum patted her leg.

"Wait until they announce your brother, then Daddy will grab some snacks."

Teagan kissed her forehead, and Tatum clapped her hands in excitement.

The doors of the school opened again, and everyone clapped while Teagan looked on in shock that Spider, Daughtrey, Gregory, and Broderick came to the game in shirts with CJ's number on the front. All the men hyped up the team and came around to the section where Teagan and Christian were sitting.

"What are you guys doing here?" Teagan leaned in to hug them.

"Just in the neighborhood and thought we'd come check out a game," Daughtrey joked, sitting next to Cole.

Gregory and Broderick sat in front of the first row of bleachers, with Spider on the opposite end of Teagan.

"You didn't have to do this."

"All your family and all Sean talked about was this game."

"He loved the kids."

"Relax and watch Daughtrey lose a hundred bucks," Spider teased, winking his left eye at Teagan.

"He did not bet on my child?"

"This is Daughtrey we're talking about."

Teagan shook her head, screaming when they announced CJ's name. This was the only place Teagan wanted to be, and she was glad to have friends and family around to keep her mind from going to that dark palace.

* * *

Monday after the weekend.

Teagan stepped off the elevator and smiled at the security guard and waved at a few other familiar faces while walking down to the conference room for her monthly meeting with the secretary of defense. Today, her hair had been blown out and was down, she wore light makeup, and she looked refreshed and ready for the business at hand. After she scanned her badge and stepped in, she walked to the table that held a classified brief on top. Only the top security clearance was allowed in this meeting, and Teagan wasn't sure if she would be back in after everything that happened.

The secretary of defense spoke on the latest cases that are on high alert for the US. Teagan sat stoic as he spoke on what each agency would handle after the crisis with Jacqueline was over, and she was home safe.

"Agent Stone, you and your team will take on surveillance for now."

"Yes, sir."

"Nothing out of the ordinary, but I want your people to monitor conversations we've recorded."

"Can I ask what the case is about, sir?"

"At this moment, we need to keep it on a need-to-know basis."

"Of course, Mr. Secretary."

Teagan took notes and waited for him to release everyone.

"Mrs. Stone!" He stopped her before she could leave.

"Yes."

"I know it's a difficult time for you right now."

"I'm fine."

"Then you know what's about to happen in London?"

"Not familiar." He scanned the room and waited for the last person to walk out of the room.

"I have reason to believe someone higher up in the London government is planning an attack."

"Has this been confirmed?"

"You're the first person I'm telling."

"My job is to know when something is going to cause an interruption to our priorities."

"Are you ready for a new case? Like mentally prepared?"

"What are you saying?"

"Dr. Falk is a great listener."

Teagan stumbled back in surprise.

"Don't worry, your conversations are strictly confidential."

"How... How did you know?"

"The notepad you're writing on; I have the same one with her logo."

Teagan looked down at her pen and pad.

"My team is ready for anything," Teagan replied.

"Agent Red, I'll be in touch." He held a hand out, and Teagan reached her palm over before watching him leave. She glanced down at her notepad, ripped off the top part, dropped the pad in the trashcan, and headed back to her office.

* * *

I hope you enjoyed Teagan's story so far. Please also check out "**Agent Red (Revenge) Teagan Stone Book 7**" **sneak peek** with a host of characters intertwined. Also, if you love mystery and suspense, check out **Mirror of Lies Book 1** or another thriller/crime fiction "**Ruined**"

Check out free short here ***"The Firm"*** https://payhip.com/b/py7S

Grab Boxset **"Agent Red 1-3"** here https://payhip.com/b/1KcxY

Sneak Peek: Mirror of Danger
Book 3

Jessica returned to work after the kidnapping and the death of her best friends. Now it was time to go back full time as a journalist and put her mind on the job. It only made sense when a story dropped in her lap to continue finding out what the police had missed. The biggest story across the news stations caused her to not only be the face in the media, but someone had other plans that derailed her into danger.

Can Jessica put her life back on track once again?

Reading Order of Mirror Series

Mirror of Lies Book 1
https://books2read.com/u/mgjEPx
Mirror of Lust Book 2
https://books2read.com/u/mVRpz2
Mirror of Danger Book 3
Mirror of Murder Book 4

Reading Order Teagan Stone Series

1. Agent Red-Fatal Memory Book 1
https://books2read.com/u/4j2PYX
2. **Agent Red-Fatal Target Book**
https://books2read.com/u/bWP8Jq
3. **Agent Red-Fatal Crime Book**
https://books2read.com/u/mZadZJ
4. Agent Red-Fatal Justice Book
https://books2read.com/u/mqo7wd

5. **Agent Red-Fatal Enemy Book**
https://books2read.com/u/bxeo1q
6. **Agent Red-Fatal Death Book**
https://books2read.com/u/mqwlRv
7. Agent Red-Fatal Revenge Book
https://books2read.com/u/3JnKyA
8. Agent Red- Fatal Pursuit Book
https://books2read.com/u/bOPowo
9. Agent Red- Fatal Attack Book

10. Agent Red-Fatal Mission Book

About the Author

Ava S. King is the debut author of thriller, mystery, suspense, and psychological crime novels.

If you want to know when the next book will come out, please visit Author Ava S. King website at http://www.authoravasking.com, where you can sign up to receive an email for her next release.

What's Next?

Want to know what happens next? Follow me at the links below to catch the next release.

Thank you so much for reading, and if you enjoyed the crazy ride and decided to leave a review, we'd truly appreciate the support. Reviews are the lifeblood of the publishing world. They're read, appreciated, and needed. Please consider taking the time to leave a few words on Goodreads or BookBub.

Sign up for updates and sneak peeks at the sites below:
www.authoravasking.com
www.bookbub.com/avasking
www.goodreads.com/author/avasking
www.Twitter.com/authoravaking
www.Instagram.com/authoravasking
www.Facebook.com/authoravasking
www.304publishing.tumblr.com

Acknowledgments

I want to thank my team, which helps me behind the scenes, from my editors to my test readers and graphic designers, and the list goes on. I truly appreciate each of you for keeping me on my toes.